THE VOICE
OF FEAR

THE VOICE
OF FEAR

B.A. CHEPAITIS

WILDSIDE PRESS

A great wind rent the mountain... And after the wind, an earthquake...and after the earthquake, a fire...and after the fire a still small voice.

—First Kings 19:9

PROLOGUE

Home Planet, Madison Square Garden, New Manhattan

His audience was with him, electric energy pouring out from them as his voice moved above their screams, scorching out the chorus of the song *Fun Gun.*

And if I can't kill you, then I'll cure you. Make you live inside your soul, he sang.

The audience sang with him, all of them looking to him, Springer Todd, the Wild One, Rank Rock superstar, their hero.

He lifted a hand over them, blessing these people he'd never know. The spotlights made it impossible for him to see their faces, but he tasted their lives on his tongue, in his throat. Thousands of people, all willing to lick the heels of his boots.

The most sardonic part of him laughed at them for it, but his better self felt compassion. Everyone wanted a god or two. He never signed up for the job, but he was in it now, up to his eyeballs. And he'd act the part. With this final song of the night, he'd give them a show they'd never forget.

At the front of the stage a fake machine gun was set up. Part of the act, this prop blasted pellets of light over the first few rows as he called out the chorus one more time, followed by the howl of joy that ended the song.

Looking for the light, he sang. *The light, the light, the light.*

He moved to the prop, his sandpaper voice rasping out an extended cry of passion. Behind him, the bass player took his solo, pulling hard at glowing strings. Springer dropped to his knees in back of the gun. The kids up front clamored close to the stage, hands reaching for the seeds of light that would disperse over their heads, always just out of reach.

They needed this like they needed air in their lungs, like they needed hope. This light, these virtual stars which disappeared before they could be grasped. They became one creature with a million hands clutching for them, as if it was the only food to sustain them. He loved them for it, because they were right. He hated them for it, because they were right.

"Are you ready for the light?" he called out, his voice reverberating through the amp.

A roar of agreement bounced back to him. They wanted this. Wanted it.

"Then let's do it," he screeched.

He pulled back on the release and laid his finger against the automatic fire button. The synth pumped out chords as stars burst out over them.

Stars rose and fell. The blossoming ping of stars. Hand reached for them and mouths opened to swallow them, to let light pour down their parched throats. But the stars didn't dissolve into ethereal darkness. Not this time.

This time they pierced the children who reached for them, pieces of star-hot fire opening like flowers inside them. Stars exploded in their throats, in their flesh. The clamoring adolescents gasped and choked, dropping heavily into pools of their own blood.

Screaming. They were all screaming, and Springer howled behind the gun, the lights lending him the aspect of a coyote racing the moon to morning, teeth bared, orange eyes catching the reflection of falling stars.

Bodies fell to the floor and went still. Blood poured from their mouths and ran in rivulets around them. The screams grew exigent with terror. The band played the song to its ending and left the stage.

It wasn't until well after they were gone that anyone realized these fallen teenagers weren't all just a part of the act.

CHAPTER ONE

Prison Planetoid 3, Zone 12, Toronto Replica City

Alex Dzarny sat at his desk, scowling at numbers that scrolled across his computer screen. He had reports to write on the latest recidivism stats, which were low, and the latest budget requests, which were high.

As he kept explaining to various administrators, there was a direct correlation between a high budget and low recidivism. The Board of Governors and legislators who doled out dollars for the Planetoid Prison system knew this, but insisted on arguing about it at endless meetings, one of which he had to attend that evening. He'd spent the last hour going over his notes for it, and he was glad when a knock on his office door interrupted his work.

"Come in," he said.

The door opened, and Rachel Shofet, researcher and team member for Prison Planetoid Three, Zone 12, ducked her head inside. Though she had years of experience in the system, her brown eyes held in a smooth, round face, framed by exuberantly curling brown hair, made her look too innocent for Planetoid work. Her continued optimism did nothing to change that.

"Got a minute?" she asked.

"A bunch, if it'll get me away from this desk," he replied. "What's up?"

She came inside and approached his desk. "It's the new prisoner. Springer Todd."

Alex knew the case. Todd was lead singer for *Rumors of Pigs*, a very popular Rank Rock band. At their big concert in Madison Square Garden he'd blown away the first few rows of his audience with a laser fire machine gun. It made for quite a show, and earned him a prison stint in Alex's zone. He'd arrived two days ago and was still in testing to determine his psi capacities, cognitive issues, and core fear. Once that information was gathered, Alex would assign a Teacher and coordinate a program to make him face and move beyond the fear that drove him to his crime. It was a high profile case, and while Planetoid Three took the worst of the worst criminals, he'd be particularly challenging. One of those cases where you wondered why you did this job.

"It's too bad," he said. "I liked his music."

"Me, too. He doesn't use all the technojunk. Definitely not Gen T."

Alex nodded. The current generation had been dubbed Gen T by the media, the T standing for trauma. They were born after the Killing Times, that massive urban violence which created the Planetoid Prison system, but their parents saw it all, and their lingering fears seeped into the children they raised. The trauma they inherited made them cautious, emotionally detached, and more comfortable with technology than direct human interaction.

As a result their music was intellectual, with performers who relied on surround screens, infrasound, nanobot relays, and H-synths. To Alex, it was repetitive and emotionally flat. Water music, he called it. Not bad, in its own way, but he preferred his music to have more heat. When Springer burst onto the scene he brought all that.

His songs were primal, full of fire and earth. He'd been compared to singers like Jim Morrison, Eddie Vedders, Rathbone Harrington. While other bands worked their technology, he danced wildly on the stage, howling and screaming. And he could sing anything from world beat, blues, classic rock, and technopoet riffs, with some of his songs having all of the above. The excitement he generated grew from passion and skill. From the music and lyrics he wrote and performed.

He'd had some controversy in the last year, but nothing that indicated he'd turn spree killer. Alex was curious to find out what went wrong. The case was first on his list, after he got through his damn reports and meetings.

"You read his file yet?" Rachel asked.

"Glanced at it. Why?"

"He wants to see you."

"What?"

"He asked to see you."

Alex's eyebrows curled down. "Me? Specifically?"

"By name," Rachel said.

"How the hell does he know my name?"

"He didn't say. Just asked to speak with you. Some of his test results are in. You want to go over them first? I filed it under PI217."

He stared at his computer. He noticed she didn't ask if he *would* go. She already knew the answer to that.

Rachel had once been Jaguar's prisoner, and had long since become a very good friend to both of them. She was their best researcher, their best hacker, and one of the few people who knew he was Jaguar's lover as well as her supervisor. One of the few people they trusted with that information.

His hand moved toward the keypad, then stopped. One more file might kill him right now, and sometimes it was better to go in cold, let the situation dictate action. "I'll see him first," he said.

"Okay. Just so you know, he's in and out."

"Meaning?"

"Sometimes he talks nice. Other times he howls and rolls around on the floor."

Alex sighed. One of those. Some prisoners acted out, hoping for a test result of insanity to get off their Planetoid sentence. Others just howled because of who they were. He'd find out soon enough which category Springer fell into.

"Where is he?" Alex asked.

"Observation. 42C. Need me there?"

"No. I can deal with howlers."

"Yeah," she said. "You think you'll give this one to Jaguar?"

He eyed here. "Why would I?"

"Looks like her kind of case. A musician. Highly vexed. Lots of press interest. The usual."

She was right on all counts. Jaguar was trained as a ritual singer for her Native Mertec people, and she frequently sang with the Planetoid band, *Moon Illusion*. She understood the mind of the musician, in aspects both sacred and profane. She was also the first person who came to mind when a case looked complicated. There was only one problem.

"She's on assignment, Rachel."

"I know. Samantha Huran. A tough one."

Samantha was a financier who embezzled ten million dollars from the various companies she consulted with, then killed three people to cover her tracks. Smooth, self-assured and without the usual fear of powerlessness associated with this crime, she was proving to be a challenge.

"But I'm hearing rumors she might get a reprieve—something wrong with her trial," Rachel said. "And sometimes you move Jaguar around when you need to. How's she doing, anyway? I haven't seen her since this assignment started."

"Me neither, Rachel. I've been chained to my desk, and she's been chained to a prisoner."

It happened periodically. Their work made it so. Jaguar, a Teacher who created and ran prisoner programs, was currently on an assignment that required her attention 24 and 7. They'd seen each other only in stolen moments in his office, where they met to review the case, keeping to their most professional aspects. There were no complaints from either side about it. They were both passionate about their work, as well as each other.

And they knew that after a prisoner was deemed good to go, there would be rest leave for her, down time for him, and they'd revel in a long stretch of time together. After this assignment, he had vacation coming. Maybe they'd take a shuttle to the home planet, go to New Mexico and see Jaguar's people, Jake and One Bird. Maybe they'd just stay in bed for about a week.

"Love stinks, huh?" was Rachel's only comment.

Alex grinned. "Love is fine. Work stinks." He rose to leave. "And I'll think about your advice for Springer. You may just be right."

He left his office and walked down the hall, where the business of Prison Planetoid Three proceeded in its daily round. He passed administrative offices where staff did the work necessary to keep the place running smoothly. He went by rooms where Teachers conducted interviews with new prisoners. On the floors above him were conference rooms for meetings to deal with the legal and political issues that sprouted like weeds around this prison system. Below him were banks of secure computers for researchers and Teachers. At the end of the corridor he took a left and got on the elevator for the floor below him, where prisoner testing occurred.

He got off the elevator, moved down the hall, and stopped at the observation window for 42C. Within the room he saw the new prisoner for the first time. Springer Todd was leaning back in a plastic chair, his long legs stretched out under the table, his infamous orange eyes closed. He was supposed to be filling out a questionnaire, but from what Alex could see the page was blank. They still used paper for this part of testing, gleaning information from handwriting, even testing the chemical composition of residue left by the prisoner's hands. The process was thorough.

Monitors blinked on the wall behind him, recording his inner state as he either answered, or refused to answer, the questions asked. In spite of his pose, he wasn't relaxed. He looked like he was waiting, full attention, for something important to happen. At least, Alex thought, he wasn't howling. He pressed a hand against the window and inside the room Springer shifted slightly, lifted his head and sniffed the air. As if he sensed Alex's presence. As if he could smell it.

"Interesting," Alex muttered. He moved away from the window, entered the room, closed the door behind him and waited.

Springer didn't open his eyes or shift his pose. "Took your time, didn't you?" he asked.

Alex had no idea what he was talking about, so he didn't answer. He just observed, reading the space around this famous and charismatic young man.

If he was standing, he'd be almost as tall as Alex, who stood over six feet. But he was less broad in the shoulders, lanky and lean, rangy as a hungry coyote, an animal he'd been compared to more than once. The Wild One, media called him, his chiseled features and raucously curling light brown hair, his slightly slanted eyes, a strange combination of brown and hazel that made them look orange, known ubiquitously, even here.

And for reasons he wouldn't state, he'd turned what everyone thought was a light gun on his audience and sprayed them with laser fire instead. 23 were killed, 42 others wounded, and given the size of the crowd, they were lucky it wasn't worse.

After he shot his wad, he left the stage with the rest of the band, who apparently had no idea what he'd done. Security thought nothing of all the screaming, normal for this kind of concert, until riotous attempts to exit left three more trampled to death, a lot more wounded. When security went to the Green Room, Springer was crouched on the floor, singing a line about death being a lover. A new song, he said.

He pled guilty, but at his allocution he only reported what happened. In response to questions about where he got live fire, he said he couldn't remember. When asked why he'd done it, he started singing one of his songs—*Bury Me Deep*. It was about the Killing Times, and what it meant to carry the burden of the dead through time. One of his best.

His lawyer tried for an insanity plea and didn't get it. All his preliminary tests judged him free of psychosis, morally and legally responsible for his crime, and not under the influence of any drugs. Reading him empathically, Alex also sensed nothing of psychosis or drugs, but a great deal by way of psi capacities. The air around him crackled with it.

"Well?" Springer asked. "Don't you know me?"

Alex was about to say of course I do, then realized Springer meant something more personal. Had they ever met? If so, he had no memory of it. "Should I?" he asked.

In response, Springer's face grew taut, and a low moan of pain rumbled in his throat. He pushed his palms against his temples and held on as if trying to keep his head from bursting apart. Alex, waiting for him to start howling, instead felt the unmistakable energy of empathic contact. Okay, he thought. He's an empath. Let's see if he's got any chops.

He allowed the contact, and attended to it. It was rough and gritty as his singing. He had the chops, but no discipline. None of the finesse that, for instance, Jaguar used in her contact. Alex wasn't sure he was even aware he was making contact. That happened sometimes with untaught empaths. Information spewed out of them, and what they felt was a kind of madness. But he was strong, the shadow of remembered experience layered and rich with clarity.

Alex saw a child, breaking a lamp. Then, the child listening, hearing the sound of breakage as a sequence of separate cadences, rhythms, and pitches. In his mind, it wasn't anything as simple as a crash. He heard the flow of air around an object of specific size, followed by the rise and fall of pitch from breaking glass, and the rain of glittering glass singing its own tune.

Then, in quick succession, a series of images of the same boy listening to running water, to windshield wipers on a car, to a tree. Alex perceived the sound as Springer did, each layer combining to create small symphonies. Sound was a living thing he pursued, which pursued him beyond any boundaries Alex could fathom. No excuse for a killing spree, but the information would be useful for his program. Gently, not wanting to disturb him, Alex moved away from empathic contact.

"Springer?" he asked out loud.

He startled, dropped his hands from his head and lifted burning eyes toward Alex. "Now I do what's next," he said.

"I decide what's next," Alex replied.

"Not anymore. It's all in motion."

Normally, Alex would take that as a threat, but Springer spoke with a sizzle of fear. Before Alex could respond his cellcom buzzed. He took it out of his pocket, flipped it open. "Supervisor Dzarny," he said.

The man on the other end, a Planetoid lawyer, talked, and Alex listened. Samantha Huran's case was going wrong, he said. Her lawyers claimed tainted evidence and the courts agreed. She was to be released. Jaguar would be pissed as hell when she found out, but it also meant she was free to take on Springer.

"Got it," he said. He closed his cellcom, tapped at it thoughtfully.

"See?" Springer said. "No stopping it now." He closed his eyes, humming softly to himself.

Alex was about to ask him what the hell he meant when he was unceremoniously tossed into Adept space. He glanced at Springer, then away. A reaction sparked by Springer's empathic contact? Could be. Sometimes it happened that way. But the reason didn't matter. When his own gift of precognition called him, he had to answer. If Springer noticed, he could do nothing about that.

He let himself be carried into brief blips of disconnected images—Springer, laughing, talking with Jaguar. Himself, caught in tight embrace with a woman whose face wasn't visible, though he knew she wasn't

Jaguar. Then, a gun pointed at Jaguar's head. Immense grief poured through him, and he and saw himself standing on the roof of a skyscraper, looking down. Then, Jaguar again, on a mesa in New Mexico, shining like the dawn while he knelt nearby, gutting a deer.

It spun itself out quick as dreaming, a wash of time he'd learn to bear in stillness, disciplining himself not to resist or direct, only to observe. The images made no sense, because they hadn't happened yet, and might never happen. They were either metaphors, or possible futures, yet to unfold. But all of them related in some way to this prisoner. Later, when he had time, he'd consider what they might mean, how he might manage them toward the best possible end. That was his core art, and the reason Jaguar sometimes called him Spider Magus.

When it dissipated, spitting him back into the present time and place, he pushed a fingernail into the palm of his hand, moved his feet against the floor. His skin was numb, his mind slack. The emotional quality of the visions lingered like the hangover from a bad dream.

He took in breath slowly, and released it. Became aware of himself standing in the room with Springer, who continued to hum.

A shudder coursed its way down his spine. He turned and left the room.

* * * *

Schulman Enterprises, New Manhattan, Home Planet

"We'll want a new video for Chain Gang within the month," Ron Schulman told his daughter, Jeral, who was sitting across the desk from him. "Before their tour starts. That should help."

"I don't know if anything can help Chain Gang," his daughter replied.

Ron bristled. Though she'd worked with him for all her adult life and understood the music industry as well as he did, she was still the daughter, and he was still both the father and the CEO. He knew best. "Get it done," he said. "And get some interviews for Jack. Tonight Show, Morning Hour, Heat Wave."

"Sure," she said, though she didn't sound it.

Ron sighed. She was right. Chain Gang was a new Faux band under management with Schulman Entertainment Enterprises, the kind of group that didn't so much make music as create musical experiences, using H-synth to establish feedback loops between audience brain waves and sound machines, infrasound to shift moods, nanos to tap into things like the sound of cold metal, and their own brain waves to control light shows. It was a big deal in the industry these days, and lots of groups were making lots of money with it, but Chain Gang's sales were flat, their profile not drawing the interest he'd anticipated. He wasn't sure why. Everything he knew indicated they'd do well, and after all his years in the business, he knew a lot.

He'd built Schulman Entertainment into one of the largest production and management companies in the world, his success growing from knowing how to make the public buy what he was selling, and his willingness to stay diverse. Though his primary interest was music, he was also a show runner for TV and web, owned racing teams in Nascar and F1, had a football and baseball team to call his own. The only thing he stayed away from was publishing. Books in any form were just too chancy, no matter how you padded your assets.

But he'd called a few bad ones in the last year. The sitcom he backed was a flop. His football coach had to be fired for beating his wife, even though he was still the best coach around. He'd gotten him a great legal team, and thought for sure they'd discredit the woman, but medical records said otherwise, and the new coach wasn't getting the team anywhere near the Superbowl. Personally, he thought it was a damn shame to let a good man go just because he wasn't nice to his wife.

And now, Chain Gang going flat, even though he funded them for any toy they wanted, and ran one of the heaviest publicity campaigns he'd ever done.

"What do you think the problem is?" he asked his daughter.

She brushed back her wealth of red hair, regarded him with her large hazel eyes. Doe eyes, he thought. She had the eyes of a doe, and they bothered him. Deer were prey animals, and he didn't like prey. Predators were much more reliable. But then, her red hair, inherited from her mother, gave the lie to that. It curled outrageously, and she wore it long, like a flash of fire running over her shoulders. The eyes might name her demure, but the hair called her something else altogether. And both aspects of her were true, in all ways.

Like her mother, she was tall—just a few inches below his six feet— and though she was large boned, she never looked masculine. That she also got from her mother. In fact, there was very little she got from him. Her face was round and except for her eyes her features small and soft. He was tall and lean, his grey hair cropped close to his head accentuating his sharp nose, narrow face, narrow blue eyes. And he took command of a room as soon as he entered it, while she somehow managed to disappear entirely, in spite of her height and wealth of flaming hair. When she went with him on business trips people assumed she was an intern or a secretary because she put herself behind him, avoided center stage as if it was the middle of a mushroom cloud.

Most people were either clearly predators or prey. His daughter seemed to be neither, or both, which meant he could never really place her, though he could place everyone else he met. Still, she knew her stuff about music. In fact, when she was young, he'd considered starting her as a singer. She had a voice, and was good with keyboards, but she didn't have the hunger. He was better off using her skills as a consultant.

"They don't really care about the art or the craft, and that makes them boring," she said. "A dozen other groups do what they do, only better. Look at Terra Cotta—they use clay for their nanos, and it makes a specific sound, which they've learned to manipulate in a specific way. And when Bend It uses H-synth, they coordinate it with their visuals to create a whole mindset for the audience, so they've got good material coming back to them, which they also know how to manipulate. Chain Gang's infrasound is just haunted house crap. They're cashing in on a trend—and your willingness to fund it."

She was probably right. He didn't actually care much about music, except as a commodity, but his instinct for a highly sellable commodity had always served him well. He was disturbed that it failed him so badly this year.

"Are you suggesting I cut them loose? After all the money we sunk into them?"

"Well," she said, "maybe you'll get lucky, and they'll kill their audience. That should bump up their sales. It did the last time."

Ron scowled. Another example of the way you never knew with her. All this time, she'd been talking about Chain Gang, but thinking about Springer Todd. "Don't tell me you're still worked up about him," he said with disdain.

Her lips pinched in. "Yes," she said. "Of course. He was—he was *ours*."

"As it turns out, he wasn't," Ron said distinctly, and took some pleasure in watching her wince. That was the problem with Jeral in her prey mode. She brought out the worst in him, and then he'd feel like crap. She should know better than to leave herself open to it. "I'd think you'd be glad to see the end of him," he added, trying to sound conciliatory. "The whole thing tore you up pretty badly."

Blood crept up under her fair skin, but she spoke with determination. "I'm not," she said. "I'm worried about what they'll do to him up there."

She glanced up, as people on the home planet did when they referred to the Planetoids, which they knew mostly as distant and dimly shining rings of light, only occasionally visible in the night sky.

"Not worried about what he did to us down here?" her father asked. "After he was featured on the show, after we pushed him as the best example of what we do?"

"How many times have you told me there's no bad publicity?" she said, staying firm. "Besides, he's more than a poster child for your charitable programs."

Years ago, he'd started a program to help talented kids who were in trouble. It was good for the company profile and good for business, because kids in trouble often had lots of drive, and just needed to direct it. He'd take them in, let them live in one of his houses and attend schools he paid for as he nurtured their specific talents. One of his boys had turned out to be a World Series winning pitcher, one of the girls was his best F1 driver, so it paid off. Both he and Jeral spent time with the kids, though Jeral was more of presence in their lives than he was. But with Springer—well, that was different. Her attachment to him was different. She hadn't been herself since he'd been arrested.

"You want to help him," he said. "And in spite of everything, you want me to help him, too. Is that it?" he demanded.

"Yes," she said. "I do."

He stared at her long enough to see if she meant it, and when she didn't back down, he reached over the desk and put a hand on her arm. "Well," he said. "The fact is, I agree that we should be involved in what happens next with him. I've made some plans in that direction."

She lifted her head, her doe eyes shining with what he suspected were tears. He tried not to be irritated at that.

"It's a matter of good business practice," he said gruffly. "We can't hide this, so we better make use of it. As soon as we get this Chain Gang stuff cleared away, I'm going to the Planetoid to talk to some people. With you, of course. I've got other interests there I can check at the same time."

Another aspect of his charitable giving—he funded post-Planetoid work programs for prisoners, and occasionally gave money for development through grants from his foundation. This, he told his daughter, gave him a better standing with the conservatives, and since the politics that controlled things like the airwaves and censorship was important to his business, he wanted all the friends he could get on both sides of the aisle.

Jeral took in a breath that was easy, maybe the first one she'd taken since this started. "You're not angry with me, are you?"

Ron released her arm. Patted her hand. "How could I stay angry with you?"

She grasped his hand in hers and squeezed hard. "Thank you," she said.

"Don't I always take care of you?"

She ducked her head down, nodded. "Yes, Daddy," she said. "You do."

CHAPTER TWO

Planetoid 3, Zone 12, Toronto Replica City

Jaguar peered through the observation window, studying the occupant of the room. "That's Springer Todd," she told Alex. "The Wild One."

"I told you that before we got here," Alex agreed.

"You said we had *a* Springer Todd. Not *the* Springer Todd."

"I didn't know there was more than one."

"Springer Todd the hockey player. Springer Todd, the asshole I dated when I was in grad school. I'm sure there's more. Why is this one here?"

"You don't know? It's all over the news."

"I've been working, Alex."

He should have guessed. When Jaguar was on an assignment, she knew nothing else, cared about nothing else except getting the job done. "Part of his act is firing light balls over his audience," he said. "At his last gig he used laser fire instead and killed a bunch of teenagers."

"Huh. Bad for ticket sales," Jaguar noted.

"Maybe, but not other sales. His music went platinum the week after."

Jaguar rolled her eyes. "Sure it did. I'm surprised they didn't resurrect the electric chair for him. That'd boost profit even more."

"There was agitation for execution, but the judge held the line and sent him here."

"Let's hear it for the triumph of morals over cupidity. And what does the prisoner have to say for himself?"

"He says he's guilty, but he's not giving any motive."

"Is there speculation about that?"

"Lots. He was a foster kid, in trouble early, so there's talk it's genetic. Also talk of drugs, of general insanity, bad morals. And he had a rough year, so it seems something's been cooking in him. He took his clothes off at a show and danced with the audience. Had a highly public affair with an older woman that ended in a highly public fight. Gave a nasty rant on stage about a Senator he didn't like, which earned him the attention of the FBI."

"Naughty boy," she said.

"We're just finding out how naughty. And naughty in what way."

They both turned to the observation window and viewed Springer, who crouched in a corner muttering to himself while the implants monitoring his neural system sent signals to the viewscreen on the wall.

He'd been in and out of coherent speech since Alex had seen him, sometimes responding with perfect clarity, other times disappearing into a world of his own. Right now he was being scanned for corollary psi capacities, and Jaguar, trained to read the screens, glanced at them and sniffed impatiently.

"They won't find out that way," she said.

The technology, she said, read only for the obvious, obscuring the subtler signals of deeper capacities and more complex intertwined capacities only another empath would pick up on. To her, those capacities were the most important in designing a prisoner's program.

With a musician, Alex knew, that was even more complicated. The study of music created different sets of neural bundles, different interactions between the limbic and cortical systems, even a different perceptual system. Jaguar, who sang the chants of her Mertec people in ceremony and sang with the local Planetoid band, *Moon Illusion*, understood this. For her, music also was a tool to create a different relationship with the spirits. Musicians moved between worlds, bringing the spark of another realm into this one and sharing it through their bodies, their hearts and their throats. It was, she'd often told him, almost as demanding as chant-shaping.

"You looking for a consult?" she asked. "What Teacher I think would work well with him?"

He scanned the length of her long and lean figure, smooth as the amber of her skin and the long dark silk of her hair. Even in jeans and the long sleeved silk shirts she preferred, her tensile strength was apparent in the way she held herself, animal grace inherent in both her motion and her stillness. He let his gaze rest on the sun-flecked sea green of her eyes. "That's not what I want," he said, and then went silent.

She waited, and when nothing more was forthcoming, she spoke. "Being cryptic," she said, "doesn't suit you."

"I know. Bear with me. You know his music?"

"I listen to it, and I like it. I went to a few of his shows, early on in his career. When he's on stage, he's...working."

She raised a hand, two fingers touching his forehead. The gesture of the empath, and her way of saying Springer used those skills on stage.

"Harmonic sympathizer?" Alex asked.

This, a term for an obscure empathic trait that few people beyond Jaguar would know about. Harmonic sympathizers connected their energy with large groups, creating a feedback loop that drew from them and fed them in return. This connection was what H-synth technology was trying to recreate. Or, more accurately, trying to package and control. But the subtleties involved, the complexity of the connection, defied any perfect technological reproduction. It was, Alex thought, like 3D movies. Fun in its own way, but it couldn't replace the real thing.

"I thought so before I saw him," she said. She clenched and unclenched her hand as if she manipulated cloth within it, her body recalling the texture of empathic space she'd experienced. "It feels like that, but there's more going on."

Good, Alex thought. She was already intrigued. "You want to take him on?" he asked.

She raised her eyebrows at him. "What about Samantha Huran?"

"She's being released. Tainted evidence on her trial."

"Oh, for fuck's sake—"

"Leave it, Dr. Addams. The Board approved. She's gone." He tapped on the plexiglass of the window in front of them. "Bend your brain to this one."

He watched as she drew in a breath, her face going dark and angry. Then she closed her eyes and breathed out. Just air, he could hear her saying. Let it go. In their years of working together he'd learned appreciate the way she let go of small anger, saving herself for the big issues she'd never relinquish.

Ready, she said, speaking subvocally. *Tell me about him.*

There's personal history, medical and psych profile. Psi profile. What do you want first?

He felt her mind playing like breath over his thoughts, the ripples of her understanding touching his.

There's more, she said. A statement, not a question. *Something you know.*

He pulled back hard, and the empathic connection was cut roughly.

"Ouch," Jaguar said out loud. She rubbed at her forehead. "Was that necessary?"

"Sorry," Alex said. "I just—"

She put a hand to her hip, tapped her foot. "You just don't want to tell me something."

There was no point denying it. "That's right."

Jaguar lifted her sea eyes to his and he saw the snap of green and gold within them, caught the swift, clean scent of mint and the slicing feel of a good knife. Then, her voice spoke within him.

What has the Adept learned?

Of course, she would sniff that out. Adept space carried a specific and unmistakable residue of charged air she'd recognize.

He blocked her as politely as possible. *Not yet*, he replied.

To his relief, she accepted it. Smooth as a sigh, she left him. Just to show him he could have done better, he supposed. "Show off," he said out loud.

"That wasn't even close to showing off. Why the secrecy? I thought we weren't doing that anymore. No more evasions."

"I'm not evading. I'm telling you directly. There's something here I can't talk about yet."

"Why not?"

"Because I'm not sure of it myself."

She sighed, and gave it up. He'd seen something he was still trying to interpret, something that asked him to remain quiet until he did so. In the slippery slope of Adept space, sometimes to speak too soon was to wreck the mountain. Though she once considered his arts among the most manipulative, over time she'd grown to trust his use of them. That, however, didn't mean she liked them.

She ran her gaze over him, and he knew she was taking in every available bit of information—the way the small muscles in his face moved or stayed still, the feel of the energy surrounding him, the scent of his words.

"Will you tell me, once you know?" she asked.

An interesting question, and one he didn't have the answer to. "If I can."

"But you're not sure."

"I'll jump off that bridge when I get to it," he said.

"In the meantime, you want me to take this on blind? Jesus, Alex."

"You'll have his files. All the information any teacher might have."

"I repeat. Jesus, Alex."

"I know. Will you do it anyway?"

"What if I won't?"

"He goes to someone else, and you take another case. No harm, no foul. Jaguar, can you trust me on this one?"

A quick smile came and went. She touched his chest, briefly pressing a finger against the scar he still had where her knife had pierced him, a reminder of his willingness to give his life for hers. "What do you think?" she asked softly.

He took a chance on raising his hand to her face and running a finger down the side of it. They avoided showing affection in public because protocol was against this kind of relationship between Supervisor and

Teacher, but her gesture needed acknowledgment. She moved toward his touch, then pulled back. They both returned to their most professional aspects. She was the first to speak.

"What's testing show so far?" she asked.

"He's positive for psi capacities."

"That's obvious to the most casual observer, which I'm not. I see empath, a touch of Adept. I suspect at least two more."

He assumed she was right on all counts. She could read a prisoner through a brick wall better than any technology the Planetoids had. He often thought they should get rid of all their technology and just let Jaguar sit in rooms with prisoners, then give a report. She was incredibly accurate, and read for the most subtle variations.

"Which ones?" he asked.

She grinned at him. "I'd rather not say until I'm sure."

If she had a paw, he thought, she'd be licking it. "Okay," he said. "I get it. Just so you know, this is a high profile case. Lots of media and home planet interest."

She turned back to the observation window. "I'll bet. Famous rock star—and he was one of Ron Schulman's spawn."

As part of his extensive charitable giving, every year entertainment producer Ron Schulman adopted a few young people from the justice system—kids in trouble, who tested gifted in a variety of realms. He'd get them educated, help them climb out of the hole they'd fallen into. And though it served the needs of the kids he took in, Schulman also got good airplay from it. Internet and TV had followed a full year of the kids' progress, splashing Schulman Enterprises across the globe and raising their stock considerably. Springer was one of the kids in that show.

"How do you know?"

"I saw the show. Then I read up on Schulman. I was curious. Schulman doesn't strike me as the type to nurture a budding young empath. From what I read, he throws money at politicians who back anti-empath reforms."

"I'm guessing that's more about money than personal ethics," Alex said. "He also funds Planetoid programs."

"Does he? Planetoid prisoners and delinquents. Guilty conscience?"

"Cynic," he said.

"Realist," she corrected. "Y'know, Springer left him for a few years. His best years, some people say."

"I'm aware of that," Alex said.

Springer went to Julliard for a year, on Schulman's tab, but then left both academia and Ron to start his own band, go out on the road with it.

Like his killing, he gave no explanation for the move, or the return to his benefactor's fold a year later.

"You think think he left because he's an empath?" Alex asked.

"It's possible. I'm guessing he has trouble with his arts. When I saw his show, I had the impression he wasn't in charge, maybe not even conscious of what he's doing. You know. Spewing stuff out, taking stuff in, making himself crazy."

That confirmed what Alex had seen in him. "The testing runs shows the usual bumps for psi use, but in a random pattern, indicating they come into play beyond his volition."

"There you go," Jaguar said. "Untaught, but highly gifted. Volatile combination, and fuck you very much for that, Ron Schulman."

Alex could tell she was as drawn to this as she was to his musical abilities. Nothing like a gifted empath to make her hands itch. But she wasn't completely convinced yet.

"Questions?" he asked.

She swiveled her face to his. "Just one. What's got you so twitchy?" she asked. He didn't respond immediately, and she continued. "I get it, about the music, and the complicated empath thing. I like that, and I'm good with it, and you know it. But usually you prefer to keep me away from cases that make you twitch this much."

All he had to offer in response was from Adept space, something cold and inevitable running through his blood. "He's pretty far gone, Jaguar," he said. "There's not another Teacher who stands a chance of retrieving him. There's—only you."

"So it's important to you," she noted.

He tensed. It shouldn't be. There was no reason for it to be. "It's a case," he said. "They're all important to me."

"Right. Anything you *can* tell me before I decide?"

"He's got a strong Thanatos drive, and it's not clear which direction it's turned. You should assume he'll get ugly."

She waved that away. "Most of them do," she said.

She'd never refuse a case on those grounds. She was godlike in her willingness to ignore her own repugnance in order to get a job done. She directed her attention away from him and toward Springer, whose movements had changed from rocking and muttering to sniffing the air. He turned his head and stared directly at her, as if he could see her through the mirrored window.

"He really does have orange eyes," she murmured. "How very odd."

His lips curled back from his teeth, and he stood, the sinewy muscles of his lanky frame stretched taut. Still staring at Jaguar, he began howling long and low, his eyes catching blips of light from the monitors, sparks flying from him to her. Jaguar pressed her hand against the glass. The tip of the retractable red glass knife she wore up her sleeve glistened like blood at her wrist.

"I'd have to create my own program for him," she said. "You know that, right?"

"Use anything you think will work," he said. "No restrictions."

She tilted her head at him. "Supervisor, I'm shocked. After you spent years trying to get me to behave. Follow the rules, Dr. Addams," she mimicked. "A little discretion, Dr. Addams. Don't sleep with the prisoners, Dr. Addams."

She was testing his boundaries, and maybe the parameters of their relationship. Certainly poking at him to get knowledge he didn't want to give. "I've never actually restricted you," he said carefully. "I don't know that I could, or would."

"So you *want* me to sleep with him? Is that what the Adept spit out?"

"Of course not," he said tersely, with more intensity than he'd meant. He tried for separation of church and state. "I never thought it was a good idea, professionally speaking."

"What about personally?"

"You really have to ask?" he said with some impatience.

"Alpha male," she said softly.

"Yes, Jaguar," he agreed. His guiding spirit was the wolf, possessive once he made a choice of mate. "Any objections?"

"None so far," she said.

"Glad to hear it. Any other questions?"

She focused on Springer with the neutral stare of a cat observing its prey. "Did the testers name his core fear?"

"They're saying Napoleon." That was the term applied to spree killers, whose terror of powerlessness drove them to take ultimate control over the lives and deaths of others.

"They think too categorically," she said. "It's not that. What about his core psi capacity?"

"They can't find it," Alex said. "That'd be your job."

"Then I'll be busy," she said.

Inevitability washed through him. "You'll take him?" he asked, already knowing the answer.

She pressed a finger against the glass of the one-way mirror. Clairvoyance was one of her gifts, and Alex was aware she was using it now, finding her own cryptic, cogent reasons for taking this on. In less than a minute, she confirmed.

"Yeah," she said. "This one's mine."

CHAPTER THREE

Alex made sure Jaguar had all the files she needed, and then made his way back to the testing room, where Springer was just unhooked from the monitors, waiting transportation back to his holding cell. He kept his head lowered but raised his eyes when Alex entered. The whites showed, giving him a feral look.

"You here to poke me more?" he demanded.

So, Alex thought. Today he was clear, cogent, and truculent. A totally different young man. He moved to the table and took a seat. "You've been assigned a teacher, and your program starts soon," he said.

"Arts and crafts? Community Service?" Springer offered a one-sided grin, one Alex had seen in his PR photos. Boyish and charming, everyone said. Arrogant, he thought.

"Facing your fear," Alex told him.

"What if I'm not afraid of anything?"

"Everyone who comes here is. That's our working philosophy. You want the short version of how we got there?"

"I know it. After the Killing Times, a new prison system was created, based on the theory that all crime grows from fear and blah blah blah."

"You don't buy it?"

"I don't give a rat's ass." He retreated back into himself, looked bored.

Alex tapped a finger on the table, considering his next move. He wanted to get something about his motive for killing those kids. Just a hint, a place to start. It might help him place what he'd seen in Adept space, which remained elusive. He debated approaches, then settled on direct. At the least, he'd learn something from his reaction.

"You haven't given any motive yet," he noted. A statement, rather than a question.

Springer's grin broadened. "Maybe I killed them because I wanted to meet you."

"I'm guessing no on that. Why won't you talk about it?"

"Because I don't want to," he said, slamming that door shut. "So what's my program?"

"That's up to your Teacher," Alex said.

Springer raised his eyes to Alex's face, establishing empathic contact. Alex allowed it, though he doubted Springer knew what he was doing. In a few ticks of time, Springer shivered, and went back to his grin. "You're giving me to *her*? Not scared I'll move in on your territory? Pretty dicey, if you ask me."

Alex avoided startling. Apparently, he picked out not only who his teacher was, but also her relationship to Alex. Untaught, but highly skilled. Much more than he realized.

"I didn't ask you," he said pointedly. "And don't kid yourself. She's the best Teacher in the system. If you work against her, you may or may not live to regret it." He hesitated, then added, "I'll be seeing you now and then, but I'll be away for a few days. On the home planet."

A tremor moved over him. "Looking up my sordid past?"

Alex didn't try to run from this insight. "That's right. I'll talk to your foster parents. The survivors of your concert."

"Don't stay away too long. I'll be guarding your family jewels."

"No you won't," Alex said decisively. "That's my job."

Springer laughed softly, and began to rock back and forth in his chair. Alex saw the contortion of his features that indicated pain, saw him disappear into himself as he began muttering, twisting his twitching hands.

Twitching hands. A bit of the Adept, Jaguar said. As before, what happened with Springer triggered something in him, and his own hand began the same rhythmic dance. He felt the opening of time that was the greater portion of his own arts. Something important here. Connection beyond his ken. In this white room, the lines of their future were joined.

Alex steeled himself for the journey. Adept space was never easy to bear, and he'd worked hard to grow into the discipline, but this was beyond him. Two Adepts in one room, all their combined possible futures dancing in and around them. And in this, too, Springer was strong but unskilled. He wasn't reading what Alex saw because he didn't know how, and his own visions poured from him with no control, a tidal wave rushing out to overwhelm the dancing play of Alex's art. Time coursed through them both, and Alex worked to stay within its demands.

First, a cityscape. Tall steel buildings with black windows glinting in the sun. He stood in front of them and felt his own despair, waiting for him in some future day. The image shimmered and dissolved, and he stood on a mesa in the canyon lands of New Mexico. Creatures moved toward him. A mule deer. A lizard. A coyote. A wolf.

Were there wolves in New Mexico? He focused on it, saw that it ran with the coyote. Then, a woman appeared. Jaguar, standing between coyote and wolf. Both animals tensed to spring, with very different goals in mind. Coyote moved first, lunging at a graceful female throat. Alex took in breath, switched his attention to what Springer was perceiving. It was no better.

There, he saw Springer's face bloodied, saw him point a gun at Jaguar's face. Alex made his hand into a fist, closed contact abruptly and thoroughly.

"No," he said, louder than he meant to.

Both visions dissipated and once again he sat in the testing room, his heart beating too hard, beads of sweat on his forehead. Springer, still caught within Adept space, muttered at him.

"Not looking good, is it?" he said.

"I'll manage it," Alex said crisply.

"That's what you think," Springer replied. He sank back into his own internal world, head bent low over the table, eyes closed.

* * * *

Paul Dinardo, in his Planetoid office, greeted his guest with all the respect due to him. Ron Schulman gave quite a bit of money to their programs, and a visit from him was an unexpected and important event.

"Your shuttle ride was okay? No trouble?"

"I took my own shuttle," Ron said. "No trouble at all. Very pleasant, in fact."

"Glad to hear it. Can I get you coffee, or water, or maybe a drink?"

Ron put himself in a chair, invited his daughter to do the same. "No, thanks. I'm fine."

"Then tell me what we can do for you today."

He offered Paul his well-known, charming half smile. It was boyish, honest and friendly without belying the strength behind it. It made him look younger than his sixty-some years. "Let's talk about what I can do for you, first," he said. "I want to increase the endowment for post-rehab programs. It's been at stasis for five years, and I'm guessing demands have increased in the meantime."

"They always do," Paul said demurely.

"Of course. I'll want to draw up some paperwork with your legal folks. Make sure the money's there in perpetuity. None of us are getting any younger, are we?"

"That's very generous. I'll arrange a meeting tomorrow—I mean, if you're staying over."

"I'm staying longer than that," Ron said. "I'll be here until Springer Todd's case is done."

Paul narrowly avoided gulping. That was even more unexpected, and difficult in so many ways. Nobody liked home-planet involvement in Planetoid cases, for one thing. For another, Paul already knew Alex had put Addams on this case, and he'd prefer to keep her far, far away from Ron Schulman.

"You got—uh—clearance for a longer stay?"

"I figured you could take care of that for me," Ron said mildly. "And naturally, I'm interested, given my relationship with Springer."

"Naturally," Paul agreed.

"You've got Alex Dzarny in charge of it," Ron said. "I've heard good things about him."

Technically, that was classified information, not something Ron was supposed to know, but Paul let that pass. Instead he agreed, with enthusiasm. "He's great. His zone has the highest success rates, lowest recidivism stats. Springer's in good hands, Mr. Schulman."

"Call me Ron. Has he been assigned to a Teacher yet? I know that's your protocol, and if you can tell me who he's got, I'd appreciate it."

"Generally we keep that to ourselves. Not the kind of thing we want the media in on."

"Of course. But I'm sure you make exceptions, when you know you can trust someone."

"Sure," Paul said, and tried an evasive maneuver. "I don't have the information in front of me—didn't realize it'd be needed. But I can get it for you, if you don't mind waiting."

"As I said, we're here for the long haul. You can let me know. I'll want to talk with whoever you assign. I can offer some good insights."

Paul hoped his face didn't look as bloodless as it felt. The idea of Ron Schulman speaking with Jaguar was terrifying. "I'll check into that, too," he offered.

"Great. In the meantime, maybe I can talk with Supervisor Dzarny?"

"If he was here, you could. He had to go to the home planet for a few days."

"Good thing I planned on a long stay," he said cheerfully. "Another thing—Springer had a counselor on the home planet. I can bring him here—a support person, you understand."

"That's—very good of you. Of course, I'll have to clear it with Alex."

"Aren't you his boss?"

Paul shook his head. "That's not how we work. Strict hierarchy, micromanaging—it's not effective here. Our idea is hire the best, and let them do what they do best."

"Wise practice," Ron agreed. "By all means, clear it with him. And as soon as he's back, you can arrange that meeting with him."

Ron stood to leave. His daughter, who had said nothing throughout, stood with him. Ron took her arm, smiled at Paul. "Know anything my daughter can do while she's here, besides hang around with the old man?"

"There's some fine restaurants and clubs," Paul said. He smelled an agenda, and waited for it to unfold. Soon enough it did so.

"I was thinking maybe there's some good men working for you. How about this Dzarny? Is he...available?"

Paul thought about how incredibly unavailable Alex was. He tried out a smile and it seemed to work. "Ha," he laughed cordially. "Ha ha. Alex is a great guy, but he's pretty much married to his work," he said with all honesty.

"Is he? But she's used to that. After all, she grew up with me."

"Ha," Paul repeated. "Ha ha."

Ron flashed him one more charming smile. "We'll very much look forward to meeting him."

"I'm sure," Paul agreed, "it'll just be a blast."

CHAPTER FOUR

Jaguar, perched on the arm of her couch, took the moments before her prisoner woke to examine him.

It wasn't the first time she'd had an unconscious killer on her couch. Her cases often required a program that brought her in close contact with a prisoner. She'd worked with bums and no-name bastards as frequently as she did with high profile cases like Springer Todd, but Alex generally threw the most difficult assignments her way. The worst of the worst. Not that she minded. She liked the challenge. And for the most part, she knew she could meet it.

With Springer, her first conclusion was that he was much more attractive in motion than at rest. In performance he had the look of a coyote crossed with a Satyr. Something sexual and mischievous, passionate and powerful, in his aspect. Lying on her couch, his long legs and arms stretched out and his wildly curling honey hair sprawled over his eyes, he had the look of roadkill, fragile and probably fetid. An animal whose limbs were about to come apart, whose belly was about to explode.

She ran her hand lightly over his energy field, where she picked up on the same random static bursts that showed in his testing report. His energy was also like roadkill, all over the place. She moved her hand closer, not yet entering his thoughts or feelings. She had some work to do before she went deeper. Alex, the Adept, said it could be rough, and she trusted him. Besides, the crime Springer committed, her reading of his full report, made her agree.

One reason it did so was his relationship with Ron Schulman. Of course it was the ultimate lottery, to be chosen by Schulman. Most artists would kill for that kind of opportunity. But Springer, even after being rejected by a few adoptive parents and tossed through the foster care system, had waffled. He left Schulman, then went back, and never said why about either.

Going back got him rich and famous, and put his music in front of millions of people who might not have heard it otherwise. A deal with the devil, Jaguar thought, but she was not averse to demons, if they worked for you. She'd made a few deals of her own that worked out just fine. But something went wrong, since he'd killed people and ended up on her couch. She'd have to find out if that had anything to do with Schulman. No. Not if. What. Everything in her said there was a connection. And regardless of what he'd done, it was her job to make sure he became someone who'd never kill again.

Her soft empathic touch, just below the surface of his thoughts, revealed only more random energy. She frowned, explored a little more to make sure she had that right. Energy should grow more consolidated under the surface. He might have an inverted energy field. She hoped not. They were hell to deal with.

Then again, performers kept most of their energy up front, reserving the center for peace and quiet. It could be just that. Yet another complication to explore at a later date. She withdrew her hand, stared down at him.

She had no idea how he'd wake up. During testing he'd danced between incoherent raving and very lucid responses to all questions asked. Not only lucid, but cogent and cool, the kind of response you'd expect from a sociopath, though he didn't test positive for that.

She was already pretty sure he was dealing badly with involuntary empathic skills. He'd go into his gifts, and because he'd never been taught containment they'd overwhelm him, toss him around, making him appear insane. When he crawled back out, he'd try to feel as little as possible, show as little emotion as possible. If that was all she had to deal with, it would be pretty easy, but there was also the Thanatos drive Alex mentioned, another layer of complexity.

None of this daunted her. "You're an onion," she murmured. "And I'm going to peel you." She flexed her hands. Briefly, testing his responses, she spoke into his thoughts.

Wake up, she said.

Immediately he stirred, woke, and stared at her. Well then, she thought. He's open. So am I. Open for business.

He stretched, sat up on the couch and took a long look around. "Nice place," he said. "I like the rocking chair." He twisted his neck this way and that, sniffed the air. "Mint?" he asked.

She nodded. Apparently he was in a lucid phase. "You know where you are?"

"I know I'm out of that fucking white room." He rubbed at his wrists and elbows, as if his complaint of the testing routine resided in those joints.

"The testers are through with you for now," she said. She swung her leg down, stood in front of him, brushed her long hair back over her shoulder and held out her hand. "I'm Jaguar Addams. You're Springer Todd, and you're my prisoner."

Springer took her hand and caressed her palm lightly with his thumb. "Not a bad gig so far," he said, his voice low and gentle, with the hint of sandpaper that made his singing so distinct.

She slapped at him lightly. "Depends how you treat your audience this time," she said. "Speaking of that, why'd you kill those kids?"

He startled, then quickly pulled it together. "Bad hair night?" he suggested.

Interesting, she thought. Not denial. Just a very large No Trespassing sign. "We all have them," she said lightly. "Want a cigarette?"

She took a pack from the pocket of her black silk pants, tapped it lightly against the end table and let two fall out. He took one, and she pulled out a lighter, lit them both.

"I'm in the ten percent of the population who doesn't get addicted to nicotine," she noted. "You?"

"Maybe. It's not my favorite drug."

"What is?"

He scratched at his neck, sat up and blew smoke out. "I had a few fine nights with X," he said. "And there was this shaman in Mexico who walked me through a mushroom thing I enjoyed."

She breathed in smoke, puffed some rings into the air. The right mushrooms, used with the right teachers, should teach an empath a lot. "Learn anything interesting?" she asked.

"Not really," he said. "The guy said a lot of hocus pocus, but I'm not into that."

"Don't believe in visions?"

He shifted, and the small muscles in his throat worked. Jaguar interpreted. Yes, he did believe, but didn't want to. Yes, he'd learned something, and wouldn't name it. Not even to himself. He leaned back and relaxed his body into the contours of her couch. No matter what was going on with him psychologically, physically he was more relaxed than most prisoners. Either he wanted to be here, or he no longer cared where he was—or he was arrogant enough to think he'd beat the system. But arrogance was as good a cover as any for despair. Something else she'd have to figure out.

"Here's another question for you," she said. "Why'd you leave Schulman's protection?"

Another startle reflex. "I didn't," he said.

"Yeah you did. After Julliard. When you started your band."

"Oh. That. I wanted to be on my own for a while."

"How come? Old Ronnie didn't approve of an empath adoptee?"

His eyelids closed and opened slowly, like a wary cat. "I don't know what you're talking about," he said.

"Liar," she said amicably. "Then tell me how come you went back to him?"

"That's easy. I wanted the money."

She turned her cigarette over in her hands, took a drag. "More liar," she said. "On all counts."

He offered no protest. "Maybe I don't want you digging in my business," he said.

"Too bad," she said. "That's my job, and I'm very good at it. I'll get answers, sooner or later. And don't bother running. You've got an implant in your leg that'll paralyze you if you try, and I've got a few tricks of my own to keep you in line. I also have a 98 percent success rate with my prisoners, and the others weren't failures. They're just dead. With me so far?"

"Sure," he said. "You'd just as soon kill me as fix me."

"Is that what you're hoping for?"

"Not really. But I heard it's an option here. Especially with guys like me."

"Like you?"

"The tough ones."

She laughed. "You're not that tough."

"You got someone worse?"

"Sure. Pedophiles."

"What's so tough about them?"

"They lie more convincingly than you, because they're lying to themselves," she said. "You're not lying to yourself. Just running like hell."

"That's easier?"

"Sure, because I run faster. I'll catch you." She paused, scanned him. "But you don't have a clue how, do you?"

"Nope," he agreed. He showed her a grin, one she recognized from the security camera footage of the moment before he released gunfire over his audience. "You don't know what I'll do either, do you?"

"Not yet," she admitted. "We'll both be winging it for awhile."

"What do we do while we're waiting to see what we do?" he asked.

"I'm putting you to work, at what you do best."

"Kill people?"

She tamped her cigarette out in an ashtray, grasped his lower jaw in her hand. "Not at all," she said, running her thumb against his lips. "For me, you're going to sing."

* * * *

Alex sat in his seat on the shuttle, headed toward the home planet.

He was thinking of the way voice can shape a body, and Jaguar. Jaguar and her voice that held and shaped the space she sang in whenever she sang. Jaguar, and the way the shape of her body felt as he smoothed his hand over it. Jaguar and her voice, which might work Springer's case to something like a conclusion of his song.

He'd read her preliminary program notes on the assignment, and knew he'd chosen well. No other Teacher would have created the program she had. She would take Springer out with the band *Moon Illusion*. Gerry Wallach, lead guitarist of the group, once a prisoner of Jaguar's and now a team member who assisted with assignments, had booked gigs in bars and halls around the Planetoid. That kind of program was always more risky than keeping a prisoner in a more contained facility, but he didn't doubt she'd manage it. Springer would be on Jaguar's leash electronically and empathically. She said she anticipated at least four weeks of initial work before she knew more. She was going slow with him.

Before he got on the shuttle, he called her to discuss particulars. He'd set up a home base for her at Normal house 23 when they were in zone 12, and booked her in the more secure hotels when they weren't. She'd have Rachel and Gerry staying with her, and extra team members in and out. He'd also gotten extra security for the gigs. Scott White, his assistant, would be there for most of them, and take care of other security tasks as needed.

"You're giving me Scott?" Jaguar asked, pleased. He was a former Navy SEAL, a skilled telepath who was coming up fast as an empath. He'd been very useful to them on a recent case, and she trusted him.

"I thought you'd like that," Alex said.

"I do. How'd you get it past the pencil pushers?"

"Ron Schulman's interest greases many wheels."

She groaned. "Deal with the devil."

"The devil," he noted, "pays."

"And collects on all debts. Anything else I should know?"

"Check your prisoner for weapons, Dr. Addams. We don't want to ruin *Moon Illusion's* career."

"Gerry will be on him every step," she'd replied.

He believed it. Gerry, who was big and crazy enough to be a little frightening, came to the Planetoids on charges of drug running. He knew his way around a tough scenario. "Good. When's your first gig?"

"Tonight. The Crab Nebula. You coming?"

"No. I'll be on the home planet for a few days. We'll be out of contact while I'm away." He waited for her response. Since they'd become lovers they had the consolation of empathic communication, even when they were apart. Each of them had enough esper to translate thought into the brief sensation of touch, and they'd shared enough passion that even small touch called back the pleasure of their time together. But now he was saying no to it, and he wasn't even sure why. Something about those threads joining in time. Something.

"What's up, Alex?" she asked.

"Just sniffing around about this and that."

"More shit you can't say," she noted. "By any chance are you curious about why Springer never got adopted?"

He silently admired her perspicacity, and responded mildly. "A little. You?"

"More than a little," she said. "A healthy white male baby boy, and every adoption somehow went wrong? Then he wins the abandoned child lottery and ends up with Schulman. All that bad and all that good. Either he has a really interesting karma, or something's up. So why are you going, instead of sending a researcher?"

"The researchers already went, and they didn't find anything, so I'm thinking they didn't ask the right questions."

"Okay. Will you tell me what you find out?"

"Yes," he said. "On that, I will."

"And whatever else you're looking for?"

He said nothing. Avoidance was often the better part of valor with Jaguar. Besides, he wasn't sure what else he was looking for. Not yet, anyway.

She made a tsk sound. "Just so you know, whatever it is, I'll be looking for it my own way."

"Of course you will," he answered.

"Good. Also, I don't like this. Not at all."

"Me neither, Jaguar," he replied, and signed off.

He turned his thoughts back to Springer. He'd already gone through records from his earliest years, and learned that Springer was abandoned at a hospital by an unnamed birth mother. As Jaguar pointed out, he was prime for adoption, but it all went quickly strange.

His first set of adoptive parents backed out at the last minute. They claimed it was a personal decision, a change of heart, but that was unusual for those who went through the trouble of wending their way through the adoption process. Springer was placed in foster care, and his foster parents considered adopting him, but then asked that he be placed in another home. They had a change of circumstances, they said, and could no longer be part of the foster system.

He stayed in foster care with another couple until he was seven, and they stepped up for adoption until the foster father was killed by a mugger, and his wife turned him back to the state. Thus, Springer remained in the permanently swinging door of foster care until he was eleven, by which time he'd already started getting in trouble—fights, mailbox bashing, absenteeism. Nothing major, but enough to show he was an angry young man who might someday do worse. Fortunately, he came to the attention of Ron Schulman before it was too late.

Alex let all this sift through his fingers like stars, which might fall anywhere. He asked himself if it connected to what he'd seen in Adept space, and followed the energy where it led.

Back to the beginning. Failed adoptions and a dead person were fine, but the most interesting beginning was with his biological parents, who remained unnamed. Alex knew someone who might help him with that. He'd start there.

CHAPTER FIVE

"Smell this," Gerry whispered, raising his arm so Jaguar was staring directly into the fuzzy region of his armpit.

She grabbed his earlobe between two fingers and pulled it to her. "I decline your gracious invitation, Gerry," she said, then pushed him away.

She turned from him and began poking at buttons on the synthesizer, setting it up for the opening of the second set. The first set went well, and it was a good crowd. Thick, attentive, and willing to cram themselves in front of the stage to dance. Good energy.

This was their second gig, and so far, so good. They only let Springer sing back-up, do some guitar work, while Jaguar kept an eye on him. He kept his energy low and tight, directed at the music rather than the audience. Nobody recognized him, either. They made him tie his hair back and wear contact lenses that turned his eyes a muddy brown. Tonight, in their gig at the Silver Bay, near the shores of the Lake Ontario Replica, they kept him in this disguise, but let him sing one solo in the first set. He remained low key, laying back into the music rather than reaching out to the people who crowded the stage.

Jaguar wondered if he was hustling them, or if full out performance sent him back to the moment he'd snapped, something he wanted to avoid. Either way, for now they had no problem, except for Gerry's sweat.

As Springer sat on a stool upstage, his fingers working the strings of an old acoustic guitar, Gerry drew his bulky frame toward her again, pursuing his topic in frantic whispers. "No, Jag—I mean it. My sweat stinks."

Jaguar rolled her eyes. He was one of the few people who could call her Jag without taking a punch. She figured her full name was sometimes too many syllables for him. "Welcome to the human race, Gerry. Are we starting with the vampire song?"

"Yeah. I think. Don't you? Either that or Bloody Rag."

"Vampire," she said. "Definitely. I'm in the mood for it."

"Okay," he said, then leaned over and whispered again. "Listen. Really. About Springer. I know he's good, but something's going on with him. I mean, my sweat don't smell like this unless something's making it, and the only thing around is him."

Jaguar looked up at his bulging eyes, the wispy, light blonde hair that stood out around his head. "You mean that, don't you?"

He blinked in surprise. "Why else would I say it?"

She resisted the urge to explain the many reasons why any human tells conscious or unconscious lies, and instead replied, "So why do you think Springer makes your sweat stink?"

"I don't know. Maybe he's a meat eater?"

"Gerry, he kills teenagers. Why wouldn't he eat meat?"

"Then something else. Drugs, probably. That's what I'm thinking."

Gerry came to Planetoid Three on multiple counts of drug running, the last of which led to a dead undercover cop. In that realm, he knew what he was talking about.

"What kind of drugs?" she asked.

"Not something I ever used. I know most of the smells."

"But you think something?"

"Yeah," he said. "And, y'know, I don't want this one messed up."

"Really? Why not?"

Gerry rolled his shoulders around, and ground out some words. "Because he's good. I mean, *really* good. And I like him. What he does—he means it."

Jaguar wasn't surprised. They had a lot in common—troubled pasts, dancing brains, and difficulty articulating what they felt. The brain of the musician often experienced a great deal of emotion, and lacked words to put around it. But Springer went through all the usual drug testing routines and came up clean, though clearly he'd used them in the past.

"What if he's in withdrawal. If his body chemistry's changing because he's not taking drugs? Could that be it?" she asked.

"Maybe?" Gerry asked.

More complications to consider, and she'd consider them. Gerry had good instincts, even when he was functionally nonverbal. "Okay," she said. "I hear your sweat, and I honor it. Now can I—" she tapped the synth, and he shrugged, went to help Pinkie with percussion.

When Jaguar felt a hand on her shoulder shortly afterward, she spoke impatiently. "I *heard* you, Gerry."

"But did you hear the night lady sing?" a low and raspy voice said.

She raised her head, turned it slightly. Springer. "How's it going?" she asked.

"I'm good. Did you say we're starting with the vampire song? I back that up, don't I?"

"Yup. Just a low E thump thump. Remember?"

He leaned over and picked up a the guitar leaning against the synth, palmed the monitor set-up, and pulled at the right chord. "Like that?" he asked.

"That's it."

"And how about if I do this?" He rang a few changes, She tried the upper line to them with her voice, liked them, nodded.

"Nice," he agreed. "Keep singing."

She did, because it felt good, the lines pouring out of her throat easy and smooth. At the same time, she saw how he listened to everything—the synth, her voice, the riffs he was picking out. Their percussionist, Pinkie Horton, lover to Rachel, stopped paying attention to Gerry and grabbed an African drum, began beating out a rhythm. Then, Springer started to sing.

There's a hole in my soul and it goes real deep. There's a hole in my soul won't hold no air. It's a hole in my soul to never.

Not the vampire song. She knew this one. *Bury me Deep.* The song he sang in court. The lyrics reverberated within her as well as in the room. He was singing now, really singing, with rising passion, his voice a rough breath of emptiness. The sound of it called the audience back to their seats, all of them caught in the air that changed around him as he sang.

Jaguar kept the sweet synth progression going and sang with him, her voice a high and careless whirling breeze above his. He moved to the audience, energy pouring from him to them.

There's a hole in my soul and the raven drinks there. A hole in my soul for swimming. Swimming. Swimming.

The audience stood, swaying with the music. When did he hook his voice up to sound? Or did Gerry take care of that? He was making love to his bass, away from them. As she sang, Springer circled her like a wild dog, a coyote, carving spirals around her. He was outside himself, his entire being acting without his volition. It ran strong in him, the gift he carried.

Swimming. Swimming. Swimming, he sang, and she was swimming with him, in a pool of deep, dark nothing. He would pull her down into it, if she let him. Pull her down until she drowned in him.

She wouldn't let him. She touched him empathically, but kept her touch light, kept part of herself firmly in the world. A fine balancing act, to hold the inside and the outside of someone at the same time, but she could manage it. And it was worth the effort.

Within him, she found only dark nothing, but outside him, the air changed shape. She recognized the distinct feel of a psi capacity. Harmonic empathizer? Yes and no. Something else was mixed in. More than one thing. A complex conglomerate of gifts. A complex case. A complex young man, who killed people.

She resisted the change he created by looking beyond it, out to the audience, wanting to know what they perceived. As she did so she saw they were altered, their bodies shifting like sand in hot wind, bodies shaped by the air he moved with his music. Some of them were snake, and some were hawk. Some were trees and some were rivers. Rachel, in the audience tonight, was shifted into the aspect of a swallow piercing the early evening sky.

"Okay, then," she murmured, and brought her attention back to Springer. He remained himself, outside of them, but he was the source of all they perceived. No wonder they love him, she thought. A magus of a different kind, letting them speak with their animal selves, most of them for the first time. And as far as she could tell, he had no idea that's what he was doing.

She tried something Alex would have scolded her for—a risky empathic move, but one she could manage. She reached for contact not with Springer's experience, but with the essential energy of the psi capacity he was using. She could not yet name his gift, and she needed to.

She couldn't get there. Instead, all she got was his frantic fear, and a desperate searching. He was creating this, but had no idea how or why, and it terrified him. It wasn't something he did so much as something that happened to him. What he sought in his fear was comfort, a safe place to rest in, and he seemed to think he'd find it out there, in his audience. Disparate parts of him ran like wild dogs through a war torn village, hungry and afraid.

And then the search stopped. There.

She looked where he looked, and saw a woman, mid-thirties or perhaps a little older, with a mass of curling red hair, a tall and generous frame, the stature of a queen and haunted, hunted eyes. How long had she been here? Jaguar had the uncanny sense she'd only appeared through Springer's will. That if he hadn't seen her she would remain invisible, camouflaged by her own will not to be seen.

But when Springer looked at her she stared back, with longing and immense love. Jaguar let herself linger in this feeling, curious about it. Groupie? Former lover? Wannabe? She was about to explore her empathically when all connection was sharply severed as Springer whirled to her.

"Pick it up," he snapped, and the band and went into a stomping version of *Night Lady,* one of his biggest hits.

He grabbed Jaguar by the wrist, pulled her away from the keyboard and dragged her to him, his grip so tight that later she would find bruises.

Right now, she was too filled with the untamed pleasure of music to notice anything like injury. She fell into his music, singing with him, his strange eyes holding her to his demands for harmonies, for dance.

The song played itself out in bliss and sound, with no room for any other concern. When she next looked toward the audience, she saw no sign of a woman with great stature and red hair.

CHAPTER SIX

Home Planet, New Manhattan

Alex's first stop on the home planet was the 23rd floor of a tall building in the park district of New Manhattan. The stones of the building were white, as was the lobby, and most of the rooms beyond. There were quite a few offices here, some operating as technical forensic consultants, some as medical concerns. He took the elevator up to Hanson Labs, and when he opened the glass door to yet another white room his friend, Mike Pierson, was waiting for him in the reception area. He smiled, greeted him.

"All this secrecy," he said, his eyes glinting with anticipation. "What do you have for me?"

"Nothing that interesting," Alex said. "Just some DNA comparison."

Mike's face showed disappointment. "You could do that through your office."

"I could, but I didn't want to," Alex said.

"Any reason why not? I mean, anything I need to know?"

Alex shook his head. He wasn't sure himself. Just a sense that this was information he wanted to control, outside the boundaries of Planetoid protocol. He handed a vial to Mike. "Tell me who the biological parents are. Any way you can find it." He knew Mike wasn't above hacking to get information he wasn't supposed to have. That almost got him arrested at one point in his varied career, but Alex had stepped up and made use of his skills in better ways. He wasn't as good as Rachel, but he was damn close.

"Okay," Mike said. "Good to see you, and I'll be in touch."

Alex left him to it, and emerged back onto the streets of New Manhattan, a place he and Jaguar found disturbing. They were both in the City during the Killing Times, she as a teenager, and he as a young man, though Jaguar had it much worse than he did. She'd seen her family killed, was raped by the man who killed them, and ended up living on the streets for almost a year before she made her way to her people in New Mexico. He'd been here as soldier when the Army was finally sent in, trying to save those he could, working in shelters to care for those he managed to drag in off the streets.

He was nineteen, and it was his first trip to the east after a life spent on a horse ranch in Montana, where the most brutal action he saw was when an old or injured horse had to be put down. It was the first time he'd been in a big city, the first time he'd seen murder, the first time he'd saved a life, the first time he'd killed someone.

He'd also met his first mentor in the empathic arts here, an old Russian woman named Sophia, whom he rescued from the streets, and who taught him how to manage his own arts—particularly his art as an Adept. And he'd had his first love affairs here, all very different from the adolescent gropings in the barn at the Montana ranch. There was Anna, fresh from the German countryside, whom he'd found handing out food to those who roamed the streets. When he asked what she was doing here, she said simply, "They need me."

He had other work to do, so he left her, but later that afternoon he found her weeping over the body of an old woman, in front of the broken window of Tiffany's. Her face was fierce with rage.

"What did we do? We did nothing wrong," she sobbed.

He'd taken her by the arm and led her to the nearest shelter, where he planned to drop her off. But she clutched at him in anger and grief, so he stayed. In the night, she tore at his clothes, ran her hands over his body as if it would save her. In the morning she was gone, and he'd never seen her again. He had no idea if she'd survived.

His other couplings were brief moments of light in a time of great darkness. There was Plain Jane, who had the look of someone either escaping or running toward death. She was physically strong, beautiful and compelling, but her eyes were a study in fragility. They met when he was bringing survivors into a shelter where she was volunteering. She assisted him with a boy who'd been pretty cut up, the two of them working hard to staunch his wounds while they waited for the medics to arrive.

The boy survived, and when he was taken away for further care, he thanked her, put out his bloody hand to shake hers, then pulled back. She'd held her hands up. "Just as bad," she said. They shook hands, and in that small meeting of flesh, what would happen next was clear to Alex.

"Call me Jane," she said.

Something in the way she said it aroused his suspicion. "That's your name?" he asked.

"It's who I want to be. Just—plain Jane."

He called her that teasingly, and in response she called him Farm Boy, after he told her about growing up on a horse ranch. Their affair was intense, but it lasted only a week. One night as they were lying naked together in the back room of the shelter, he told her he was an empath, an Adept. She hadn't said a word. She got up and left, and he never saw her again.

He was just beginning to name his arts, and her rejection came as a shock. But he was young, and had a fundamentally healthy self-esteem so he'd recovered. He even had another affair in the City, with a woman named Phoebe who was looking for her sister, but he never again mentioned the empathic arts to the women he slept with. Not until Jaguar came along.

Now, as he walked down the clean and bloodless streets, he wondered where those women were. Did Anna return to her family farm? Had Phoebe ever found her sister? And Plain Jane—did she ever get over her fear of empaths, or whatever drove her to risk her life on the streets of Manhattan during the Killing Times? He hoped they'd all moved on to better things, as he had. He hoped they felt as he did—that their time together was a reminder of joy within despair. Then he moved on to consider his current job, which was all about Springer Todd.

This was where Springer started his life, born into the ashes of the City's death and rebirth. He was second generation from the Killing Times, Gen T. His first set of foster parents still lived in SoHo, his second and third in Queens and Manhattan. Alex had set up appointments to meet with all of them. He was closest to SoHo, so he started there.

Their building was in a good part of the city, and when he got to it, he was surprised to see only one name on the door. He looked up. Three floors. They owned all of it?

"Rich folk," he mused. And yet, during the time they fostered Springer they were both public school teachers. Educators were great, but they weren't rich folk.

He pressed the buzzer and waited. When a bright female voice came over the intercom he gave his name and was invited inside. Already he was surprised to hear children's voices in the background. He was more surprised when he entered the cool space of a well-appointed hall, and a woman greeted him with three children clustered around her, ranging in age from 12 to maybe two years old.

He stuck his hand out. "Alex Dzarny," he said. "Good to meet you."

"Greta Bergen," she answered, took his offered hand, shook it. "These are my kids—Danny, Beatrice, Greg."

They eyed him with the particular stares kids have for strange grown-ups, the littlest one giggling wildly for no apparent reason.

"Danny, you and Bea take Greg upstairs, okay? I have to talk with Mr. Dzarny," Greta told them.

"Can we watch a movie?" Danny asked.

"Which one?" she asked.

"Haunted Castle?" he tried.

She shook her head. "How about Ben's Journey?"

He sighed, and relented. "Okay," he said. "Fine."

They skittered away, already arguing about who would make popcorn.

"Well," Greta said to Alex. "Come into the kitchen. You want coffee?"

"That would be lovely," Alex said, and they proceeded down the hall.

The kitchen was like the rest of the house—clean, fresh looking, everything in it up to date. "You must have quite a time with your kids," Alex noted, as she saw to the business of coffee. "I was an only child, and my mother could never keep her kitchen this clean."

"Oh, I have help," she said brightly. "I could never do this on my own. Cream and sugar?"

She moved toward him with a cup, gestured for him to take a seat at the island in the center of the room, and he did so. "Black is fine," he said, and caught the scent of rich, smooth coffee. Nothing cheap there, either.

She brought her own cup to the counter and sat across from him, settling down. "Now, how can I help you? You said it's about Springer?"

"It is. You probably know he's on the Planetoids."

She tsked mildly. "Terrible thing. Danny—my oldest—he actually tried to talk me into letting him go see that concert. Of course, I told him he's too young. Thank God, right?"

"Yes. He's—adopted?"

"They all are. We couldn't have our own. But they're ours now, so it's all good."

"I'm glad. But you didn't want Springer," he said, keeping his voice neutral, nonjudgmental.

She bridled anyway. "There was something—*wrong* about him. We saw it right away. He wouldn't look at me. Wouldn't look at Pete. We thought maybe they lied to us and he was born with some defect. I guess that makes sense now, right?"

Everything she said might make sense, but he smelled a lie. Partly that came from the nervous gestures she used. Partly it came from her house, the expensive coffee, the help, and the fact that their adopted children all went to private schools.

"It sure does," he said. He showed her a smile. "You probably noticed because you're both teachers. Are you still teaching?"

"The kids are my job. They're enough, right? My husband—he went back to school, and now he teaches at Columbia."

"Then you had some good fortune after Springer left you."

She lowered her head, ran a hand across an eyebrow. Shame, he thought. There it was.

"I had an uncle who left me some money," she said. "Of course, it all goes to the kids."

"Of course," he said. He took a stab in the dark. "The money Mr. Schulman sends must come in handy."

Her face flushed a deep red. "How do you know about that?" she demanded.

"We know a lot on the Planetoid," he lied. He'd seen no reports of money from Ron Schulman.

"Well," she said, still truculent, "we wouldn't have done it, but Mr. Schulman said he had a better place for him, and he'd compensate us for our trouble. It costs a lot to try and adopt—lawyers and psychologists and everything. There's nothing wrong with it, is there? I mean, we were trying to do right by the kid."

"It never occurred to you that he was lying?"

She showed genuine surprise. "Of course not. Why would he?"

Alex gave her a tight smile. "No reason I can think of," he said. "But we have to ask about everything. Did you keep track of Springer?"

"We signed papers, saying we wouldn't. Also saying we'd never talk about it." She leaned forward, and now she was afraid. "You're not going to tell him about this, are you?"

"No," he said. "Of course not."

* * * *

At the next set of adoptive parents Alex found more of the same. This couple also started out middle class, she a secretary and he in construction, then came into money after they gave Springer up. When he mentioned Ron Schulman they quickly shut him down. They weren't the kind to talk.

His third stop was a penthouse on Fifth Avenue, where Ariel Dondre still lived alone, and quite elegantly. She invited him in, offered him a martini instead of coffee, and curled herself on a white silk couch while they talked. Her nails were manicured, her hair expensively highlighted, and her clothes were Sax.

Alex went through his spiel again, how he was looking into Springer's background as part of his program on the Planetoid and so on.

"What can I tell you?" she said. "He was lively, you know? Full of energy and ideas. We really liked him. A lot. We started adoption proceedings, but then Charlie—well, he was killed. A drug addict mugged and shot him. You know about that?"

"I do, and I was sorry to hear it," Alex said. "And after that? You felt you couldn't keep Springer?"

"I tried. I was muddling along, and it was pretty tough. One income, no family to help, and Springer was a handful. Then this man came to see me."

"Ron Schulman?" Alex asked.

She blinked at him. "Who?" she asked.

Her surprise was authentic. "I've heard he helped some of the other people involved. He didn't contact you?"

"No. It was a lawyer. Guy named Gary Halifax. He was with a foundation, he said. One that helped women in my position. He had these other people ready to adopt Springer—a really good home. I talked to them, saw the house. It was better than what I had to give, so I let him go."

She shook her head sadly. "I never would have, if Charlie didn't die. We actually had an offer from someone before we started the adoption thing, and we said no. And the awful thing is, about a year after he left, all this money came through—something from the city, because of Charlie. A victim's compensation fund. Now I'm loaded. If I'd known, I would've hung on."

Again, authentic. She'd acted for the good of the child, under duress. "You never adopted any others?"

"I couldn't face it." She leaned close. "What Springer did—is it because I let him go?"

"No," he said. "It's not your fault."

Her relief was immense, and honest. "That's good to know. It was so hard. I still see his face, looking at me with those funny eyes."

"Not your fault," he repeated. "What he did had nothing at all to do with you."

* * * *

His next stop was the cop shop, to read over the files of Charlie Dondre, who was mugged and shot dead by Jason Becker for the fifty dollars in his wallet. Becker, a drug addict, was apprehended and arrested quickly. But to Alex's disappointment, he wasn't available for interviewing. His current address was the cemetery. He was also dead.

He was cursing about this quietly when he heard a voice behind him. "Something wrong?" it asked.

Alex twisted around, saw a tall man in uniform, big at the shoulders with arms like tree trunks, standing behind him.

"Someone I want to talk to is dead," he noted.

The man glanced at the file. "Becker," he said. "Pissed me off, too."

That was interesting. "How come?" Alex asked.

"My first collar." He stuck a hand out. "Manny Cruz."

"Alex Dzarny. Planetoid Three."

Manny eyed him with a mingling of respect and suspicion, the usual reaction to someone who worked 'up there.' Alex anticipated questions about his job, but Manny was more interested in his own work. "What's Becker got to do with you?" he asked.

"I thought he might be witness to a crime we're working," Alex answered. "How'd he die?"

"Smash and dash," Manny said. "I went after it, but I never caught the bastard."

The story, as Manny told it, was simple enough. Becker was out on bail, waiting for his trial. He crossed a street just outside his apartment and was hit by an oncoming vehicle, which immediately took off. Nobody go the license plate, and the descriptions of the car varied wildly from witness to witness. What they all agreed on was that the driver had pulled out of a parking spot and gunned the motor before he ran him down.

"I kept digging, trying to find out more about the victim," Manny said. "Maybe he had something else going—gambling, loan sharks, something. Then something funny happened."

"Funny?" Alex asked.

"I was out walking the beat, and there's this kid across the street from me, crying. So I step out, going to him, and this car shoots out of nowhere, almost clips me." He held up a hand to forestall any comments. "Which would be nothing, but then I get a phone call—a guy who calls me by my name and says, 'people who work too hard gotta keep their eyes open.'"

"Huh," Alex said. "They mention Jason Becker by any chance?"

"No such luck. Nothing reportable, though I did report it and got laughed at for my trouble. Anyway, I couldn't trace it, and kept at the hit and run for a while, but my heart wasn't really in it anymore, if you know what I mean."

Alex certainly did.

CHAPTER SEVEN

Prison Planetoid Three, Zone 12

After their third gig Jaguar took Springer and the band back to Normal House 23, though the situation seemed anything but normal.

Gerry, Pinkie, and Rachel were all staying tonight. Pinkie wasn't officially on duty, but she wanted to stay with Rachel and Jaguar saw nothing against it. They were all tense, uncertain about what they were experiencing when Springer sang. When they'd seen Springer safely into his room, Rachel grabbed at Jaguar.

"What's he doing?" she demanded. "It has to be him. Some empathic thing?"

Jaguar tilted her head at her. "You were a swallow, I think. Is that what it felt like?"

Rachel ran a hand through her thick, dark hair. "Well, yeah. But, I mean, how?"

"One of his gifts," Jaguar said. "You okay?"

"You tell me. Am I?"

Jaguar lifted a hand, read the space around and within her friend. "You're fine," she said. "It doesn't carry over. It's just part of his act."

"Quite an act."

"Go tuck Pinkie in," Jaguar suggested. "That'll reset your barometer."

Usually that kind of comment made Rachel blush and Jaguar would laugh at her for it, but not this time. Instead, Rachel grimaced. "I don't think so," she said.

When they were on a job, Jaguar didn't pay attention to personal details, but this seemed meaningful. "Trouble in Paradise?" she asked.

"Pinkie got a job offer. With a band on the home planet."

"Oh," Jaguar said. "Hell."

"Yeah. I mean, not that it matters, really. We had other problems."

"Like what?"

"I want kids. She doesn't. Let me not get into it." She walked off toward Pinkie's room anyway. Jaguar bit at her lip. The last thing she needed was a team member with romantic troubles. Complications continued. It was the main theme of this case.

She went to her room, hoisted her foot on the bed to get her stiletto heeled, thigh high boots off. It was one of her favorite singing outfits—leather pants and jacket, long boots, her hair slicked back hard from her face. She had the zipper halfway down when Springer entered the room. She'd deliberately left his door unlocked, hoping he'd show so she could work on him.

"Those must be hell on your feet," he said.

She sat on the bed and stuck her foot out. "Pull," she said, and he did, flinging the boot aside when it came off with a sucking sound. He squatted down and took her foot in his hands, began to massage it gently.

"That's nice," she said.

"Thought it would be," he replied. "Hey—you're quite a singer. I liked what you did for *Night Lady.*"

"Thanks. You're not so bad yourself. Do it again tomorrow?"

He chuckled. "You're the boss."

"Sure," she said, "but you can't really make someone sing unless they want to. You want to."

He shrugged it off. "Give me your hand, I'll massage that, too."

"No. Not the hand."

"Then let me brush your hair."

"No hand. No hair. I know where my power lives."

He squatted back on his heels and looked up at her. "Then where can I touch you? I wouldn't mind having a little fun. You got something against fun?"

"I like my fun," she admitted. "But you're not here for fun. Besides, I prefer men to boys."

"Am I supposed to resent that?" he asked.

"Only if you resent the truth." She leaned forward, rested her chin in the palm of her hand. "Let's try something else," she suggested.

"Like what?"

In her worldview, the opposite of fear wasn't courage. It was love. If she couldn't find his fear, she'd try poking around the other end of the continuum. "Tell me what you love," she said.

He cradled her foot in the palm of his hand. "I love this, sometimes," he said.

"But not all the time."

"There's nothing I love all the time," he said.

"Not even music?"

"I don't love music. It's just—there. Always there."

Something of pain in his words, a sharpness at their edge. She ran a hand over his curling hair, making empathic contact, the warm hum of it spreading around him. Not shadowed, she thought. Something, though. A corollary capacity, stuck in a bad place.

He twisted his face up to hers and held her gaze, making his own contact. She shifted her attention to what he was seeing in her, and got one of the biggest surprises of her life. Her hand stopped moving, and everything in her went still.

Within him she felt not thoughts, but sound. An ocarina, giving short, sharp whistles, like a random bird in a jungle. Joining it, the low call of the conch. Flutelike sounds joined in, all of them moving together to create a sense of place and creature rather than a specific scale. Birds and howler monkeys in a deep rainforest, their conversation laying sound over sound in a progression that was both random and natural. Mayan music, which replicated its environment, honoring and calling to the spirits they followed. Then, a growl, and she tensed. The Jaguar drum—two rasping sticks joined by a string to amplify a drum with a 't' carved in front, a glyph that meant both blood and vital breath. A jaguar drum? How the hell did he know about that?

Against her volition she was pulled into the sound. She was Mertec, her people once part of the Mayan culture, though they'd left it to go walking in the world in different ways. This music was part of her blood and vital breath. Did he know that? Before she could ask, she heard a pulsing, tonal, drum ride over the rest of the sounds. Seven beat, with an eight beat underneath. A swiftly walking sound, focused as a jaguar on the prowl. Then, the drone and melody of a Mayan triple flute, all of it joining to create a song as compelling as any she'd ever known.

She had everything she could do to keep from dancing. Everything she could do to keep her attention on Springer, whose song ran through her on a cellular level, as if he was taking her measure in sound and rhythm. His hands made small motions, lifting and falling. He began to sing, his voice moving within her in the chanting scales of her ancestors.

Shadow land, eye of the deer, white tail of the deer made of moonlight. She takes darkness in her stride, running the earth to morning. And I follow where she goes. Move with her to sunset glow. I follow blood and breath, I follow beyond death, and she stays.

He was reading her skin like sheet music, translating her into song. She'd never experienced anything like it before.

The drums picked up, and Springer's voice moved into howls, sharp calls and laughter rolling through her like water, until the sound crashed down in rain and thunder, with one final growl from the jaguar drum.

When it was done he sat back on his haunches and rocked slowly, unaware of her. Whatever he was doing, it occurred beyond his conscious intent. She smoothed her hand over his head, spoke to him in her native tongue, calling him back to the land of the living. He jerked his head up, blinked at her.

"What did you say?" he asked.

"Nothing important," she answered.

She took her hand off his head. He didn't remember, though she wouldn't be surprised if at some point he wrote this song. He hid the most important aspects of his life deep inside himself. He was an enormously gifted empath with skills she couldn't yet name, and he'd never been taught the discipline he needed to use those skills properly, or learn how to avoid being used by them. Any virtue could turn into its own vice if it was flipped on its back. Springer's case might turn out to be as simple as flipping him over again. She hoped so. She was beginning to see him as a true and passionate artist. Under his fear he might be a true and passionate man. But digging that out of him would take some work.

Already he was back into his customary arrogance, grinning at her. His hand moved up her leg, toward her thigh. She kicked it away from her. "That's how you treat a lady?" she asked.

"Is that what you are?"

"Some days," she said.

"I'll bet that's not what men want from you," he noted.

"What men want from me is that they can't have me. I'd be glad to give you some of that."

"Funny. That's what most people want from me." He breathed in deeply. "You smell of mint. Not perfume. Fresh mint. Why is that?"

"Because I carry it with me."

"Why do you carry it?"

"To block the scent of death."

"Mint? That won't cover it."

"Not physically, but empathically it does. That and sage are the best cleaners in the world. You want to know more about managing empathic gifts, I can teach you."

He ignored her opening, went somewhere else. "Nothing wrong with death," he said. "Too many people afraid of it these days."

Okay, she thought. He found it easier to talk about death than his empathic gifts. "I didn't say death. I said the scent of it. The empathic scent."

He worked on this. "You smell that on me?" he asked. "From all those kids I killed?"

"No. It's not their death. It's yours. We call it Thanatos drive. A will toward death, either your own or someone else's. And just so you know, I won't make it mine."

"Maybe you won't have a choice." He stood, stretched, made another shift. "Why're you called Jaguar?" he asked.

"Because it's my name," she said. "The name my grandfather gave me."

"Like Kanima?" he asked.

That surprised her. The Kanima was a South American creature, a werejaguar who hunted and killed murderers. "How do you know about that?"

"Not sure. Probably someone I met on the world tour. We went to Peru, Chile, lots of great places. Are you Kanima?"

There was a real question in this, and she knew what it was. His way of asking about her empathic skills without asking. Perhaps an opening she could use. "No," she said honestly. "I'm not a shapeshifter, but I'm lots of other things. So are you. Wanna talk about that?"

He didn't answer. Instead he reached down, put a hand to her face. At first his touch was a caress, but quickly his hand pressed into the bones of her jaw. She opened herself to contact and felt death moving in him. Death, like a lover he yearned for. Thanatos drive. Kill or be killed. Kill *to* be killed. Is that why he'd killed those kids? She thought not. Thanatos wasn't primary in him. It was something that happened to him.

"If you want to die, I've got no objections," she said, "but there's part of the program you have to complete first."

"What's that?"

"Restitution. Amends."

He released her face, turned away from her. "There's no restitution for what I did. No amends. Just punishment and payback."

She heard remorse and shame, along with clarity of purpose. Not something most spree killers felt. "Then we'll start there, work our way up," she said.

"How?" he asked.

"I'll figure it out and let you know. Tell me about Ron Schulman. What's he like?"

"He's like a rich guy," Springer said. "Wants to control everything."

"Were you happier with him, or without him?"

"There's no without him. Once he's got you, he owns you. Ron always wins." This last said with bitterness, deep and abiding. She thought of how often Thanatos was just a symptom of unspoken rage.

"Let's talk about something else," he said. "Ron bores the hell out of me."

"Sure. Tell me why you killed those kids."

"No," he replied.

His tone was flat, but she saw his throat working, a sure sign of distress. Again, not something you saw in most spree killers. They were proud of what they'd done, justified it, bragged about it.

"Let me know when you're ready," she said. "I'd like to hear it."

"I got a better idea. Let's run away."

Jaguar laughed and he put a hand on her arm, held it hard. "I mean it," he said. "There's places we can go. Places you go when you need to run away."

In her own mind, as soon as he said run away, she'd seen an image of 13 Streams, the New Mexico village where she'd learned to refine her own gifts, under the auspices of her mentors, Jake and One Bird. She'd run there to escape Manhattan during the Killing Times, and he'd plucked the image from her, seeking his own escape.

She sniffed the air, caught the familiar scent of the Adept at work. This place, her place of safety, fit in with something he meant to do, something he saw occurring in the future. He saw it, in Adept space. And he didn't have a clue that he'd done so.

He showed his lopsided grin. "Let's go," he said. "You and me. You can even bring Dzarny."

Not a name she expected to hear in this context. "You know him?" she asked.

"I met him when they brought me in," he said. His aspect was dark and glowering.

"You didn't like him?"

"He's okay. You can bring him if you want."

"Did you see him there with us? At 13 Streams?"

His brow furrowed down. "What the hell are you talking about?" he asked.

Whatever he'd seen, it had left him. He didn't remember at all. At least, she thought, he's consistent in his inconsistency. "If you could go anywhere," she asked, "do anything, where would you go, and what would you do?"

He dug into himself, turned away from her. "A place where it's all singing. No people. No bullshit. Just—singing."

The ping and spark of truth rang through his tone, his words. And that was as much as she needed to know for tonight.

"Go to sleep," she told him. "I don't want to look at you anymore."

He offered her an elaborate, fake bow, and left her alone with her thoughts. She stayed perched on the bed, considering what she'd learned. He was a powerful empath, who had no idea what he was doing, or how to manage it. It might be the reason why he killed, and why he wouldn't, or couldn't, talk about it. Maybe he'd done it in an unmanageable empathic moment. But no. That couldn't be true, because the killing was planned, which didn't fit with his impulsiveness, his random moments of brilliance or madness. She'd have to get to his core to find out what was going on, though he'd spent all his life learning how to keep everyone, including himself, barred from that sacred space.

She'd go slow with him. Let the music do its work. Music, not Thanatos, was primary with him. He mediated all his experience, articulated his soul, through music, whether he liked it nor not. That's how she'd find who he really was.

CHAPTER EIGHT

New Manhattan, Home Planet

When Alex left the cop shop he put a call in to Planetoid attorney Jill Polk, the most discrete and astute legal mind he'd ever met, the only lawyer capable of managing the complicated issues Jaguar landed in, and someone who remained unflustered by any strangeness.

"I've got a situation, Jill," he said.

"Jaguar?" she asked as a matter of course. It usually was.

"Not this time. I'm on the home planet, tracking Springer Todd's background. I found out one of his potential adoptive parents was murdered by a mugger, who ended up dead shortly before his trial. In case you don't know it, Springer's with Ron Schulman's outfit."

"I knew that," she said, and then was silent for a while. Alex waited it out. "Are you accusing Schulman of something?"

"Not yet. I Just want to know if there's more bodies piled up around him."

"Besides his wife and son? You know about them, right? Killed in a car accident. Drunk driver, rainy night. He was coming home from a wake. An Irish wake."

"I know that. Do you know if the driver's still alive?"

"Not a clue. Who checks on that kind of thing?"

"You do," Alex said. "At least, you do now."

"Right. I'll get on it. And tell me if you find anything else."

"You bet," he said.

Jill wouldn't move fast, Alex knew, but she'd be thorough. If she found anything at all, she'd make sure it would stick. So far, he thought, so good. Then, his cellcom buzzed, and he saw Mike's ID on it. His hand twitched, and he stared at it. The sensation subsided, but he knew fair warning when he felt it.

He answered the call. "Mike," he said. "How's it going?"

"For me, fine. For you, it depends on what you were hoping to get."

"Just an answer. You got one for me?"

"Sure do. Find a cigar and light it up. You've got a son."

He paused, not understanding. "You'll have to explain that," he said.

"Really? Well, when a man meets a woman—"

"Cut the crap, Mike," Alex said sharply.

A slight pause. "You didn't know?" he asked.

"I still don't know," Alex confirmed.

"Right," Mike said. "I put the DNA sample through the mill, and it came up flat until I hit the Planetoid files. You said go where I want with it, and that was the last place. It rolled up as a match with your DNA. Shared alleles. Paternally shared."

Alex's heart gave a small lurch. A son. He had a son? None of that appeared in Adept space, but then again, why would it? It was past, not future. But he had a son? A young man who killed children? Their was nowhere in his brain he could fit this information.

"Sure about that?" he asked, trying to sound casual.

"Not a doubt. Sample A is daddy to Sample B—which I suppose stands for bouncing baby boy."

A thousand and one random thoughts meandered through Alex's mind. He was a father. What did that mean? He had no connection to Springer except the accident of biology, so why should the world be shifting under him? Why the strange combination of elation and terror? He tried to match Springer's face to his own, but saw nothing of himself written there. Though, of course, other genes also rolled in his blood. He thought of his own father, a taciturn man who preferred the company of horses. There was something hard in his jaw, something sad in his eyes. Alex saw the same in Springer.

"What about the mother?" Alex asked.

"She did not make an appearance, my friend. You'll have to dig out your old address books and start thinking."

"You tried medical files?"

"Well, yeah. Once I found out about you, I tried all files, bar none. I was curious as hell. Whoever she is, she knows how to hide. Listen, is this bad news?"

"It's—interesting."

"Like the Chinese curse?"

"Kind of," Alex admitted. "I appreciate your help. And you'll keep it quiet, right?"

"Of course," Mike agreed, and Alex believed him. He appreciated not getting arrested, and the funds that continued to come his way for consulting on special projects like this one.

When he signed off, Alex stood in the middle of his hotel room, trying to think. But he had no thoughts. Only feelings.

Fear, from the Adept space he'd shared with Springer. Horrifying guilt, because he'd put this killer into the world. Anger at Springer for finding him, for not finding him sooner, for being who he was. Also an inexplicable, irrational sense of joy. He had a son.

His first impulse was to share the news with Jaguar, but that was quickly followed by a colder reality. She was a Sunwatcher, ritual keeper of the sun ceremonies for her people. They relinquished childbearing, retaining their energy for the empathic arts. How would she feel about him having a child by another woman? She wasn't the type to castigate him for past affairs, but it might touch off some pretty complicated emotions in her. And could she work with Springer if she knew who his father was? Could he ask that of her?

No. She couldn't know. The burden on her would be too great in an assignment that was already highly vexed. In fact, he should reassign the case. But both his reasoning mind and Adept space made him certain no other Teacher could deal with it. There was no one else to give Springer to.

That decision told him something else. As Jaguar had realized intuitively, this was important to him. He had a son, and that son needed healing. Complexities moved through him at the speed of light, encompassing his culpability and his hope, what he'd seen in Adept space, what he feared he'd done, and what he feared he'd do.

He shifted, called himself away from emotion and back to discipline. He'd take one step at a time. He had another task to complete, and maybe that would illuminate this chaotic darkness.

* * * *

His final stop in the city was a meeting with a group of young people who survived Springer's last show, and went to court to make victim statements. Two of them had been hit and lived. The others weren't hit, but saw their friends killed.

Preliminary researchers had already interviewed them, but he wanted to do his own check, see if anything they had to say could explain what Springer did. Especially now, that seemed like his most important task—to find out why his son became a killer. He made his way to the conference room at his hotel, where they'd arranged to meet.

When he entered he saw almost a dozen young faces turn toward him, none of them older than twenty one. Some were seated, toying nervously with the pads and pencils he'd had put around the table in case they felt more comfortable writing than speaking. Others stood in groups of two or three, talking in whispers. He introduced himself, took a seat, and invited them to do the same. He sent his glance around and attached names to their faces from the report on them he'd requested, and picked one to start with.

"You're Ange, right?" he said to the young woman with blonde hair, cut spikey and sporting a pink streak.

"Yes, that's me," she said. He moved his glance to the boy next to her, skinny and dark skinned and suspicious. "David?" he asked, and the boy nodded.

Across the table from them was Daryl, and Gretchen and Hope, then Melissa and Craig and more. As he greeted each he noted the dilation of their pupils. PTSD, he thought. Just coming here made them relive what they'd been through, and he was sorry for that.

"As you know, I'm from Planetoid Three, and right now Springer Todd is with us, as part of his sentencing."

"We know," Gretchen said. She twisted a piece of her lanky brown hair around her finger nervously. "Will you kill him?" she demanded with some ferocity.

Alex kept himself quiet, calm. "We don't do executions as a rule," he said.

"Then why the fuck are you talking to us? We want him dead."

"Do you?" he asked. "Really?" He held her at gaze. She shifted in her seat, looked to the others, then down at the table.

"I thought not," he said. "You've already seen enough death, for one thing. For another, it seems to me death is a little too easy for what he did. One minute and it's over."

"Yeah, well, at least he'd never hurt anyone again," Daryl chimed in.

"He won't, either way," Alex said. "We pretty much guarantee that."

Gretchen again pushed forward. "So—what're you doing to him?"

"He's with a Teacher. She has to make him face what he did, why he did it. You know how tough it is to own up. You can imagine what that means when you've killed a bunch of innocent kids. It's no picnic."

At this, some murmurs of approval. They liked it.

"Then what?" David asked. "I mean, after he's faced it?"

"If that's successful, he'll have to make reparation in some way." He held up a hand to ward off their protests, which he'd anticipated. "I know. He can't bring your friends back. Can't undo what he's done. But he'll have to figure out how to make his life useful rather than destructive."

Saying this hurt more than he'd expected. His son had done this irreparable thing. His son. He shook it off. Not the time or place for it.

"What if he can't face it?" Ange asked. She had a quiet voice, low and gentle.

"Then he'll probably die," Alex said, and again pain sizzled through him. Not good, he thought. None of this was good. He ran his teeth over his lower lip, went back to business. "Right now, we're trying to determine his motive, and that's why I'm here. What you saw might give us a lead."

Daryl's high forehead creased. "He's not saying?"

"No," Alex said. "Not a word."

David brought in breath and huffed it out. "Well, we don't have a fucking clue. I mean, all we know is we were having a great time, then people started dying. And it's not our fucking job to figure it out."

"It's not. But anything you tell us becomes part of our research. It might help us prevent something like this from happening again. So if you want to talk about it, I'm here to listen."

Ange looked to Gretchen, who looked to Daryl and Dave. Clearly, they were the leaders of the group. They turned to the others in the room, and in some imperceptible way, permission was passed among them.

"Okay," Ange said. "I'll go first."

She did so, telling him how she was there with her boyfriend, a new boyfriend, who got these tickets to impress her, and it worked. She was happier than she ever remembered, here at this show she'd always wanted to see, with a guy who knew what it meant to her. And it was as great as she thought it would be. They were right up front, and she could look right into Springer's face while he played.

"Did he seem in any way different than you expected? Did he look anxious, or angry?"

Ange shook her head. "He looked like he does on his vids. Really into the music. And when he got behind the—the gun, he was smiling, had his arm out like—like this." She extended her arm full length, palm up, an invitational gesture.

"And when he started firing? I'm sorry, I know it's difficult to go back."

She lowered her arm. "I wasn't looking at him then. I kinda turned, to look at Lex—my boyfriend. We were all leaping around, trying to grab the stars, and Lex was smiling. Then he looked surprised. I—I saw blood, like, at his throat, and he fell down. I didn't understand, but I had this feeling, like someone—some kind of monster—just showed up. Like he was standing right behind me, so I started screaming. I wasn't even sure why, but I just kept screaming. Inside myself, I guess I feel like I'm still screaming. All the time. Always screaming."

She stopped speaking, and Gretchen offered her narrative, not that dissimilar. Everything seemed normal, and then she saw her friend fall, had the same sense of someone behind her, meaning her harm. One by one, they all told their stories. As they spoke, he made light empathic contact with each one, feeling their confusion, followed by cold, cold terror, the shadow of an unnamed horror taking shape behind them. He saw no images, but sensed maleness in the shadow, bigger than life or death. When they were done speaking, they stared at him with their wide, wide eyes.

"Now what?" Daryl demanded.

Alex sent his glance around at them again. It was out of their ken, and nothing in their lives had prepared them for it. Unlike Jaguar, who grew up with violence, they were raised by those who survived the Killing Times, and their parents had done everything they could and then some to keep them safe and unafraid.

In each one, Alex felt the same questing shock that asked how this could happen, why it would happen to them. And their grief at lost friends, lost trust, and more. All this, caused by a child he'd sired. A part of him thought it would be best to just shoot him and move on, a very late term abortion. Another part of him hoped the case would fail and Jaguar would kill him. Then he'd never have to deal with the rest of it. Never have to tell Jaguar. Never again have to feel what he was feeling right now.

"Does it matter?" Ange asked mournfully. "He was supposed to lift us up. Like, our souls. His music, what it did, we *needed* that, and he knew it. So what does he do? He kills us. There's no fixing that."

They'd lost more than friends. They'd lost their belief in the magic he'd promised, and unless something changed, they'd never believe again. That, perhaps, was the greatest evil. They'd recover psychologically, but their spirits would be forever diminished. Witnessing this, Alex had an idea of one way for Springer to start making amends.

"Would you like to let him know that?" Alex asked.

They shuffled in their seats, looked to each other and back to him. "Like, how?" Gretchen asked.

"Go see him. Tell him."

Daryl shook his head. "I just want to hit him. Once. Really hard."

"I've got nothing against that," Alex said.

They showed interest. He knew he'd have to get Jaguar to agree to it, but he thought she'd be amenable. It was a good plan, one that would serve her goals as well as his. He leaned forward, and explained how it could be done.

CHAPTER NINE

Planetoid 3, zone 10, Chicago Replica City

The stand slid up, and the synthesizer slid down with a crash.

"Shit," Gerry said, and gazed around at the nobody who was with him. "Didn't anyone get that fixed?" he whined. Nobody answered, since no one was there. He lay down on the floor, and struggled to get the legs upright again.

They were in the replica city of Chicago, zone 10, setting up early for that night's show. They'd rehearse first, since they were doing a new song of Springer's, one he called *Kanima*. Gerry liked it, and so did Pinkie, though she found the seven over eight beat challenging. She was practicing it with Springer in the Green Room, and Gerry was responsible not only for setting the stage, but also for setting up for recording during the show. Jaguar had insisted on it, though she didn't say why. She was still at their hotel filing a report, which Gerry resented.

He was on the floor tightening screws, when he noticed a pair of legs very close to his eyes. He looked up them, and up them some more, and then again a little more until he reached the flame-red hair that signaled the top of this woman. They had security at the door, so he assumed she was Planetoid or they wouldn't let her in.

"Hi," he said. "Can I help you?"

Her voice, low and husky, sounded uncertain. "Springer—is he here?"

"He's busy right now." As he spoke he turned away from her and back to the synthesizer leg. "Is it important? You can wait for him, or I can go get him as soon as I'm finished with this damn leg."

No answer. He waited a little, in case she was thinking about it, then tried again. "You want to leave a name or something?"

"Sure," an entirely different voice said. "What name you want me to leave?"

"Yours?" Gerry suggested tentatively.

"It's Addams. Dr. Addams," the voice said, and Gerry turned his head, then sat up and stared at her with frank admiration.

"How'd you do that?" he asked. "And—*why'd* you do that?"

"Do what?" Jaguar asked, then without waiting for an answer, "Where's Springer?"

"That's what I mean. You were just a red-head, asking the exact same damn thing. So what's the point?"

"I was a—Gerry, was someone else here?"

"I guess so. I mean, like just a split end ago. A red-head. Great tall woman like a building, and she wanted to know if Springer was here, too."

"I take it," Jaguar said, "he's not?"

"Sure he is," he said. He jerked his head to the right. "He's in the green room, with Pinkie, working on that drum beat."

"He better be," she said.

"Chill, Jaguar. Pinkie knows what she's doing."

"Sure she does," Jaguar said, and made her way to the green room. Once there, she opened the door and saw Pinkie on the couch, a wooden drum between her legs. Her eyes were closed and she was well into the rhythm.

"Hey," Jaguar said.

She stopped, smiled. She lifted her left hand, wiggled her silver pinkie finger at Jaguar. "The big cat," she said.

"Where's the prisoner?" Jaguar asked.

PInkie pointed at the couch. 'Right—holy shit." She looked blankly at Jaguar. "He was right here. I swear he was. We were jamming good. I heard his eight beat."

"Sure you did, damn his empath heart to hell. Never mind. Not your fault. I'll explain later."

She moved out the door, pulling the implant control from her pocket checking it as she went. It showed he wasn't too far, but it should have sounded an alarm before this. At least he was close enough to be easily found. He wanted a stroll, she'd take one, too. See where it led.

* * * *

Springer walked swiftly down the street, keeping his eye on the figure of a red-haired woman who walked ahead of him. He didn't want to attract attention by running, but he could walk very fast and he did until he caught up with her, and grabbed her by the arm. She startled, then stopped, smiled, held a hand to his face.

"Springer," she said. "What are you doing? Should you be here?"

"I knew you'd come. I knew you wouldn't leave me alone."

"How'd you find me?" she asked.

"C'mon. I always know."

"Are you—okay?"

"I've had worse gigs." He gave her his grin, to show he meant it. "How about you? Everything's cool?"

Her face crumbled into sorrow. "It's all so strange—you being here. *Why* you're here."

He moved closer to her and put one arm around her back. "Let's not talk about that, okay? It's done. It's just done."

She shuddered lightly. "I'm afraid," she said.

"Of what?"

"Everything. You haven't had any of your medicine since they brought you here. And if you do anything wrong, if you—hurt some-one—they'll execute you."

"I'm okay." He reached up and touched her hair. "Maybe I don't need it anymore. Maybe I got it out of my system."

"No. It's not safe. We're getting some for you, but you have to be careful. Just stay quiet, okay?"

"Not sure I want to, Jeral baby," he crooned at her.

She winced. "Don't call me that."

"What should I call you? Hot mama?"

Jeral subsumed her repulsion under a brittle smile. "You're awful," she said. "But listen. You have to take the medicine when we get it to you. This—it's a dangerous place. That woman they put you with—I've heard awful things about her."

"She's not so bad," Springer said.

"Don't, Springer. Don't get involved with her."

"Jealous?"

"Of course not. But she kills her prisoners. Please. Just promise you'll take your medicine."

"Sure," He put a hand on her shoulder and squeezed. "Anything for you and old Ronnie."

"You're hurting me," she said.

He let go of her, held his arms out wide. "Well?" he asked. "No hug for me? Nothing?"

"Springer, you have to go."

"Just for a minute. I want you to hold me."

She moved into his arms, embraced him briefly, stroking his hair. In spite of his jokes, there was tension in all his muscles. She hoped her father worked fast.

She gave him one good squeeze, then pulled back. "Go, now. I don't want you getting in trouble."

"You're sticking around, right? I'll see you again."

"Yes. Of course."

He tipped a nod her way, and ambled off. She walked briskly away, tucked into herself, not wanting to think or to see everything that could go wrong.

* * * *

As Jaguar rounded the corner she caught a brief glimpse of a red haired woman, tall and well built, clipping away from her. She paused, stared at the form. The same woman she'd seen in the audience. Springer emerged from a Convenience store a few buildings away, holding a bottle of orange juice. He was whistling as he approached her.

"Hey, Kanima," he said amicably.

"Where the hell have you been?" she asked.

"In general, or—what?"

"You can't leave the bar without telling anyone," she said.

"I told Pinkie. I wanted OJ."

"Liar. You let Pinkie get lost in the drumming, then snuck out to see your red haired lady friend."

"Caught me," Springer said without rancor.

"How'd you slip your implant?" she asked.

He frowned at her. "I didn't," he said, and she could see he meant it. His psi capacities, acting without his volition. But overriding technology was an advanced skill. Even Alex struggled with it sometimes. That, she thought, didn't bode well for her.

"The red head," she said. "I saw her at the show, giving you her big sad eyes. Who is she?"

"An admirer," he said.

"Of your music or your killing?" Jaguar asked.

"Both," he replied. "She slipped a note to me through one of the bartenders, said she was sorry I was in trouble, and asked if she could help any. She likes bad boys."

"You didn't have near enough time to get any," Jaguar noted, "so I'm figuring you made arrangements for later."

"Maybe. Is that allowed, or do you take care of the more personal needs?"

From the look of it, he'd just as soon have one as the other. "Ever hear of old man coyote?" she asked him.

"Yeah," he said, suspicious. "A cartoon or something, right?"

"More like a god. One with a funny side and a dark side. Where I grew up there's lots of stories about him. One says his penis would leave him at night, go out sniffing in holes and come back in the morning before the rest of him woke up. The trouble was, it only had one eye, so it couldn't see very well. One night it went out sniffing around and ran into a cactus. When it came back it was all full of prickers, and coyote couldn't understand why he kept wanting to rub himself up against something soft, like a woman."

"Funny," Springer said. "Is there a point?"

"Keep it in your pants or it'll end up full of prickers, and there's nothing soft here for you to rub it up against. Got it, coyote man?"

"Sure," he said. "No problem."

He shrugged down into himself and they walked back to the bar.

* * * *

When Springer was safely ensconced onstage, rehearsing with Gerry, Jaguar pulled out her cellcom and put in a call to Rachel, who was at the hotel room, getting some paperwork done.

"Listen," she said, "I need you to do some research for me."

"Sure thing. What is it?"

"Get me anything you can find about a tall, red-haired woman in her late thirties, maybe early forties, associated with Springer. Old lover, old friend, old enemy, long lost sibling, person in the music industry—any association at all. Got it?"

"That's easy. Anything else?"

She considered. "Yeah. Tell me everywhere Alex went on the home planet. And I mean everywhere. Places he stopped to pee, restaurants he ate at, who he ate with—the works. Also any association he might have with that tall, red haired lady."

"What?" Rachel asked.

"You heard me."

"Okay, but can't you just ask him?"

"Not right now," Jaguar said, enunciating each word distinctly.

"What's wrong?" Rachel asked.

"Nothing. Not yet, anyway. Just find out for me, okay?"

A pause, as Rachel considered. She loved both Jaguar and Alex, but her first loyalty was to Jaguar. "You want me to keep it quiet, right? Not let him know?"

"No reason for that," Jaguar said. "In fact, let him know I'm looking. He should know."

Rachel sighed, thinking of the early days when Jaguar more often growled at Alex than spoke with him. She hoped they wouldn't go back there, even though she was aware they were both twitchy lately. But she knew better than to get between two twitchy wizards. She'd do as she was asked, and hope for the best.

CHAPTER TEN

When Alex got back to the Planetoid, the first place he went was his office. Once there, he sat and drummed his fingers on his desk, as he thought through his next moves.

The first one was to punch in numbers on his telecom, and when Scott appeared, he said briefly, without explanation, "Give me the latest on Springer Todd."

"Yes, sir," Scott replied. "They've been at four bars, here and in zone 10, and so far no trouble. They're due back in zone 12 today. Should be at the Normal house by now."

"You going to the gigs?"

"All but the last one, sir," he said. "I had to help out with a training."

"Okay. What do you notice so far?"

"A few things. First, the prisoner is gaining confidence, singing more. Dr. Addams is giving him a lot of room."

"Room? What's that mean?"

"He, um, gets rough, and she doesn't close him down," Scott said.

A small flame of anger pushed through Alex's veins, and he asked it to subside. She often did that, letting prisoners think they had more control than they did. She was expert at the long con. He'd learned to control his feelings around it, but this was different. His son. It was his son getting rough with her. "Right," he said. "She does that sometimes. Just—keep an eye on it. What's second?"

"There's a woman present at all the shows."

"I'd guess there's quite a few. Something special about this one?"

"She's a red head, older than the rest of the crowd, and seems more—sophisticated. She's attentive in a different way, and Dr. Addams is paying attention to her."

A red head. Older. In all the commotion of his recent thoughts, he couldn't place this at all. "Okay," he said. "I'll keep it in mind. Anything else?"

"Springer's using some kind of empathic contact with the audience," he said judiciously.

"Harmonic sympathizer, it's called," Alex said.

Scott let out a long breath of air. "I'm not familiar with that one. I think I should show you what he did," he said, "if that's permissible. sir."

Well, Alex thought. He's learning a thing or two. "Go ahead," he said, and Scott did, letting Alex witness all that flowed from Springer to his audience, opening them up to their animal kin.

"Huh," Alex said when Scott was done. "That's—new."

"Yes, sir," Scott agreed. "Dr. Addams is aware of it."

"Of course she is. Listen, when they're in zone 12 you'll need to bring Springer to this building now and then. Dr. Addams will ask why, and on whose orders. Tell her it's testing. If she asks for particulars, you don't know."

To Alex's surprise, Scott looked relieved. "No I don't, sir. It's best that way."

"Why do you say that, Scott?"

He paused, then spoke with circumspection. "She can take me," he said. "Telepathically speaking, that is."

"Exactly," he agreed.

Scott signed off, and Alex was about to try Jill Polk, see if she'd learned anything, when his telecom buzzed him. He saw the name on the screen and picked up.

"Paul," he said when he saw his basset hound face, looking even more glum than usual. "What's up?"

"Come to my office," Paul said. "A few things to go over."

"Now?"

"Yeah," Paul said. "Right now."

"On my way," Alex said.

He signed off, pushed himself up and walked the two flights to Paul's office. His mind was filled with a roiling of both emotions and possible strategies, so he had a hand on the door of Paul's office before he was aware of Adept visions moving within him. He stopped cold.

Everything he needed to know and did not want to know was on the other side of the door. The last piece of the puzzle. He tried to tell himself it wasn't that bad, but the wiser part of him smelled disaster. He took in breath, prepared himself to meet it with equanimity, and opened the door.

Paul sat behind his desk. A man and a woman were seated on the other side of it. The man was perhaps early sixties, but in very good shape, trim and fit, his gray hair cropped close to his head, his angular features tight and firm. The woman next to him sat tall, but kept herself quiet, demure. They both turned to Alex at the same time, and he stood where he was, taking them in. Before Paul could make formal introductions, he spoke.

"Hello, Plain Jane," he said to the woman.

"Hello, farm boy," she replied.

CHAPTER ELEVEN

"Alex," Paul said, "this is Ron Schulman, and his daughter Jeral. They're staying on the Planetoid, reviewing some of the programs they support, seeing what else they might do here."

Ron stood and extended a hand, which Alex took, shook, and released. "You know my daughter?" he asked.

Alex looked to her, took the hand she proffered and shook that as well. He saw her hazel eyes, large and cautious, sending clear messages to him. Don't tell him.

"We met at a Planetoid charity function," Alex said. "Quite a few years ago." Her hand lingered in his a moment longer than necessary, then released him.

"That's nice," Ron said. "Um—farm boy?"

"I was raised on a horse ranch. Your daughter teased me about it. I called her Plain Jane, to tease her back."

"That's great," Paul said cheerfully. "You're already friends. Have a seat, Alex. Ron had a few questions maybe you can answer."

He took one, but stayed on the edge of it and looked to Ron. "Ask away," he said.

"Right to the point, huh?" Ron said. "That's how I work, too. It's about Springer Todd. I've got a special interest in his progress, and Paul says you'd have all the information on him. I'd like to know what his program is, how he's doing in it—that kind of thing." Ron showed him a smile indicating they were compatriots, working toward the same goal.

Alex smiled, friendly but not compatriot. "That material's all confidential, Ron."

"To most people," Ron said. "I'm not most people. Neither is my daughter," he added, by way of understatement.

"No," Alex agreed. "She's special."

"Is she?" Ron asked.

"Any daughter you raised would be, of course."

"Sure," Ron said, though he wasn't buying what Alex was selling. "So maybe if you can't tell me, you can tell her," he suggested, his smile growing more affable.

"Frankly, it's early days, and there isn't anything to tell," Alex said. "But I appreciate that you're concerned for him. He's one of your adoptees, so I understand."

"That's right. And naturally I feel horrible that he ended here. Especially the way he—what he did. It's a nightmare, really."

I'll bet it is, Alex thought. A PR nightmare of the first order, and I doubt very much if you care personally. But your daughter does. She most certainly does. He worked his most calming aspect. "I know it's difficult for people outside the system to understand, but sometimes coming here is a beginning of sorts."

"I can only hope. And I'd like to offer my help in that," Ron said.

"In what way?" Alex asked.

"I told Paul already. Springer had a counselor on the home planet, helping him get through some of his—his issues. I think he should be part of Springer's program here."

Alex took careful note of the words Ron used. Should was a command rather than a request. Issues, he supposed, was a euphemism for psi capacities. "I appreciate it, but that won't be necessary," he said.

Ron leaned in. "Listen, lots of these musicians get—well, I guess you'd call them lifestyle problems. Too much adoration. Too many late nights and long days on the road. His counselor specializes in that kind of thing. That'll help him."

"It might not," Alex said. "In fact, it could interfere. What we do isn't therapy."

"I know what it is," Ron said, an edge of impatience creeping into his tone. "You make them face their fears. But doesn't therapy do that, too?"

"Not in the same way. Our regimen is more focused."

"Maybe," Paul cut in, "Mr. Schulman can send you information on his counselor and you can go over it with Springer's Teacher. Take it under advisement."

Alex heard the desperation in Paul's voice. Play him, he was asking. Just a little. Alex resented it, but saw the practical side. Get him quiet and out of the office, and they could all go on with their work. And it hardly mattered, since he knew the answer already. "Sure," he said blandly, as he imagined Jaguar's response. "That's a good idea."

"The Teacher he's with—Paul just told me about her. It's a Dr. Addams, right?"

Alex cast a glance at Paul. "We don't give that information out, as a rule."

"Every rule's got an exception," Paul said, twitching into a smile.

"Absolutely," Ron agreed. "And the information is safe with me. I'm accustomed to keeping confidences. But Addams—she's got a bit of a reputation."

Small fires lit themselves inside Alex's eyes. The last thing he wanted was to argue about Jaguar with Ron Schulman, in front of his daughter. "She's earned it," he said crisply. "Dr. Addams has a 98 percent success rate. She's our best."

"So I hear. But I'm not so sure a woman is right for Springer. Young guy like him, and she's a bit of a looker herself—might be risky. I also hear she's got some moves that might be a bad idea for him...." He let the rest of the sentence go away. Alex filled for him.

"The ruling against Teachers with psi capacities was lifted some time ago," he mentioned blandly. "In fact, there's a great deal of evidence suggesting they're useful." He turned to Paul, whose face tried hard to agree and disagree at the same time.

"Our Teachers are all very well supervised," he settled on, and Alex shot him a quick glare.

Ron leaned forward, spoke confidentially. "I'm not against it, philosophically. But Springer—he had trouble with it. Started about a year ago. Seeing visions, that kind of thing. We had him checked for everything—schizophrenia, brain tumor, the works."

Alex had a moment of surprise. "None of that was in his medical files."

"We had it done privately," Ron said. "Buried it good. The media's always on him, and we didn't want it hitting the tabloids."

"You should have mentioned it to the preliminary researchers," Alex said. "It's the kind of thing we need to know."

"Sorry. I thought it didn't matter, since the tests all came back negative. Then his counselor suggested he might have other, um, issues."

"He tested positive for psi capacities here, if that's what you mean, but we know how to deal with that."

"Sure you do, but his counselor has a few tricks you might find useful."

"Does he? Like what?"

"He's good at—at making them go away."

"Springer was working with a plumber?" Alex asked, struggling to keep the anger from his voice.

"Plumber? No. The guy's a counselor."

"Sorry. It's a local word for counselors who try to remove psi capacities," Alex clarified.

"Well, I don't really understand it, since I've never had any problems in that area, but Springer's an artist. They always have special needs.

I've worked with them long enough to know. And it helped for a while. No more visions or anything. I'm guessing he had some kind of relapse."

"Are you?" Alex asked, his voice dangerously quiet. Though he knew it was wrong, knew it was dangerous, he looked to Jeral, held her glance. Her fair skin turned even paler, glowing white and translucent.

"Sure," Ron said. "What else?"

"There's lots of possibilities for his motive," Alex said. "We're considering all of them, without prejudice. And as you pointed out, we're highly successful at our jobs."

Ron reined himself in. "Of course," he said. "Well, I just want you to understand the background. In case you find this particular Teacher isn't working out, you'll know why."

"I appreciate your concerns," Alex said. "I'll bring them to Dr. Addams' attention. She's best placed to know how to manage them." He turned to Paul, who looked like a deer in the headlights.

"Dr. Addams handles our toughest cases," he confirmed judiciously.

"And we'll want a full report on any treatment Springer had in the past," Alex added.

"Sure,' Ron said. "Anything you need. Right away."

Alex glanced at the clock, put his hands on the arm of his chair and levered himself to stand. "Is there anything else? I've got a meeting…"

"Nothing right now. I'll be here for the duration, so we can meet again when you've made some progress," Ron said.

Alex kept his smile on. "You're staying?"

"You bet," Ron said. "We've got a suite at the Governor's Inn." He looked to Jeral, who tried hard to be invisible and failed. "Maybe you could suggest some good places for my daughter to go, so she's not too bored with waiting."

"Places?" Alex asked.

"Restaurants, shows, music. She likes music."

Alex looked to her. She continued silent, and he felt sorry for her. The shadow of her father was too large for her to climb out of. No wonder she wanted to be just Plain Jane. He offered a smile of honest sympathy.

"I'll have my assistant draw up a list," he said. "We can't compete with the home planet city of Toronto, but we have some interesting features of our own."

"Good," Ron said. "And since you already know each other, maybe you could show her around some."

Alex found that his mouth had suddenly gone dry. Ron stared at him. He knows, Alex thought. He knows, and he's angry about it.

"That would be lovely, if I had the time," he said. "Unfortunately, I'm short of that commodity these days."

Jeral's face blanched, and Ron passed a microexpression of anger her way before he resumed his smile. "Paul tells me you work too much," he said. "Well, if that changes, you know where we are."

"I do," Alex agreed. He shook hands all around one more time, then made his way out of this particular version of hell.

* * * *

By the time he'd gotten back to his office, his mind had sprinted through more complexities than he could rationally field. He had a son, and that son's mother was here, with her father, whose agenda was beyond what he stated, though Alex had no idea what it was, exactly. He had a lover, and she was in charge of making sure his son stayed alive, though she didn't know who her prisoner was, and he had to keep that information from her.

It was all too much, and so he stayed with present needs, practicality. Once he was at his desk he went to his computer and opened his own records. He stared at them, trying to remember the rubric he'd been taught for how to block files, something only supervisors and governors could do. Something even Rachel couldn't get through. The information filtered back from memory, and he went through the protocol, which took more than an hour to complete. When he was done, he breathed a sigh of relief, rested his elbow on his desk, rested his face in his hand.

"Jaguar," he whispered, wanting the solace of her name if he couldn't have the comfort of her confidence.

Nothing about this was going to be easy. Nothing at all.

* * * *

Ron and Jeral left the building, Ron clipping ahead, walking fast to their car. Jeral knew this aspect of him. He was considering his strategy, and using all his concentration to do so. He wasn't aware of her, or anyone else on the street.

She strode next to him. "This Addams woman—she's dangerous," she said.

"I'll take care of it," Ron said, impatient.

"In the meantime, he has to have his medicine," she persisted.

"Did I say I'd take care of it? If you want to help, you can spend some time with Dzarny. Convince him to take on that counselor."

"It's pretty clear he doesn't want anything to do with a counselor or me," she noted.

"He liked the taste of you once. Make him hungry again."

She cringed at the words, and the disgust in his voice. He had many faces for many different uses, but she was the only one who got to see this one. The face that regarded the world and all its people with contempt. The one that was willing to sell his daughter to get what he wanted.

Not a soul would believe her if she told the truth about it. He'd charmed so many people, finding what they wanted and playing on it. But she didn't know if he could charm his way around the Prison Planetoid System, and that scared her. Though she loathed herself for it even more than he did, she'd do whatever she could to help him in this particular task.

"I'll try," she said.

"Of course you will," he replied. "And you'll get the job done."

CHAPTER TWELVE

In the morning Jaguar found a message on her cellcom from Alex, telling her he was back and asking her to call. Instead, she decided she wanted to see him. He might not be available for empathic contact, but she could read a face as expertly as she could read a mind, and his might have something to say. While Springer slept and Gerry kept watch, she made her way downtown, to the Teacher's building.

As she stepped inside his office he was bent over his desk, frowning down at his screen. He didn't hear her enter, which meant he was truly closed against her. Not a good sign. She looked him over quickly, then looked him over again, slowly. She closed the door and he lifted his head, stared at her.

"You okay?" she asked.

"Fine," he said. "Tired from the trip. That's all."

"No it's not," she said. "Something happened."

Of course she'd pick up on that. He had very little experience keeping things from her. The learning curve would be steep. He tried to show her a face that looked more like a wall than a window.

She scowled at him. "This cryptic thing is only getting worse," she said.

"Doesn't look like improving any time soon. How's the assignment going?

"Moving along at the rate of molasses in snow. What, specifically, did you want to know?"

"His core art, or his core fear will do."

"Can't tell either one. He's hiding both."

"From you? How?"

"Because he's also hiding them from himself. He's had no instruction, can't name any of his gifts and doesn't want to admit he has any of them. They scare the hell out of him, but something else is scaring him more. Will that do for a report?"

Alex noted the frustration in her voice. He was bugging her, but so was the prisoner. "It's a start," he said. Then he tapped his finger against his desk. Maybe he knew something she didn't that he could actually tell her. "Is it possible he's a shapeshifter, hiding in his shapes?" he asked, thinking of Scott's report.

"What makes you say that?"

"Something Scott showed me, from one of the gigs."

She tilted her head at him, and her green eyes sparked. "*Showed* you?" she inquired.

The implication was clear. Scott was allowed contact, and she wasn't. He kept his face still. "It was the most efficient way to relate the information, Dr. Addams. Is Springer a shapeshifter?"

She bridled, but didn't pursue it, which he was thankful for. "I don't believe he is, Supervisor. At least, not in the traditional sense. He's got images of animals moving internally, and they *may* be from Adept space or they may not. And he *may* be projecting them onto his audience, using some variation of harmonic sympathizer I've never seen before, or he *may* be a young god come to earth to mess with the people."

Alex tried to parse his way through all that and failed. "Try again," he said.

"He projects a sense of animal spirits onto the audience, but he doesn't shift. Not at all," she said.

This time, Alex got it. He gave a whistle, soft and low. Shapeshifters physically assumed the form of animals, imbued with both human and animal knowledge. What she was talking about was a trick he'd never heard of.

"You ever see that before?" he asked.

"Only in ceremony, and it wasn't a projection. It was a connection. Not likely it'd turn up in a killer, but I'm considering it, among a bunch of other possibilities. In the meantime, I can confirm he's an Adept."

"You're sure about that?"

She lifted an eyebrow at him. "You have to ask?"

"No. Of course not. What'll you do next?"

"More of what I've been doing, until I get somewhere. Unless you got a better idea?"

"Just keep him alive," he said, before he could stop himself. Immediately, he regretted it. They had their share of prisoners who would rather die than face their fear. He'd never been directive about it before.

Her slow gaze took him in. "Sure," she said quietly. "I can do that."

He reined it in. "I mean, watch the Thanatos," he corrected. "It can turn on a dime, and he's the kind to go for the throat."

"How do you know?"

He smiled. "Just a hunch."

"Right," she said, not buying it. "What did you find out about the foster parents?"

He was glad to give her something to chew on besides his flesh. "There's a body trail."

"One of his foster fathers, right? Killed by a mugger. It's in his file."

"The file doesn't say the mugger was also killed before he went to trial. Hit and run."

"Really? Any chance of tracking that?"

"I met a cop who tried. He got a phone call, warning him off it."

"Better by the minute." she said. "You want Rachel to root around?"

"I've got Jill Polk on it. Let Rachel focus on what you need."

"Good idea," she agreed. "In fact, she's digging into a couple of things for me already. So—what else did you do on the home planet?"

Her way of telling him Rachel was getting that information, which meant he might as well give her some version of it now. Rachel would find it soon enough on her own, and a reasonable explanation might forestall further digging. "I saw Mike Pearson," he said. "Brought him Springer's DNA, thinking maybe he could track the biological parents."

"You think that's important?"

"They're invisible. It might mean something, or it might not."

"You should've put Rachel on it," Jaguar said. "Mike's good, but she's better."

"I didn't think it would be that tough," he said. "If you want, you can put her on it now. Let me know if she gets anywhere. He didn't."

He kept his face steady while she looked him over for any sign of prevarication. Her shoulder lifted and fell. She'd seen nothing of interest. "Listen, at the gig the other night, I saw more than Scott did," she said. "You want it, I'll show you."

Several curse words banged around inside Alex's head. She hadn't dropped it. She just bided her time until the mouse got closer, and less wary.

"Let's keep it verbal," he said. "It's best if we avoid contact for the time being."

Her eyes glinted. "The time being how long?" she asked pointedly

"For the duration of this assignment," he said.

She studied him some more. What she said next surprised him. "You took me off leash for this case, said I had no restrictions. You want your own time off leash?"

"What?" he asked, not understanding.

"Off leash," she repeated. "Activities you don't want to share with me. Bedding down elsewhere. Fucking around."

He blinked at her. The notion was so far from his own thoughts, his response still expressed bewilderment. "No, Jaguar," he said. "Not at all."

"You sure?"

She had a very short history of trusting men, most of which started with him. Nothing he said would make a dent in her suspicions, so he didn't answer. Instead he pushed himself out of his chair, walked to her and wrapped his hand around the back of her neck. He drew her close and kissed her, with full attention to the task. Her body against his was warm and good. He'd missed it like a drowning man misses air. It would be easy to get lost in this pleasure. Too easy, if he let it go on. He released her, moved back to his chair and sat.

"Very sure," he said.

"You have an interesting definition of no contact," she observed.

"I like it," he said. He allowed her to study him until she was satisfied. On this front, he could afford to let her read the truth in him. She did so, easily, and they returned to business.

"Jaguar, there's one other thing I need to know, and two things I have to tell you," he said.

"Go," she said.

"Scott says Springer's getting physical with you. Is it the Thanatos?"

"No. He's an emotional roller coaster. Gerry thought he smelled drugs on him. He was tested, right?"

"Thoroughly."

"I thought so. I suppose it could be a protracted withdrawal, but I'm guessing some of it's the empathic problem, and some is just plain old rage. He's got a ton of it."

"He's a bundle of fun," Alex noted. "Why are you allowing it?"

"I'm hustling him."

Jaguar, master of the long con. Let them see her as weak, until the moment she fought back. "Just—be careful," he said.

"Always am, in my own way. What else?"

She wouldn't like this next bit, but it would be easier to manage than everything else so far. "Ron Schulman's here," he told her.

"Schulman? Why?"

"Protecting his investment. He asked if he could send up Springer's counselor to help you out. Perry Delgardo by name."

Jaguar's face went through a variety of changes before it settled on pissed off. "Xipe Totec flay him," she said.

"I take it that's a no?"

"You know who Delgardo is? Always on the news, saying empaths are in league with satan and so on. He's a plumber. Sticks his thing down empath throats and fills them with his waste product. So that's a no. No way. No fucking way. No *rat* fuck way."

"You're sure about that, Jaguar?" Alex asked, amused.

"If it smells like a rat, walks like a rat and fucks like a rat, what is it?"

"Rat fucked," he replied.

"So how the hell you can even ask me—"

"Paul begged me. I wanted your response in a secure recording for him, to impress him with the magnitude of your feelings."

"Oh," Jaguar said. "Should I say more?"

"You did just fine," he said.

"Let him know if any of Schulman's people get near me, he'll live to regret it. Just barely."

"Yes, Jaguar," he said, and smiled for real. This was familiar territory, their wrangling part of the love song they sang to each other. They were still together in spite of current difficulties. It felt almost as good as kissing her.

She apparently agreed, because she relaxed and returned the smile. "I like this better than cryptic," she said, and leaned toward him. "Alex, if there's nothing else on the agenda, I've got an idea for something to do with Springer."

"Tell me," he said.

"I want to bring up some of the kids who survived his last concert. To meet with him."

Not only together, but thinking along the same lines. "Funny you should mention it. That was the other thing I wanted to tell you. I met with some of them on the home planet, and I thought the same thing." He told her about the meeting, the impression they all had of a menacing shadow figure behind them.

She tapped at her lip, considered. "Springer's projection?" she asked.

"Could be. I didn't get anything other than very big and male. When you see them, maybe you can pick up more. How do you want to do it?"

"Bring them to a show," she said. "Meet with him in the green room after. Tell him a thing or two about their experiences."

He nodded. That echoed his idea. "We can do that. You'll have Scott there. I'll set up a testing run on Springer's psych status for afterward."

"Why?"

"Because I'm the Supervisor, Jaguar."

"You're pulling that card a lot lately."

"That's my privilege. Come over here and look at my list of kids. I'll tell you what they had to say, and we can talk details."

She moved to his side of the desk, and as they worked, her hair brushed softly against his arm. He made no move to touch her, though everything in him wanted to do so. They went through the list, and figured it out.

* * * *

Paul Dinardo was unusual as a governor in that he spent as much time actually on the Planetoid as he did on the home planet, working senators and fielding the media. It wasn't a hardship for him to stick around as long as Ron Schulman did, but he was already tired of standing between his interests, the danger of Jaguar's involvement, and Alex's unusual reluctance to play nice with the money. He especially felt that today, as he sat in his Planetoid office and took Alex's call.

"Dr. Addams just left," he said, "and I asked her about bringing in a counselor. Mr. Schulman will have to accept disappointment. She won't go for it."

"Alex, I'm sure if you reason with her," Paul started to say, but Alex cut him off.

"Before you say anything, I've got something for you to listen to."

He pressed a button and played back Jaguar's reaction to the idea. Paul stifled a groan, but it was way too late to stop Jaguar's rant. The recording played out.

"Just so you know," Alex said when it was done, "even if she said yes, I wouldn't approve it. I only asked because you insisted. We can't have that level of interference with a case that's already damn difficult. If you want, I'll tell him so. Or I could just play the audio for him."

Paul, wondering if he looked as pale as he felt, shook his head. "That won't be necessary," he said. "I'll take it from here."

Alex signed off and Paul turned his pale, apologetic face to Ron, who happened to be there for a chat, and had heard the entire call. "I'm sorry. Dr. Addams can be—um—too outspoken in her opinions. But she is the best for the job."

Ron was unexpectedly sanguine. "I get it. I don't let other people tell me how to run my offices. But really, assure her I only wanted to help. Maybe I can do that some other way."

Paul's relief was immense. "Sure," he said, ready to agree to just about anything offered. "What did you have in mind?"

"I could put a couple of crew members on board with the band, just to give them a hand with the equipment lugging and so on. Let your team members focus on what's important."

"That's very generous."

"Not a problem. I've got some kids who're looking for a little extra work. Always good when you can make these kinds of connections, isn't it?"

"Sure," Paul said. "Sure it is."

Something in him wasn't quite so sure, but he brushed it away. It was an easy way to satisfy Ron, and what harm could it do?

"I'll have them up here right away," Ron said. "Should be on the job by tomorrow." He stuck out his hand and Paul took it, shook it firmly.

"It's always a pleasure doing business with you," he said.

CHAPTER THIRTEEN

Jaguar chose to walk back to the Normal house, glad for the time on her own. The sky was cloudy, the air cool, moving into Planetoid autumn. The mass generator that sustained their atmosphere and environment had created a hot, dry summer, but tomorrow it was supposed to rain, and she was glad. A brooding sky would match her mood better.

Something was wrong with Alex, and she wanted to know what. At least, a part of her did. Another part of her would just as soon stay the hell out of his way and let him solve it on his own. But she couldn't. Not anymore. This, she supposed, was the down side of having a lover you actually cared about.

Today, she'd decided she'd consult with some old friends about him.

Just outside the secure area of the Normal houses the Replica city of Toronto had a zoo. In the back portion of that zoo was a breeding complex, which housed two jaguars, Chaos and Hecate. Sometimes she stopped by just to visit with them. Other times she went to them for a consult, seeking help in the company of her people.

She made her way through the public portion of the zoo and put her palm against the scanner, breathed out the password that got her into the breeding complex. Here, Marie Camposi established a breeding program that was incredibly successful. Under her care, animals that would never breed in captivity raised young that would later be released into the wild, keeping alive quite a few species that might otherwise be lost. The jaguars were among them. Their two kits now ran free on the jaguar reserve in Calakmul. Marie was hoping they'd have more by next year.

Other zoos were emulating her methods, which were pretty simple. She'd decided to let the jaguars out at night so they could hunt small animals like rabbit and squirrel. Hunting, she said, encouraged breeding. Jaguar concurred.

Sometimes she'd come late in the night to follow them as they hunted. Once she brought Alex along, and taught him how to establish empathic contact with them. He was the only man she'd ever met who wasn't afraid to do so. In fact, he welcomed the chance, and sometimes in their lovemaking he shared what they'd both felt in their contact with animal joy. She remembered it viscerally, and with great pleasure.

"Stop thinking about that," she scolded herself. She needed a clear mind and calm heart to do this work.

She approached the jaguar habitat, large and equipped with trees and plants and running water designed to make them feel at home. It was surrounded with laser fencing, but she disabled that easily and stepped forward to put her hands on the metal bars beyond it. They were cool and smooth against her skin.

She peered in, but didn't see the jaguars, so she began a soft crooning in her native Mertec, praising their beauty and power, letting them know she was here and had need of them.

A rustling in the plant life told her they'd heard, and soon enough they came into view, sleek black Chaos and his mate, golden, donut spotted Hecate strolling toward her, leisurely. She quieted herself for a conversation that would include more energy than words. When she sensed resistance in herself, she breathed into it, asked it to leave her. She wanted answers, but was afraid of what they might be. Chaos and Hecate halted where they were, waiting for a clear sense of direction from her. She pressed her hands more firmly around the bars of the cage, made an effort to get out of her own way.

Before she could do so, she heard the sound of approaching footsteps, quiet talk behind her. She cursed quietly, turned and saw Marie, saw her plodding forward in her shitkickers, her sturdy frame dressed in its usual flannel and khaki, her short white hair covered by a bandana. She carried a bucket with contents redolent of roadkill, even from where Jaguar stood. None of that was unusual, but to her surprise, Marie wasn't alone.

A man walked with her. Dressed in t-shirt and jeans, he was tall, broad of shoulder and girth, his mahogany skin showing creases around eyes and mouth, his close cropped hair lightly grizzled. About Marie's age, Jaguar thought. And he looked familiar.

"Hey" Jaguar said as they drew closer. "Feeding time?"

"Not for them," Marie said. "The hyenas. I saw you on the cameras and thought I'd stop by to say hello. It's been a while."

"Too long. Too many prisoners."

"They just keep showing up, don't they? Am I…interrupting?" Marie, not an empath, knew that Jaguar was, knew why she came here and approved. Animals to her were the best connection to the divine.

"Not yet," Jaguar said.

Marie nodded. "We won't stay long. I wanted to introduce you to Junius. He'll be volunteering here."

As Marie said the name, Jaguar remembered him. He was a teacher in Zone 10. She'd done a training there with his group, on how to manage prisoners with psi capacities. Junius had asked some good questions. He was smart, attentive, and definitely an empath himself.

She put her hand out. "We met before," she said. "Training on psi capacities."

He took her hand in his firm grasp, shook it and released it. "How could I forget? The way you took down Shayla Corning was…pretty."

"Shayla, who tried to claim there's no such thing as psi capacities?" Jaguar had dispelled her skepticism quickly by moving into her mind and plucking out her first sexual encounter, then describing it in detail to the rest of the class.

Junius gave a wicked chuckle. "I didn't know a face could turn that many shades of red."

"You did training with Jaguar?" Marie asked. "And yet you live?"

"Just barely. I think there were two or three other casualties that day."

"If they can't stand training with me, they have no business working here."

"I'm pretty sure that's why you get that job. You still working with Alex?"

"The only supervisor who can put up with me. How about you? Who're you with?"

"Frank Dennis. Not too bad. Not much imagination, but he don't get in my way."

"He won't be there long," Marie noted, and looked at Junius with something like pride. That made Jaguar sit up and take notice. Marie was having a fling? If so, she'd picked well.

"She's bragging on me," Junius said. "I just passed the Supervisor test."

"With high honors," Marie added.

"Something like that. I'm waiting for a post to open up."

"If you need my recommendation, you got it. From Alex, too, I'm sure. As long as it's not his post."

"As if I'd ever try and supervise you. How is Alex? I haven't seen him in a while."

He's good," Jaguar said. "Busy. You know."

Junius's dark eyes considered her. He'd heard something wrong in her tone. Like most skilled empaths, he was also an excellent listener. "You need anything, you let me know. Same goes for Alex," he said, trying to sound casual.

Marie, beaming, touched his arm. He gave her a wave with his large hand, and they ambled on. Jaguar again turned to the big cats, ready to work, but was interrupted again, this time by her cellcom buzzing.

"Hell," she muttered, but she answered it. Could be some emergency with Springer. But it wasn't. It was Rachel. Her face on the small screen looked excited.

"Something?" Jaguar asked.

"A few things," Rachel said. "Thing one—the red head. It's Ron Schulman's daughter. Jeral."

"Oh, for fuck's sake," Jaguar said. "Him again?" If she'd known that when she saw Alex she would have told him. As it was, she didn't even think to mention the incident. It seemed too normal, not worth it. Then again, maybe he already knew, and it was one of the things he couldn't talk about. Something going on with him and the suits? She hoped not. She'd prefer it if Jeral was just trying to seduce Springer for some nefarious goal Schulman had in mind.

"Any connection between her and Alex?" she asked.

"None I could find," Rachel said.

"How hard did you look?" Rachel had a certain prejudice in Alex's favor.

"As hard as I could, Jaguar. Why would you even ask?"

"Sorry," Jaguar said. "I'm a little edgy. Is there a thing two?"

"Two and three. There's no correlation with Springer's DNA anywhere."

"Did I ask you to check his DNA?"

"Well, no. But you asked me to find out everything Alex did on the home planet, and I learned he spent some with Mike Pearson, at Hanson Labs. Mike's speciality is DNA, so I figured Alex was looking into it, and you'd want to know, too."

"You're getting too good at this," Jaguar noted.

"Look who trained me. Anyway, Mike's records showed a blank, and I couldn't find a damn thing on my own. Not through means legal or illegal."

"That's ridiculous," Jaguar said. "He's got to be related to someone in the world." The Planetoid itself had one of the biggest and most sensitive databases of any agency. Sometimes it was a problem because it turned up too many second and third cousins, muddying the field.

"I know," Rachel said. "So that means—"

"Somebody's hiding it," Jaguar completed for her. "And doing a damn good job."

Wiping out a prisoner's DNA connections would take considerable resources, or considerable skill. And she knew of only one person involved who had both. Someone who'd gone to the trouble to get here, and who wanted to give Springer away to Perry Delgardo. "I'd start digging around Ron Schulman if I was you," Jaguar said.

"I thought the same thing, but I ran into a problem, and that's the third thing. Ron's DNA is in a bauble.

"A bubble?"

"Bauble, Jaguar."

"Cheap bauble, expensive bauble, what?"

"You don't know what a bauble is? Never mind. It's a digital construction, a holding place for information you want to keep separate from any connection. A digital brick house, so to speak. The info is there, but not visible. *And* it grabs and hides any connection to related info from any and all available sources."

"I don't get it," Jaguar knew little about technology except how to make it cease functioning. "Why not just delete the information, if you don't want it known?"

"Not easy—at least not for civilians. We've got a few protocols for supervisors and governors even I can't bust. But in most cases, the bauble works better. Really obscure, and if you don't know how to spot them, they make your search protocol believe the information is available, but not connected to what you're looking for. I almost missed this one, but I happened to notice a small spike in—"

"—Good for you," Jaguar interrupted. Rachel could go into infinite raptures about the details of code, making Jaguar's head spin. She wasn't up to it today. "So now you can do something about it."

"Sure. What would you suggest?"

"Pop it, Rachel," she said.

"What?"

"If his DNA is in a bubble, pop it."

"Bauble, Jaguar. And they're really tough because the spike I was telling you about always pushes you back to—"

"—C'mon," Jaguar cut in. "Just give it a little prick."

Rachel's eyes went wide. "Oh," she said happily. "Oh, that's brilliant, Jaguar."

"Is it?"

"Very."

"Okay. If you say so."

"I do. Gotta go," Rachel said, and did so.

Jaguar had no idea what she'd said, but thought Rachel's reaction was a good sign. When she was on the track of a hacking possibility, she was pure bloodhound. She'd leave her to it.

She turned back once more to the jaguars. They regarded her with eyes that saw everything, and gave nothing away. Eyes like her own, sometimes.

She sighed. "Whatever you have to tell me, I guess I'm not ready to hear it," she said.

Chaos made a low growling sound. Hecate leaned over and licked his ear.

She turned and walked away. Regardless of bubbles and baubles, regardless of her fear, she had a prisoner to deal with. And they had a show coming up in just a few hours.

CHAPTER FOURTEEN

"Oh, yeah," Gerry said. "Vamping on a groove would create such a very hip foundation for any verbiage."

He picked his beer up from the bar and took a long swig from it. Springer did the same with his. They were relaxing at the bar of the Crab Nebula, waiting for Jaguar and Pinkie to finish going over the set list for tonight's show. They stood on the stage, not too far, and seemed absorbed in their work.

"So try it like this," Springer answered, and picked up the guitar resting near his barstool, starting a riff that was more rhythmic than tonal, his fingers plucking swiftly at strings, interspersing that with slaps to the wood while Gerry spit out words that were his tribute to styrofoam, a substance he had a thing about. His foot tapped out time, the two of them lost in rhythm and words, working their craft.

When the song reached its inevitable conclusion, Gerry threw his hands up and gave a whoop. "Man," he said, "you are so good at that. You just pick *up* on what a song wants to do, and you *do* it. It's great."

"Thanks," Springer said. "But it only works because you do the same thing."

"Appreciate it," Gerry said. "Hey—on my next vacation I'm doing some home planet gigs. You wanna sit in?"

Springer's face twisted into amusement. "Not sure they'll let me," he said.

"Oh. Right. Y'know, sometimes I forget why you're here. It's like—well, like that was a different you. Maybe that's just what happens here. I guess it's what happened to me."

"Did it? What got you here anyway?"

Gerry shifted, moved his shoulders around, took another sip of beer. "Drug running. I killed a cop. Shot up a bunch of other people." He tossed a nod toward Jaguar, on stage. "I was one of hers."

Springer moved his beer around. "How come you stuck around?" he asked.

He gestured around the room. "I can play what I want, hang out with people like Jaguar who can howl in four or five octaves. No worries about the crazy makers in the music industry. There's a good recording studio nearby, and if I feel like it, I can do some gigs on the home planet. I like it."

Springer looked in Jaguar's direction, then brought his orange eyes back to stare at Gerry's face. "She helped you?"

"Sure. She's—well, she's over the edge."

"I got that," he said.

"So go with it, right? Just go with it."

Springer shook his head. "What I did is different."

Gerry experienced an emotion he couldn't name, though he knew it sent something soft and sad moving through his muscles. A blues tune, probably. Deep blues. "Why'd you do it?" he asked.

Springer ducked his head down, raised it again. "I don't talk about that," he said.

"Yeah. Okay. Just—well, you can trust Jaguar. She won't lead you wrong."

"Yes I will," another voice cut in, and they both looked to it. Jaguar, in her black leggings and a red silk shirt, standing next to Gerry, with one hand on her hip, tapping the toe of her well-heeled boot. "Wrong is one of my favorite directions."

Springer pulled up a grin. "What's the Kanima want?" he asked.

"Some help with the set up, if you don't mind," she said, and they followed her to the stage.

Jaguar watched them as they worked, adjusting the synth for the first number, dealing with the recording equipment. In spite of his concerns about the smell of sweat, Gerry was liking the music, the time to be with a musician like Springer. And it was good for Springer to be with some- one who'd done as much damage as Gerry had and moved on to a better life. When she saw them talking together she'd left them alone, hoping Gerry would tell something of his story. Later, she'd fill in the parts he wouldn't say—how he sent a good deal of his money to the widow of the man he'd killed. How he'd gone to each person he'd wounded and done what he could for them. That would also be good for Springer to hear.

She was mostly pleased with the progression of the case. They'd had five good gigs, connecting as they played together. Springer had remained calm and lucid throughout last night's gig, and when the music started he folded himself into it, content just to be playing. It all went easily and well, though Jaguar noticed Springer didn't use any of his em- pathic gifts. Gerry was also happy because they'd been given two new team members for road crew—Arni and Phil, two big guys who grunted more than they talked. That luxury wasn't usually in the budget, and she supposed the extra help was homage to Schulman's interest. Wherever it came from, she appreciated it as much as Gerry. It made their lives easier, made everyone more relaxed.

But after last night's gig, when they got back to the Normal House, for reasons Jaguar couldn't determine, Springer stopped dead in his tracks in front of the door, clutched at his head, and started screaming. When she moved to him he made a dash for it, and it took her, Gerry, and Pinkie, to restrain him and drag him inside. They'd given him a shot of rezonine, enough to knock out a small elephant, which reduced him to muttering and, finally, to sleep.

"What the hell was that?" Gerry had demanded. "I mean, it was a good night."

"You know how it goes, Gerry. One step forward, two steps back." After a breakthrough, prisoners often went through retrenchment. She figured the more Springer opened, the closer he came to feeling what he'd done, and the more it hurt, and the harder he'd run away. But the steps back shouldn't take him as far as he'd been before he got here.

They didn't. The next morning he was mellow again, though he seemed to have no memory of what happened the night before. That suited Jaguar just fine. He should start the gig mellow. There would be enough to challenge him dead ahead.

Alex, reliable as death in spite of his recent dive into the cryptic, had brought four of the kids to the Planetoid. Tonight, they'd do their part in Springer's program, with a slight change from the original plans. Jaguar and Alex wanted the kids talk to Springer after the gig, in the contained arena of the greenroom, but Daryl and Gretchen said they had a better idea.

"We want to do to him what he did to us." Gretchen said firmly.

"We can't let you kill him," Jaguar had pointed out. "Against protocol."

Daryl unbent enough to laugh. "Not that. But he—y'know, caught us off guard. We want to catch him off guard. So we'll rush him after the song. Scream at him, call him a killer. That kind of thing." He gestured toward the others. "Right? That's what we agreed on?"

They all nodded. Jaguar had looked to Alex, who turned a hand toward her. "Your call," he said.

"Okay," she'd agreed. "We'll do it your way." It was riskier, required extra security, but Alex took care of that as well.

Jaguar was going over the set list before the show started when she saw him enter the bar with the four kids they'd chosen. Ange and Daryl. Gretchen and Dave. They looked nervous and grim, ready to do battle. She was in the same frame of mind.

She looked toward Alex, who nodded at her, held up a hand with five fingers showing, as he sent his glance to particular tables in the room. Five extra team members, he was telling her. She scanned the tables, got their faces in her head. Among them she saw Scott, who managed to acknowledge her glance without moving a molecule. Of all the people involved, she trusted him the most. She greeted him subvocally.

You ready?

Yes, ma'am, he replied, and she smiled. He'd never gotten over the habit of using ma'am and sir for people he respected.

She turned back to Alex, tapped the side of her nose, indicating she got it, thinking how much easier this would be if they could use empathic contact. She considered telling him as much, empathically, but didn't like being blocked, so she scowled at him instead. He lifted a shoulder, let it fall. He got it.

She turned back to the set list, which included two songs for Springer that he knew about, and one he didn't. More people came in to the bar, a bigger crowd than usual. Moon Illusion's new singer was beginning to draw attention, even among those who didn't know who he was. When she went to the synth to set it for the first song, she felt a hand on her shoulder. She turned. Springer.

"What's up?" she asked.

He looked out into the rapidly filling bar, directly at Alex. "What's he doing here?"

"What's it to you?"

Springer shook his head, kept his eyes glued on Alex, who stared right back at him. They'd taken his contacts out, and his eyes glowed orange under the bar lights. "Nothing," he said.

She brushed his thoughts empathically, but he was totally closed. Adepts, she thought. Fucking Spider Magus men. "I think you two have a lot in common," she muttered.

He turned and stared at her hard. "What's that mean?"

"Nothing I want to go into right now."

"Something's going on, isn't it?"

"Yup," she said.

"What?"

"You have your secrets. I have mine."

He looked at Alex one more time, gave him a nod. Alex returned the nod and left the bar. As if they knew each other, Jaguar thought. As if whatever meeting they'd had was more than just Supervisory intake. A tingle coursed through her, but she didn't have time to delve into its meaning. Gerry started to play. The night was hers, now. The night, the kids, the music, and the prisoner. All hers.

Springer was fully on, fully in the music, singing some of his best work and giving it away as if he had a stadium of thousands in front of him. *Night Lady*, and *Raven Call* went like magic, and she found herself falling into it with him, caught up in the ecstasy, the power of his voice. When he grabbed her wrist and pulled her stage front to sing with him on *Better Not Be*, she was partner in that power, and she had to make an effort to stay detached enough to keep her peripheral vision on the audience, on the kids, on Scott, who would be the first person she'd call in case of trouble.

The kids from the home planet stood apart from the others, and though they'd remained grim through the first two songs, by the third their moods seemed to shift. Ange started singing along with *Raven Call*. Gretchen began to sway, and then to dance. Daryl and Dave cast disapproving looks at them, then started moving, too, as if they couldn't help themselves, as if they had no choice. When they finished *Better Not Be*, while the audience was still screaming, Springer pulled her close, his arm around her waist, his voice in her ear.

"What's next?" he whispered to her.

She leaned in, whispered back. "Fun Gun," she said.

Every muscle in his body went tight, his arm at her waist clutching hard. "What?" he asked.

"You heard me," she said.

He licked at his lips. "I don't have a gun," he said coolly.

"You'll sing it anyway," she said.

She signaled Gerry, who started the opening riff. She stood stage left, one hand pretending to work the synthesizer while she watched the audience, the extra security who were prepped to anticipate trouble. They were only a few bars in when the audience caught on. Jaguar heard a gasp or two. *Fun Gun* had been played endlessly on the news, video showing Springer's face contorted in madness as he howled. She saw people leaning in, talking about it. Then, amidst all the other sounds, she heard one that stood out. It sounded like a sob. She looked toward it.

Not one of the kids. Springer's red haired lady, Jeral, daughter to Ron Schulman. She was standing at the back of the bar, near the door, and her hand was firmly over her mouth to keep any more sound from escaping, her eyes wide and glassy with tears, her gaze glued to Springer. Their attachment was clearly more than casual. Maybe she'd had an extended affair with him. Springer was known to like cougars.

But he hadn't even noticed her presence. He was at the mike, not singing yet as Gerry repeated the opening riff. He squinted at the people who stared at him, and he spoke.

"Gonna do a song about light," he said. "It's called Fun Gun. In case you didn't know."

And he started singing.

Jaguar watched him, watched out for the trouble she'd called down on her own head. But it never happened.

Instead, Ange closed her eyes and swayed with the music. Daryl put an arm around her and did the same. The other two closed in and swayed, singing, tears streaming down their faces. She raised a hand and made contact with them. She expected to find animals, as happened before, or maybe the image of someone stalking them, but she saw and felt only light.

They were filled with pulsing light, as if the stars they shared matter with came alive inside them, offering consolation and strength to their long estranged children, these humans they'd given birth to. Jaguar swiveled her head to Springer, who moved his hand toward one, and then the other, as if he knew them, as if he'd called down stars just for them. Then he moved his hand over the rest of the audience, sharing his light with them as well.

No killer she'd ever dealt with offered such extravagant consolation, such immense richness. Why was Springer doing so? And what the hell was he doing, anyway? Not hypnopath work. She saw no illusions in the room. There was only one gift she knew of that could do this, but she couldn't believe he owned it. She had to see, had to understand.

She moved across the stage, stood behind him, wrapped her hands around his head and made empathic contact, swaying with him as he sang. He didn't break stride. He just kept singing. Kept doing what he did best.

A thrill of power ran from his song to her hand. She lived inside it, and felt it as a creature of power. It changed the shape of time and space, healed all that had happened, made everything that had not happened possible, made everything that should have happened true. She thought of what he'd done with her, pulling a song from her skin easy as breathing, easy as walking on water, if you knew how.

It had to be, and it couldn't be. She'd have to test it, but that was impossible while music held them both captive. For now, she just experienced his relationship to the harsh mistress he served beyond any other demand. His blind devotion was born into his being, something he didn't even name as love, because you don't love breathing. It just is.

And the audience who clamored for him felt that. They were so alone, unless he showed them what they couldn't find on their own: their wild selves, animal selves blocked out by too much technology, too much everything. The heart of the stars living within them. They couldn't see it without him, and he couldn't not see. He couldn't not deliver.

She kept her hands on him, probed deeper, and felt the turmoil of what this did to him, like opening a wrist and pouring out blood. She took a chance and went deeper still, seeking anything that smelled of fear. And she saw something she never expected. Someone she knew.

"Alex?" she asked out loud.

Springer whipped around to her, grabbed her arm and pulled her tightly against him.

"You're hurting me," she hissed as his fingers pressed into her flesh. He just kept singing, and she heard the whispers inside him. *Find the light. The light, the light.*

In her peripheral vision she saw Scott step forward, ready to intervene. Heard the kids singing the final chorus that had been the death of all their friends. They raised their hands high, rocking and keening to his song, tears in their eyes, light a living thing within them.

Springer flung her away so hard she slammed into the back wall of the stage. He fell to his knees and gave the final howl. Nobody moved, all held still in the memory of death, waiting for death to find them, though he'd given them only light, and renewed life.

"Not this time," she whispered.

The audience screamed for what he gave them, forgetting what he'd stolen. Springer rose from his knees. Without looking at anyone, he left the stage.

* * * *

Jaguar found the kids in a group at the back of the bar, all of them looking simultaneously confused and somehow, more peaceful, perhaps confused at the peace they didn't want to feel.

"What happened?" she asked. "I thought you were going to rush him."

Gretchen spoke first. "We couldn't," she said.

"Why not?" Jaguar asked gently.

"I don't know," she said. She lifted a hand and ran it through the air, as if she could grab an answer that eluded her in a more ephemeral space. "He killed my boyfriend, my best friend. And when he sang, everything changed. *Why* couldn't I?"

She made a fist and pounded at the side of her head. Jaguar reached up and stopped her, held onto her hand. She looked to the others. "Quiet, now," she said. "We'll figure it out."

Gretchen's hand unclenched, and Jaguar released her, looked to the others. "The rest of you?" she asked.

They all spoke at once, but each of them had the same experience. They wanted to go after him, and couldn't. Wanted to hate him, and couldn't.

"It's what Gretchen said. When he sang, it all changed. *We* changed. We turned into people who can't hate."

"That's probably good," Jaguar said. "Hate won't answer your questions, or soothe your grief. What you need is to understand. Right? Understand how it happened, why he did it?"

A sigh of recognition. Yes. That's what they needed. To know why they'd been so horribly betrayed. What would make him do so.

"You want another shot at it? Might be easier when he's offstage, not singing."

They were uncertain, ashamed of themselves. "The thing is," Ange said, "it felt like a different person. Like the Springer here wasn't the one who killed our friends. Not really."

"What do you mean?" Jaguar asked.

"Don't know," Ange said. "It's just a feeling. How could he sing like that, and kill us?"

"Did the same thing happen as last time—that feeling of being stalked by someone else?"

Ange shook her head. "No. Nothing like that."

"Yeah, but we know he pulled the trigger," Daryl said, working hard to stir up some anger in himself, in the others.

Dave shook his head. "Man, don't try. You felt it too. We all felt it."

There was an uncomfortable shuffling of feet. Heads ducked down.

"Maybe," Jaguar said judiciously, "you can help me find out what that's all about."

"How?" Daryl asked.

"Like I said. Go see him. Do your thing."

"We tried, and we couldn't."

"Success is all about what you do the second and third time around."

They looked to each other, back to her. "Okay," Ange said. "Let's go."

She led them to the green room, noticed that Scott was on his feet, following her far enough behind that they wouldn't see him. He'd park himself outside the Green Room door, ready if she needed him. She hoped she wouldn't. She hoped like hell she got somewhere closer to understanding all this herself.

When they entered the green room, Springer was slouched on the old couch, his long legs stretched out in front of him, his head leaned back, his eyes closed. One of the new crew guys—Arni—was with him. He stood when she entered. She tossed a nod toward the door. He rose and left the room.

"Hey," she said to Springer. "Wake up. There's some people here to meet you."

He opened his eyes. Saw the kids. "Fans?" he asked.

"Former fans. They didn't like your last show so much. You killed a bunch of their friends and they want to know why. Maybe you don't owe me an answer, but you sure as hell owe them. So you ready to talk?"

His strange eyes sparked. He said nothing. He was terrified. That was good. Jaguar turned to the kids, curled a hand, calling them over. "Go ahead," she said.

Ange stepped up first, holding out a photo of her boyfriend. "This is Lex," she said. "*Fun Gun* was his favorite song. He used to imitate you singing it." She raised the photo to his face. He glanced at it, then away.

"That's what he used to look like," she said. "This is what he looked like after you were done with him."

She held out another photo, which showed him splayed on the floor, his eyes open, blood trickling out the side of his mouth. Springer stared at the photo, unable not to look, and remained silent.

Jaguar nodded to Gretchen, who moved forward and dropped her photos at Springer's feet. "I won't tell you anything about my friends. You can just look at them. You did this," she said. "You killed them. Ruined my life. I *believed* in you."

When he evaded eye contact she reached out and punched him in the chest. Startled, he stared up at her. "Look at it," she said through clenched teeth.

Springer wrenched his gaze away from her and down to the photos on the floor. Daryl and Dave came forward with their photos and their stories. As they did, Jaguar made empathic contact between them and Springer, making sure he felt everything they felt, making sure that transfer of emotion was complete. As she did so, she kept track of his response, visually and empathically. His face twisted in revulsion and he subdued it, went cool. All shields up. But he had no practice that allowed him to block her or these children. Each photo hit him full on. And, to her surprise, each photo came as a shock, as if it was news he was just hearing.

How could that be? He admitted his guilt. She should perceive shame or satisfaction in him, or both, and he had none of that. Within him, she found only the horror of someone viewing a tragedy never seen before. But why? She stepped over to him, put her hand on his chin and raised his face to hers. "Now that you know what it was like for them, show them what it was like for you."

He jerked away, but she pulled him back. "You planned it. You watched them die. Tell them how it felt."

"It didn't feel like anything," he said, his voice stoney and toneless.

She pushed harder. "C'mon, Springer. All those kids yearning for a taste of hope and getting fire down their throats—did it make you laugh?"

His hand shot up, grasped her wrist. "It didn't *feel* like anything," he growled.

"Not up to an essay question? Then let's try multiple choice. *A*—you did it so you could feel death and write a song about it. *B*—you did it because your ticket sales were flat. *C*—you did it to give a thrill to Jeral Schulman, who's following you around."

He released her, stood and roared out wordless rage, then swung at her hard. She caught his hand, kicked him neatly at the back of his legs and laid him flat. When he tried to rise she kicked him again, this time in the jaw, and he went out cold.

At the sound of turmoil, Scott came crashing in, Gerry and Arni right behind. They all stood and stared. She held a hand up. "Stay back. I'm not finished."

She knelt next to Springer, put a hand on his heart and moved into his thoughts. She was surprised at what she didn't find. No memory at all of what he'd done. "Son of a bitch," she muttered.

She released him, looked to Gerry. "Get him back to the house."

As Gerry hefted him up, Gretchen grabbed at her elbow. "Thanks," she said. "That was—that was real."

"Yeah," Jaguar agreed, though she wasn't sure what reality it came from. A prisoner who had no memory of his crime. No feeling associated with it.

"Were we right?" Ange asked. "I mean, it's like he wasn't there, isn't it?"

"You were right," she said.

"So what the hell does that mean?" Daryl asked.

She thought of all the official answers she could give them, and discarded them. She shook her head. "I haven't got a fucking clue."

CHAPTER FIFTEEN

Scott showed up first thing in the morning to bring Springer back to the Teacher's building. It took Jaguar a moment, and then she remembered why.

"Oh. Right. Testing run," she said.

"Yes, ma'am," Scott agreed.

"Christ. I've got work to do with him today. Listen, when it's done, call me. I want him in an observation room. With these." She went to the desk and gathered up the photos of the kids he'd killed, gave them to Scott. "He had a rough night, so keep an eye out. He might kick."

They'd all had a rough night. The new crew guy offered to stay in case Springer went off again. She said sure, why not, but around 3 am she caught him skulking outside Springer's door. Low on patience and sleep, Jaguar deferred words and instead pushed the heel of her hand hard against his solar plexus.

"What the hell are you doing?" she'd barked at him.

His eyes went wide. "I—I heard sounds. I was checking on him."

"You don't enter that room without another team member. You hear something, you get me."

He'd been very apologetic, and she let him go. He was new, still learning. But it shook her up, made her realize how tense she was about this assignment. Her instincts were buzzing, which meant she was working her own gifts, currently beyond conscious knowledge. She'd have to take some time to check in, see if she was ready to know what was down there.

The rest of her night was comprised of restless half sleep, and when Scott showed in the morning she was groggy, ill-tempered. She went to Springer's room, opened the door. He was up, dressed, ready to go.

"You've got testing. Teacher's building."

"I know."

Of course he did. He was an Adept. He knew things.

Scott moved to him, and Jaguar touched his arm. "If you see Alex, tell him he can call me for a report."

Scott left, Springer in tow, and Jaguar went into the kitchen and started coffee brewing. As she did, Rachel entered the room.

"Coffee's almost done," Jaguar said.

"Sure," Rachel replied.

Jaguar, attuned to the fine points of vocal tone, heard discouragement in this small word. She looked at her friend and noted the tension in her face. "What is it?" she asked.

Rachel sighed, grabbed a coffee mug and got the cream from the refrigerator. "Pinkie's leaving," she said.

"She can't leave," Jaguar said, testy. "She's on assignment."

"Not that. I mean, she's resigning. As soon as this one's done. Going back to the home planet. Remember? I told you."

"Oh," Jaguar said, the fog lifting slightly. She subdued her irritation that other people had problems too, and offered what consolation she could. "I'm sorry, Rachel. That just bites."

Rachel took her mug to the table and buried her face in her hands, muttering something. Jaguar reached over and touched her hand lightly. "Okay," she said, "but if you want me to hear you, you'll have to emerge."

Rachel gave a rough groan, lifted her face. "Is it wrong? Wanting kids?"

"Of course not. It's just—Pinkie doesn't. Nothing you can do about that."

"I *hate* that," Rachel said. She wiped at her face. "I hate not being able to do something."

"Yeah," Jaguar agreed. "Not my favorite thing, either."

"Do you want them? Kids, I mean. You and Alex?"

The question raised an unexpected punch of pain. It shouldn't. She'd relinquished it long ago. But it was something she'd never shared with Rachel, so maybe it just resonated against all the secrets crowding the room lately.

"I can't, Rachel," she said. "I'm a Sunwatcher. We don't do that."

Rachel's forehead knit into a frown. "Oh. I didn't know."

Jaguar waved it away. "Alex knows. It's not a big deal. At least, I don't think it is. Anyway, that doesn't matter. What're we gonna do with you?"

"I'll get through it," Rachel said. "I mean, I guess I will. People do, right?"

"Sure. It's like the flu. You'll feel like crap for a while, and then you'll be scoping out women all over the place. And if you don't like any of them, Adrian'll be glad to jump your bones."

"Jesus, Jaguar. You trying to flip me or something? Now?"

"Of course not. But he would jump."

"Well, how would you like it if Alex left, and I threw a woman at you?"

Another unexpected punch of pain. "Don't," she said.

Rachel frowned. "What is it? Jaguar don't even tell me—"

"Not," Jaguar said firmly. "Just something he's working through. It's fine, Rachel. Really."

Rachel sighed, propped her chin with her hands and looked glum. "Love sucks," she said.

"Sometimes it does," Jaguar agreed.

* * * *

Scott knocked on Alex's office door and entered when Alex invited him.

"Sir, the prisoner's in interview room 5."

"Did she say anything?"

Scott didn't ask who she was. He knew. Dr. Addams. "She said he might kick, and I should take appropriate precautions."

"So will I," he said. "Anything else?"

"She said to call her for her report. And she made a request," he explained it.

Alex listened. Springer, and the photos the kids brought, in an observation room. "I'll take care of it," he said. "You go get some breakfast. I'll send for you when he's done with her."

Scott exited, and Alex took a moment to focus. Then he pushed himself up from his desk and walked the hall toward the interview room. As soon as he entered, Springer lifted his face and narrowed his eyes. Alex noted that his energy field was humming, his eyes sparking.

"Couldn't stay for the show?" he demanded.

Alex walked over to the table, took a seat. "Dr. Addams asked me not to."

"Yeah? You always do what she wants?"

Alex lifted a hand, let it fall. Springer was angry, but not about that.

"Where the hell have you been?" he demanded next, as if he had a right to know.

"On the home planet," Alex answered.

"Not all this time. You got back a few days ago."

"I needed a few days to absorb what I learned," he said.

Springer gave a small, guttural chuckle. "What's that?" he asked.

"That I'm your father," he said.

Springer's hand unclenched and he leaned back, satisfied. Apparently, that was all he wanted to hear. An admission of guilt. When he spoke, it wasn't about his parentage. "Bringing those kids here—was that your idea? Teaching your son a lesson?"

"Dr. Addams and I thought of it at the same time," he said, staying neutral.

Springer's lips twisted into a leer. "*Dr.* Addams. You call her that when you're doing her?"

Doing her. A term Alex hated. It smelled of use and misuse, murder and rape nothing to do with relationship. Certainly nothing to do with the emotional landscape he'd traversed with her.

"Nobody does Dr. Addams," he said, meaning it.

"What do you call it? Love? Was it love when you did my mother?" His voice held the maximum contempt possible. He might kick, Jaguar said. And here he was, kicking. Alex, pissed off for many reasons he couldn't name, kicked back.

"It's a mark of my respect for Dr. Addams to use her title," he said. "And if I hear you talk about her or your mother that way again, I'll beat the shit out of you. How's that?"

Springer laid a hand flat against the table, pushed his face toward Alex. "Okay, then, Daddy-O. What do you think of your baby boy now? Glad you made me?"

Alex grit his teeth against anger. Anger at himself, at this man-child who threw his ego around like it mattered. An empath who couldn't control his arts. A crazed young man who killed children, and was shoving Jaguar around. His son. Yet, in some ways, he was only doing what he'd never had the chance to do before. He was acting like an adolescent, testing his boundaries against his father. In any other set of circumstances, it would be healthy and normal. What the hell was it here, and how should he respond? He thought of the answers he could give, all generated by anger. Then, beneath them, one that was the unadorned truth, one he hadn't expected to find. He gave it voice.

"I wish I'd raised you," he said quietly.

Springer's eyes flashed fire. "Goddamn you," he growled. "Where the hell were you when my mother needed you?"

Oh, really? Alex thought. That, of all things, touched him where he lived? "She didn't tell me," he pointed out reasonably.

"What if she did? You wouldn't marry her, would you? Get her the hell away from Ron fucking Schulman?"

Alex frowned. "Did she need to be rescued?" he asked.

As he asked, his hand begin to twitch. He stared at it, saw the lines in his skin and how they wove through time from past to present, moving toward inevitable futures. He tried to push it away. Not now, he thought. Not now. But the demands of Adept space would not be denied.

"Ah, Christ," he said, just on the edge of a moan.

Springer sat up, paid attention, his truculence suddenly gone. He stared at Alex's hand, saw it twitching. "It hurts you, too?" he asked, his voice quiet and surprised.

Alex jerked his head up, aware of Springer sitting just beyond the watery edge of vision that wanted to occur. "Sometimes," he said, his own voice sounding muddled and distant to him. "If I don't agree to it."

"What's that mean?"

Alex worked to slow his breathing. Almost impossible to converse inside the dance of time. Better to show him. He reached out, grasping Springer's wrist. "Like this," he said.

He made empathic contact and let his son feel what happened when he resisted his arts. Springer closed his eyes, allowing the contact. Alex shuddered and released his resistance, let Adept space open within him fully. Better. It was always better when he didn't fight it.

"You—take it in," Springer whispered.

"That's right," Alex said. "That's how you do it."

He was unable to say more. Time danced in circles within him. No vision accompanied this moment. Just energy in motion, trying to get somewhere, trying to do something. A problem to be solved. A way to move from dark into light. Alex surfed it, maintaining his contact.

Springer gasped. "I'm like you," he said. "What I see—it's real."

Alex blinked up at him. Suddenly, Springer started shrieking, his voice a slashing fire of sound. He tossed Alex's hand away, and Alex was thrown out of Adept space. Springer was out of his chair, up against the wall and clawing it as if he had to escape, get out, get away.

Alex went to him, put hands on his shoulders, but Springer whirled on him, fists ready to punch. Alex, trained in combat, caught the punch well before it landed, tweaked Springer's arm and brought him to his knees. He went down with him, drawing him in, holding him tight and close. Then security was in the room, two large men with billy clubs and restraints. Alex waved them back and they moved to the door, but remained at attention.

"I'm *like* you!" Springer shrieked. "It's all true, all true, all true."

Alex held on. "It's okay. It's okay to be that."

"No, *no!* I *saw* it. What he did to her. And I can't make it stop."

Springer's scream of agony was a long crescendo of sound reverberating against the inside of Alex's chest. He held on. Then, complete silence, as sudden and permeating as sound. He heard Springer's voice, speaking within him. *I'm sorry. I didn't want it to be you. But it's the only way to make him stop.*

Words that made no sense, but spoke only the truth. His son, empath, Adept, killer, speaking his truth, and Alex had no idea what it meant.

What do you need from me? he asked, hoping he didn't sound as desperate as he felt. *Just tell me. I'll do it.*

Springer jerked away hard, leaned back on his haunches and stared ahead, seeing beyond this place and time. He rocked back and forth and covered his face with his hands, as if that would close out his visions. Alex took a deep breath, touched his shoulder lightly. "Springer?" he asked out loud. No answer.

He pushed himself to standing, gestured toward the guards. "Get a medic to check him over. When he's okay, bring him to Observation room 23 and let Dr. Addams know he's there."

Jaguar had requested it. He'd see it done. She had a way of shifting the universe toward the most unexpected light. Right now, any results would be better than the ones he'd felt moving in his son.

CHAPTER SIXTEEN

Jaguar stood outside Observation room 23, watching her prisoner.

She'd gotten the call telling her he was ready for her later than she expected, and it came from an anonymous security guard. Alex either didn't know, didn't care, or wouldn't get involved. Any one of those bugged the hell out of her, but she had work to do, and she attended to it. Attended to Springer.

He sat at the table, the photos spread out in front of him, and for a long time he did nothing. No motion. No response. Then he touched a photo, his forehead creased. He looked up, away from the photo, shook his head lightly. Jaguar, reading his energy, sensed only frustration, an attempt to get at something beyond him.

"Go ahead," she murmured. "Look at the others."

He did, one by one, each time with the same confusion. Good enough, she thought. It confirmed what she'd seen last night, clarifying her thoughts and complicating her case enormously. The whole fucking assignment was a confabulation of clarity and complexity.

She turned away from the window, only to find herself staring directly into Alex's face.

"Jesus H. Christ," she said by way of greeting.

"Dr. Addams," he replied.

There was more than a hint of satisfaction in his tone. He was the only man who could sneak up on her. He enjoyed that a lot more than she did. Her face furled itself into the aspect of a stormcloud.

"Why are you here?" she demanded.

"Scott told me what you wanted, but not why you wanted it. I'd like a report. On this, and on what happened last night after I left."

"Oh? Scott didn't *show* you?"

"He told me what he saw. I'd like your take on it." A few flashes of lightning showed in her eyes, then the storm moved away. She was angry, but she'd relinquish for the sake of the job. She always did.

"Springer doesn't talk about why he killed those kids because he doesn't remember," she said. "He has no memory of what he did."

He took this in. "Why doesn't he?" he asked.

"Don't know yet," she said. "Given what the kids said about the concert, I checked for an ephemeral, but I got none of that. Also no sense of him projecting anything malevolent. That could've been infrasound, which a lot of faux bands use to create that good old haunted feeling, but I thought Springer avoided that shit like the plague. So possibly he was deep in a really fucked up empathic space during his killing spree, which he blocks when it's over. Or maybe Gerry was right and he was on drugs. Or, he didn't do it."

Alex felt blood leave his face. He hoped to hell it didn't show, but Jaguar narrowed her eyes, telling him that was a wasted hope.

"You seem to have a preference," she said.

"My preference is for the truth. How will you get it?"

"Dig it out," she said.

"It's pretty damn complicated. Sure you can handle it?" he asked.

"No," she admitted, "but I never am, really. Not until I actually do." She appeared unruffled, smooth as a summer lake. She was all about the job.

"Ever worked with anything like this?" Alex asked. "Shapes, held internal, a ton of psi capacities you can't identify, all that?"

"Twice," she said. "If it's shapes, I have to hold on 'til I find his core. Jake taught me how. It's not too bad, if…"

If. He knew the end of that sentence. If the prisoner wants to find their core and rest in it. If he has a core to find. But if his core art was bigger than just being an empath or a shapeshifter, she'd find a powerful engine driving a car with no brakes, and no steering.

"And if not?" Alex asked.

"Then," she replied coolly, "I'll hold harder. Meantime, I'm stopping the gigs. I'll do a studio recording with him."

"Why?"

"You know. See who you are. Be what you see," she said.

He gestured to her. "Elaborate, please."

"Most of his recordings are live. It's easier for him to hide from himself when he's got an audience. But he's all about the music, so somewhere in it, I'll find his core." Her eyes were bright with anticipation.

"You suspect something, don't you? Tell me what."

"Sure," she said. "I'll show you mine, if you show me yours."

Alex felt the push to tell her, and the pull to hold back. His own emotional prejudice ran so deep, he couldn't trust his impulse either toward silence or talk. If she had to trust him, he had to trust her.

"Right," he said. "Just don't hold so hard you fall into his hole with him."

She raised her eyebrows high enough that he didn't have to read her thoughts. She was hardly going to make what, in her terms, would be a kindergarten level error. If Springer's core was damaged or absent, hers was as clear as sky, strong and clean as the scent of mint under summer sun. Hardly any chance Springer could undo that, and he knew it.

"What I'd like to know," she said softly, "is what's got you running so scared."

He didn't answer. He had no reasonable answer he could give.

CHAPTER SEVENTEEN

Jeral met her father in his hotel room, at his request. When she entered he was seated at the desk, staring down at a computer screen, probably at reports from one of his businesses. His face had the aspect she associated with anger, something she was always careful about.

"What's wrong?" she asked.

He looked up from the screen, stared at her blankly. "Nothing. Why do you ask that?"

"Because you look upset," she said.

"I'm not." He turned on his smile, which had won so many people, gotten him so much investment money and so many political friends. He was about to talk her over. "You've got some work to do," he said.

"What kind of work?"

"Get that woman off Springer's case," he said.

"I don't know how to do that."

"Sure you do. Get Alex to take care of it."

She bit at her lip. "I called him, but he won't call me back," she said.

"That's too bad," he said. "From everything I hear, he controls her. She'll go if he says so."

"I think he's involved with her," she said uncertainly.

Ron's eyes turned bright and narrow with anger. "That'd be your problem to solve. But if you don't get her off the case, Springer will probably end up dead."

She blanched. She believed him. He had a way of knowing things. She often wondered if he had psi capacities he hid from her, from the world. He was so often right. She pulled herself up tall and straight.

"All right," she said. "I'll think of something. I'll take care of it."

Her father's eyes gleamed with satisfaction. He waved a hand, dismissing her from his presence.

* * * *

Jaguar walked Springer through the recording studio foyer, quiet and empty, past the reception area and the posters of bands, the potted plants and racks of brochures on services offered. She'd requested total privacy for this recording session and got it, though Friday was usually a busy day at the studio. Alex had done it, made sure the sound board was set so she could operate it easily, made sure all other appointments were cancelled. Whatever else was going on with him, he was giving her every chance at success with her prisoner.

Springer remained quiet as she led him to the engineering room. He surveyed the equipment, ran his hand lightly over the sound board. "You got twenty loops? That's fun," he noted.

"Fun isn't what you're here for," she said. "Remember?"

"Yeah. Then what am I doing?"

"You're going to record some music."

He lifted his gaze to hers and it showed both fear and anger. "Can't make me," he said.

"Don't want to," she replied. "But if you aren't drooling to record something, why are you making love to the equipment?"

He grunted, kept his hand where it was. She moved to him, touched his arm, spoke to him subvocally.

This is what you love. Music.

Quicker than lightning his mood shifted and he turned angry eyes to hers. "Don't you get it? Music is what's making me crazy. I hear it in everything. Trees talking. How water sings when it turns into ice. I can tell you the pitch of growing grass. I hear the *earth* breathing. I hear everything, and it's all music. I can't stop it."

All this fed her suspicion of what his core psi capacity was, but it wasn't proof. For that, he'd have to sing. But the more she pushed him in that direction, the harder he'd run away. So she'd try turning around, running in the other direction to see if he chased her.

"Then maybe you'd rather I took it away from you. How about that?" she asked.

He eyed her with a mingling of hope and suspicion. "You can do that?"

"You bet. A little neurological fiddling and the music's over. Just say the word."

He lifted a hand, let it drop, then lowered his gaze.

"Go ahead," she coaxed him. "Say you want to get rid of it."

He remained silent, staring at the floor. "Look at me," she said, and he raised his face to hers. "Music chose you, Springer. Now you get to decide if you'll choose it back."

His orange eyes were lit from within, with fear, with exigent joy, with the push and pull of desire and fear. He turned away, looked toward the recording room, back to her again.

"It's up to you," she said. "I can take the music away, or you can go in there and make a song. One for all those kids you killed. For the kids who survived. Or a song for yourself and nobody else. The kind you used to make before it mattered a flying fuck."

He licked at his lips and stood where he was.

"Call it, Springer," she said. "Right here. Right now. No take backs."

His motion toward the recording room door was so fluid, she wasn't sure he'd moved at all until he had his hand on the knob, had the door open, and one foot inside.

She bit her lip to keep from grinning. "That's what I figured," she murmured. "And I'm damn glad I was right."

When he was firmly inside, she closed the door behind him and took up a post in the engineering room, turned the knobs that were marked for her. She could see him, but he couldn't see her. At first, he paced the small area, a caged animal. Then he picked up the headphones, put them on and closed his eyes. She worked her own arts, calling on her ancestors to help this young man, born with his eyes open and his skin one layer too thin. Calling on them to help her name and know what he was. She lifted a hand, moving her thoughts around him, encouraging him to do what was necessary for his soul to find its truth, though it might hurt like hell.

Springer Todd, she intoned into the room, into him. *See who you are. Be what you see.*

"You ready?" he asked her through the intercom.

She pressed the button that let him hear her. "Go," she said.

He bent low, drawing in. And then he began to sing.

He took his time, letting a musical phrase enter the world. It was one she didn't often hear. A hexatonic. The Prometheus scale. A root, major second, major 3rd, flat 5th, major 6th and flat 7th. Perfect for use over the thirteenth chord. Filled with the tension of possibility.

He nurtured it, cupping his body over it, weaving a thread of sound to move beyond his life. It was simple, really. No words, and just one musical phrase, repeated like wind over the stones of the mesa. It had longing in it, a search for others who might share this folly and joy, and what it meant to be embedded in both. It reached toward whoever listened, joining them to the music, telling them they carried all that, all that, within them.

He stepped on the synth that would loop his phrase, and sang a different one, the new layer adding passion to the longing. He repeated it two, three, four times, then looped that phrase as well, to remind the listener that no emotion was pure or perfect or without the tangling of many threads, all binding the heart. He took his time with it, calling eternity into the room, telling the listener they were part of that as well.

Then, he added a phrase that howled above the others, like stars above the horizon, and with it he named himself in the fullness of his soul, his passionate, joyful soul which drank sky and poured out its darkness and its light. His voice, his being, touched distant galaxies and translated them into sound that told of ancestry among the stars. The beginning and end of the universe moved along Jaguar's neurons, rushing through his song to her. And with this, she confirmed what she'd suspected. With this, she knew how to name him.

She pressed her hand hard against the soundboard to hold herself steady. "K'aayul," she whispered, and a shiver ran down her spine. Whatever he'd done, whatever had happened to him, he wasn't broken, nor would he ever be. Not even death could take him. His core art was singing. He was K'aayul.

She'd felt it from the start, but it was such a precious commodity, she never thought to find it in a killer. To call someone K'aayul was the highest praise she could offer. The word was a verb and a noun, indicating both the person and what they did in the world. In Mertec, it meant to grieve and praise, to remember before birth and know beyond the grave. It was the title given to those who sang the ritual songs, traversing worlds, healing the deepest wounds, finding the most profound truths and making them visible.

This, she thought. This was his core, his central art, the binding thread of his life. He protected it like the gold it truly was, intuitively shielding it from the mercenary profession he'd fallen into. And it was rare. So rare, and so difficult to negotiate without instruction.

Those who were K'aayul lived with a foot in each world. They threw themselves into the spirit realm, opened themselves entirely to what they felt there, then returned and translated it into sound, the most powerful medium. Sound, that created everything, the first sensation we know and the last we let go of. Sound contained the first perception of love and fear, the complete emotions of lovemaking and death. Singers held all that in their throats, their hearts and mouths, then gave it away. It was a form of insanity, a willing relinquishment of self into worlds way too big for the human form to bear. And it was bliss of the ultimate kind, making any other state of consciousness pale in comparison.

Singers had to bear up under it somehow. Without instruction or support, many of them melted down into drug addiction or permanent insanity, unable to keep their footing as they straddled two canoes moving down separate rivers, each one coursing forward at the speed of light. She knew only two others whose lives were devoted to that art. They were both immensely wild and incredibly balanced, their lives conducted within the consort of the gods, but both had instruction from their elders, the kind she'd had from Jake and One Bird, from her grandparents, who taught her how to transition between worlds and stay sane. She'd had the protection of people like Alex, a community of eccentric sanity as a bulwark against the void. What did Springer have? Ron Schulman? The music industry? Jeral? She shuddered at the thought.

She didn't wonder that he'd lash out and kill in a moment of exigent terror, but it made no sense to her that he'd plan a killing. Singers didn't do that. Their gods would not let them stray so far from home.

How and why had that happened to him, and why didn't he remember it? She'd have to figure that out if she was going to lead him to a better path, but it was impossible to think of right now. Springer was singing, and as she listened, she felt water on her face, tears forming and falling. All he was, all he knew, formed in her eyes and fell as salt water onto her flesh.

She bowed her head, unable to see, unable to think of anything except the song he sang. She continued silent and still after he took off his headphones and tossed them aside, looking at nothing, utterly spent.

CHAPTER EIGHTEEN

When Alex got to his office the next morning he found a message from Jeral, asking him to call. He tried to remember what he once felt for her, the sense of connection, passion and hope. Impossible. It was so long ago and he was so young. Just about Springer's age now, a thought that gave him a jolt. And while he'd been honest with her about who and what he was, she hadn't returned the favor. He hit delete and her voice went away.

It was a temporary solution. Sooner or later, he'd have to see her. She was potentially a source of important information about Springer, about Ron. But not right now. This morning, he had another task.

Scott knocked on his door, stuck his head in. "Sir? Springer Todd is in holding."

"Thanks," Alex said. "Take a break. I'll let you know when I'm done." He'd asked to see him, wanting to know how he fared after his recording session. Scott told Jaguar only that Springer needed another test done.

Alex made his way to the holding room. Just outside, a young man with a crew cut and tattoos sat in a folding chair, reading a magazine.

"And you are?" Alex asked.

He looked up. "Arni Stevens. *Moon Illusion* Crew. Dr. Addams asked me to tag along, give Scott a hand."

That made sense. Smart of her. "Okay," he said. "You can wait here or go get coffee as you please. I'll send Scott back around when I'm done."

Alex entered the interview room, sat across the grey table that separated him from Springer. His hands were folded on his lap. The air around him was quiet. He looked up at Alex, very present, and very scared.

"Is it real?" he asked. "What I am. What she says I am. Is it?"

There was nothing of arrogance or anger in his tone. He looked as if he'd just seen a new color and didn't know how to name it. Alex felt a tingling in his spine. Jaguar had done it. She'd reached into him and wrapped her hands around his heart. Jaguar, working her magic.

"Dr. Addams only deals in what's real," he said.

Springer lifted his hands, considered them, then dropped them in his lap. "It hurts," he said. "Like what I hear. The shit I see. I'm not in charge. It just goes through me. That's who I am?"

"At your best, that's who you are. Now we have to help you learn to live with it."

"See who you are," he murmured. "Be what you see."

Jaguar must have said that to him. And he remembered. A good sign. "That's the idea," Alex agreed.

Springer gazed beyond Alex, who waited patiently. This was a delicate moment. Springer had to integrate a whole new perception of himself. Not everyone could manage it.

"I chose it," he said at last. "The music. I chose it. No take backs."

"I'm glad," he answered.

He offered a wry smile. "I'm not so sure, but it's done. Will you stay? I mean, after I'm through with all this. You won't disappear on me, will you?"

"Never," Alex said. His voice sounded rougher than he wanted. Too much too feel. Not enough words to cover it. He tried again. "Whatever you need from me, I'll give it."

"Yeah? You sure about that?"

"Like you said, no take backs."

Springer absorbed this. "What happens next?" he asked.

"That's up to Dr. Addams. She'll come up with something good. If you want to see me, let her know. She'll get you here, or I'll come to you. Okay?"

"Sure," he said.

Alex scanned him one more time. When a prisoner cleared, sometimes remorse drove them into an emotional crash and burn. But Jaguar knew that. She could handle it.

"I'll send Scott in for you," he said. "And I'll see you again. We've got a lot more to talk about."

"Yeah," Springer said. "That's good."

Alex was at the door when Springer called to him. "Hey," he said. "Thanks."

Alex felt his hand tighten on the door knob. "You're welcome," he said. "Always welcome."

* * * *

When Alex was down the hall and out of view Arni rose from his chair, glanced around, then entered the observation room. He didn't have much time.

"Hey," he said.

Springer raised his head. "Hey yourself," he said.

Arni tossed a nod toward the door. "He giving you bullshit?" he asked.

Springer shook his head. "No. Just—talking."

"Don't let him fool you," he said. "He's a dangerous man."

"He didn't kill anyone."

Arni laughed. "Sure he did. Quite a few people. He just found a job that lets him get away with it." He winked, and handed over four small white pills. He'd been making sure Springer had more than enough of this. That was his job, paid for by Ron Schulman. Not the kind of job he normally took, but Ron paid a lot.

"Double dose," Arni said. "Do you good."

Springer eyed it. "Maybe I shouldn't. The last few times, it made me worse."

"You didn't have enough."

"I'm feeling okay right now."

"Yeah? How's the voices?"

"They're strong, but they're just music. Just singing. She says that's good. So does Alex."

"And you believe them? What if the voices tell you to kill someone? What if they tell you to kill her? You want to risk that, especially now when things are going okay?"

Springer frowned. Took the packet. "Okay. I don't want to mess it up. How much should I take?"

"All of it. I can get as much as you need, for as long as you're here." He picked up the glass of water near Springer, handed it to him. "Go ahead."

Springer put them in his mouth, took the glass of water and swallowed.

"Thanks," he said.

"No problem," Arni replied.

He rose and quickly, silently, and went back to his post.

CHAPTER NINETEEN

While Scott took Springer for yet another testing run, Jaguar went back to the recording studio, on her own. Scott would bring her prisoner here when he was done. She'd grumbled about the testing, but in truth she could use the time to decide where to go with this assignment.

Once she was in the studio, she listened to Springer's song again. It packed as much power in the recording as it had when he sang it live. Listening to it put her deep into sacred space, where only essential truths ruled. As she listened yet a third time, she became aware of inflections, timbre, phrasing of breath and voice that seemed familiar. She knew this voice, or one like it. Where had she heard it before?

The association was as elusive as light on water, not something she could grab with her hand or track to its source. She filed it, made a mental note to see if she could place it as she heard other voices, in other contexts. For now, she'd wait until Springer arrived and make him listen to the tape he'd made, see how he reacted to hearing his own truth.

When Scott entered, Springer on his arm, she lifted her head to him, and he offered his most arrogant grin.

"Hey, baby," he said, and lunged for her, wrapped himself around her. "Let's have some fun."

Her shock at the change in him held her still only briefly. She disentangled herself, pushed him toward a chair. "Sit there," she said, "and shut up."

"Ha," he said. "Ha ha ha."

"I said shut up," she repeated. He blew a raspberry at her. Jaguar looked to Scott.

"What the hell?" she asked.

"I'm not sure. He was fine this morning." He looked around. "You're alone here, ma'am?"

"Not now I'm not. What did they do to him?"

"I don't know, exactly."

"Was Schulman there, by any chance?"

"I didn't see him. Maybe Arni did. He stayed at the testing door."

"Where is he?"

"Back at the Normal house. Helping Gerry move equipment to the van."

"Okay," she said. She eyed Springer. Always anticipate relapse was the first rule of her work, but it didn't feel like that to her. If she didn't know better, she'd say he was high as hell. Or maybe something they did in testing stirred up dust.

She leaned over, put a hand on his shoulder and read him briefly. Just as quickly, she withdrew her hand as if she'd been burned. The only image she saw was Alex, talking to him quietly in the interview room. What the hell was *he* doing with her prisoner?

"More rat fuck," she muttered. Whatever was going on, her plans for the day were shot. "Let's bring him back to the Normal House," she told Scott. She'd see if she could find out anything else from him there. And sometime before the day was out, she'd have a talk with Alex. This time she'd make him come clean.

She tapped Springer's leg. "Coyote man. Wake up. We're going home."

"Your place or mine?" he asked, leering at her.

"Spare me," she groaned. "On your feet, and let's walk."

He did so, but he kept at it. "Good. Let's get the hell out of here. I want an audience. Take me back on the road."

"The only road you're taking is back to the house," she said. "You're a piece of shit right now."

"I'm what?" he demanded.

"Piece of shit," she repeated. "Not even steaming."

In a flash, he was on her, roaring with rage, one hand at her throat and the other grabbing her shirt. But he was clumsy in violence. Unpracticed. She used the heel of her hand against his nose and brought a knee quickly to his groin. Just as quickly, he was on the floor, groaning. She looked to Scott, who was already at her side. Though she'd managed him easily enough, she felt better for his presence. If nothing else, it meant she wouldn't have to drag him home alone.

"You okay, ma'am?" he asked politely.

"Better than he is," she said. "Help me get him out of here. What a fucking wreck."

* * * *

Alex's cellcom started buzzing as soon as he went back to his office. His private line. Assuming it was Jaguar, one of the few people who knew that code, he flipped it on. To his surprise, Jeral's worried face appeared on the small screen.

"Hi," she said. "I hope I'm not interrupting your work."

She'd called on his private line. He didn't ask how she got access to it. Paul. Ron. Either man would do it for her.

"Not right now. How can I help you, Ms. Schulman?" he said, staying formal.

"Alex—you don't have to—"

"—Yes I do," he cut in, still courteous, but very firm.

She bit at her lip. "Okay. Well. Are you surprised?"

"No. I've been expecting it."

"You have?"

"I'm an Adept, Jeral. Did you forget?" He spoke deliberately, a part of him hoping to hurt her. Not something he wanted to know about himself, but there it was.

"No. I just—I didn't think. Then you know about Springer? You know what I want?"

"I know about Springer. And I know you want to talk to me. Without your father present."

"That's right. Can we meet somewhere?"

"I'm in my office, and I don't have any meetings today. You can come here."

"I was thinking of somewhere less official. I'm at the Governor's. Room 310."

"Not your room. I'll meet you in the bar after work. Eight o'clock?"

"Alex—"

"That's as unofficial as it gets with us."

"All right," she said. "At eight."

* * * *

As soon as Alex signed off Jeral turned to her father.

"Was that okay?" she asked.

"No," he said. "You need something more private than a bar."

Jeral waved a hand at the telecom. "You heard him."

"That doesn't matter. Go to his place, around seven. You'll see I'm right. I always am."

Jeral felt her stomach tighten. "It's—it's hopeless," she said.

"You'll go anyway, if you want your son to stay alive."

It was the only possible option open to her. "Sure," she said. "Anything you say."

* * * *

Alex went home to change before he went to the bar. He thought about eating, but he wasn't hungry. Instead, he poured himself a glass of whiskey and swallowed it. Then he sat and stared at the walls of his apartment. He stared for no more than fifteen minutes when there was a knock on his door.

He stiffened. He knew what came next, and he was prepared for it. Still, preparation only tells you what to do. It doesn't make the emotions you have about doing it go away. He went to his door and opened it. On the other side Jeral Schulman stood framed in the doorway, her eyes like a deer in the headlights, her shoulders held tightly.

"We were supposed to meet at the bar," he said.

"It's noisy there. Crowded," she said.

He knew better. Her father changed her mind for her. "Come in," he said, stepping aside.

She entered and he closed the door, turned back to her. She smiled at him, then held out a conciliatory hand "This is awkward, isn't it?"

"Very," he agreed. "Which is why I thought we should meet at the bar."

"Here is better. It's more...."

"Awkward," he repeated.

"Private," she amended.

"You relinquished private a long time ago."

"Alex," she said, and he cut her off.

"Just tell me what you want."

She moved closer, turned her doe eyes up to his face. "Springer. You have to save him."

Whatever her father did or didn't want, those words came only from her. She was a drowning woman clutching at him, even if he was only a straw man.

"He's got the best teacher, the best program possible," Alex said. "He's making progress."

"I want *you* to help him."

He could use her desperation, and he would do so. She was certainly willing to use his. "I'd like to, but he won't even say why he killed those kids. Do you know?"

She licked at her lips. "I don't. I wish I did. All he'll say is that it's his fault. Alex, that woman he's with. She's not good for him."

"Because she's an empath?" he asked.

"Yes. No. Because she's not you. Can't you take him through his—his program?"

"I'm not exactly objective."

"Then get someone else. I've heard things about her. That her prisoners die. That she sleeps around. With her prisoners, and—and other people."

"Been listening to rumors, Jeral?"

Her eyes went nervous and wide. "No. I—just—he should be with people who love him. He should be with—with *us*."

Every muscle in his body went tight. "There is no us, Jeral."

"There was. And we made something together. Springer. He matters to you. I can see that. Can't we help him together? I know about the Planetoids. You use all kinds of programs here. If you took him away from her, we could help him."

Another piece of the agenda. A reformation of the nuclear family, under pressure. Is that what she wanted, or what Ron wanted? If so, why?

"What did you have in mind?" he asked.

"The two people who love him best in the world are both in this room, and we should take care of him." She moved to him, put a hand tentatively on his arm. "I'm right. You know I am."

Old anger rumbled inside him. "I'm surprised you'd trust an empath. A freak."

Her hand tightened on his arm. "You're still angry about that. I'm sorry. I was young and stupid. Now—can't we help him? Can't we at least comfort each other?"

"For what? Choices you made twenty years ago? If you'd told me, I'd have done whatever you needed. Whatever he needed." His voice was sharp with bitterness. Strange to realize how much this still hurt.

"How do you think I feel?" she asked. "I had to live with the choices. You didn't even know about them."

"Because you preferred the advantages your father gave you over anything I had to offer," he pointed out, and part of him was glad to see her wince. Somehow, that made it easier for him to let go of his anger. He'd moved on to better places but she was still stuck, and in that he could feel some pity for her.

"I'm sorry," he said more gently. "But it's not my place to comfort you. I've got other commitments now."

Small frown lines formed on her forehead. "You're not married or anything, are you?" He shook his head. She smiled. "I'm surprised. I'd think some woman would've snapped you up by now. You're a good man. I should never have let you go."

"You didn't *let* me go. You ran like the hounds of hell were after you when you found out what I was."

"That was a mistake," she said. "I see that now." She moved her hand, resting it on his chest, looked up at him and pressed closer.

He kept himself from shuddering in horror, but just barely. That she'd try this move, and the reasons she'd do so. But he was no better. They were both using each other, to get to Springer.

"If you really want to help, I need to understand a few things," he said. "About Springer, and your father."

"Anything," she said. "Anything at all."

He put his hands on hers, ready to move this toward the best possibility he'd seen in Adept Space. But he'd forgotten the one thing he could never accurately predict. The 13th thing. The random, inexplicable, unaccountable something.

His apartment door opened, and Jaguar entered the room.

"Hey," she said. "I have to talk to you. Something's going on with my prisoner." She stopped with her hand still on the door and her words trailed to silence as she took in the tableux before her: Alex, clasping another woman's hands while she gazed at him with all the intensity of a lover. She closed the door hard and glared first at one, then the other.

Alex startled, pulled his hands away from Jeral. No matter how he read it, this was not going to be good.

"You sure do get around," Jaguar told Jeral.

Before she could say more, Alex cut in. "Ms. Schulman came over to ask about Springer's program—how it's progressing." He turned to Jeral, stayed formal. "Ms. Schulman, this is Springer's Teacher—Jaguar."

"That's Dr. Addams." Jaguar snapped. She turned to Jeral. "You and Springer still trying to get some private time?"

Jeral didn't answer. She gave Alex a smile that implied intimacy, put a hand on his arm and squeezed. It was, he thought, the worst possible response she could make.

"You have to work," she said. "I'll call tomorrow. We can talk about this more."

He nodded. "I'll be in my office."

She breezed to the door and made her exit. Alex stayed where he was, anticipating further unpleasantness. He wasn't disappointed.

"Okay, then," Jaguar said. "I'd say it's been real, but clearly it hasn't, so I'll just say ta-ta."

She turned toward the door. She wouldn't fight. Catlike, she'd walk away. And he couldn't let her. Not like this. He made a grab for her elbow and caught it. She jerked it back.

"Don't," she hissed. "Don't even touch me."

"Too scared to talk it out?" he shot back.

She stood where she was, the best he could hope for. They were clearly about to have a hell of a fight. It wouldn't be the first, and usually they fought hard but clean, two alphas butting heads. She came at him with her horns out and her head down and he had no doubt he'd be gored, but every time it happened she opened up a new space in him, a place where he became, somehow, more himself, a better self, more capable of loving well, of working well. He doubted that would happen this time. She wasn't into clarity right now. She was out for blood.

He reached for the only part of her that overrode both her pride and anger. Her curiosity. "Don't you want to know what Jeral's up to?" he asked.

"That's pretty obvious," she said, her voice a promise of impending rage. "Also obvious what you're up to. It's not the first time I walked in on you and a redhead. You got a thing for them?"

She was referring to his brief affair with an FBI agent. It happened before they were lovers, but that didn't stop her from not liking it.

"Carolan was strawberry blonde," Alex said, "and that was different."

"Not so different."

"Completely different," he said decisively. "I'm not in bed with this one."

"What if I showed up half an hour later?"

"Still wouldn't be, Jaguar," he said tightly.

"Sure," she said, not meaning it. "Well, if you can't keep your hands off her, maybe you can use them to make her stop stalking my prisoner. I don't need her at Springer's gigs."

That sentence was too laden with land mines to traverse. But she was still here, and that was something. He stayed formal, stuck to business. "I can't limit her legal choices. She's not under Planetoid jurisdiction."

"Looks like she's under yours." She licked at her lips. "Taste good?"

"Don't," he said, the word emerging through clenched teeth.

"Don't what? Name the truth when I see it standing in front of me?"

"You're naming fears, not truth," he said.

She slewed her eyes at him, and her voice was a knife slicing flesh from bones. "I'm not the one who's afraid."

Impossible to deny that. She was right. He was terrified, which meant his only defense was a good offense.

"You're pissed off for no reason at all," he said.

"I've got lots of reasons. Like I find you holding hands with a love-sick red-head who's messing with my prisoner. Reverse the situation, Supervisor, and tell me how you'd feel."

He knew how he'd feel. More than pissed. But he could only repeat the truth. "There's nothing going on, Jaguar. This is just work."

"Huh. And you used to give me shit about sleeping with the prisoners."

"Let's be really clear. I am *not* having sex with her. She has information that might be valuable for your assignment. I'm trying to get it."

"What kind of information?"

"I—can't say."

"That's convenient. Can't say that you've had enough dark meat and want a juicy piece of white for a change?"

His hand at his side clenched into a fist. "God*dammit*, Jaguar. You know better."

"Then why do I smell sex?"

"Not a clue."

"Okay," she said amicably, something Alex recognized as a danger signal. "Then show me who she is to you, because she's not chopped liver." She strode over to him and lifted a hand to his forehead, pressed hard and made contact. He took hold of it, pushed it away, blocked her.

"No," he said sharply.

In all their years together, she'd always been the one to deny admittance. Now it was his turn, and she didn't like it any more than he had. She jerked away, making the disconnection as painful as possible. The empathic equivalent of a slap in the face. She rubbed her hand against her hip as if wiping off germs. But she'd picked up one bit of understanding in her quick foray because she had an even angrier gleam in her eye.

"She knows, doesn't she?" she said. "All the stuff you're hiding from me. *She* knows, and you won't tell *me*?"

A truth he couldn't deny. One that would hurt like hell if she did it to him. "I'm not at liberty to talk about that," he said, staying cool, staying professional.

"Ron Schulman won't let you? Too busy protecting the suits?"

He appreciated the irony of that. Once upon a time, she'd referred to him as a suit. "You might think so," he said.

"And you'd rather play tiddlywinks with Ron and his daughter than do our job?"

"Of course not. You agreed to this, Jaguar. You said you'd trust me."

"That didn't include trusting you to fuck around with red heads and mess with my prisoner."

"I'm not fucking around, and I'm not messing with anyone. What the hell does that mean, anyway?"

"I saw you with Springer, Alex. In *his* thoughts. In *his* mind. Go ahead and say I'm wrong."

He couldn't. Instead, he rubbed at his face, and knew she read the gesture as a tell.

"I see," she said. "Then let's try another question. What's *your* fear, Alex?"

Though he'd blocked empathic contact, he felt her spreading her considerable energy field around him, felt her probing wherever she could for the answer she knew would automatically appear within him.

He jerked away from her, opened his mouth to say he carried no fear, but couldn't even start the sentence. She observed his response, and kept talking.

"You know the routine," she said. "You can avoid it, but it won't go away. You can live with it, but not for long. Or you can name it and work it out."

He raised his head, looked into her beautiful eyes, saw a turbulent ocean breaking on his shore. This was Jaguar, going for the back of the neck, ready to crush a skull.

"My fear isn't relevant," he said at last. "What matters is finishing this assignment."

She laughed softly, dangerously. "You're such a goddamn hero, so willing to face *my* fears. You don't have the balls to look at your own?"

He tried his last line of defense. "This is a case, Dr. Addams. Your case. Don't vent your frustration with it by taking pot shots at me."

"Hecate," she muttered. Then, louder, "And *fuck* you."

"Stop it," he said.

"Fuck you, white man. And the *fucking* horse you rode in on."

He stood where he was and watched her go. There was nothing else he could do.

CHAPTER TWENTY

When Jaguar left Alex's apartment she went directly to the Teacher's gym, where she kicked hard at the punching bag, and ran for an hour on the treadmill. She knew how angry she was because she improved her running time by a full minute.

The workout only lowered her level of rage from a ten plus to a nine, so she was still fuming as she walked back to Normal House 23. Jeral's big sad eyes staring at Alex stayed in her mental vision, obscuring all else. Not fucking her, he said. Didn't want to fuck her. What pissed her off most was that neither his face nor his voice showed signs of lying. In fact, he wasn't the type to play in that particularly ugly way. He was more likely to man up, declare himself, and take the heat. So what the hell *was* he up to, because he was certainly lying about something.

Something he'd told Jeral, which he wouldn't tell her. Something about the train wreck her prisoner had become. Was he in league with the suits, feeding Springer drugs? Or was he messing with Springer empathically? He was the only man she knew who was skilled enough to mess with a K'aayul. But why would he do that, or why would he give Springer drugs? And how the hell could she find out if it was drugs or empathic shit messing him up?

About halfway to the Normal House she passed the Zone 12 Infirmary, and in a moment of welcome empathic clarity, was given the image of a woman's face, broad at the cheekbones, with large, bright blue eyes. Her thick, reddish brown hair always stuck out here and there, as if she'd just rumpled it. Her voice still carried the thick drawl of her southern upbringing. Karen Hackett, a Physician's Assistant. Someone Jaguar had dealings with in the past, because she was a practiced empath, who'd set up a ward designed specifically to deal with those who had psi capacities, knowing their needs were more complicated. Jaguar shifted direction and moved toward the infirmary.

Once inside, she went to the front desk, where she asked the receptionist for Karen Hackett. A bright young thing, blonde and perky, told her Karen was on her own ward, fourth floor. Jaguar took the elevator up, and when she got off, she stopped and looked around. She hadn't been here in over a year, when she'd brought one of her prisoners, a Telekine who needed help in controlling his gifts, to Karen's attention. She'd forgotten how different this place was from the regular hospital. The walls were painted in bright colors—sun yellow, robin's egg blue, crimson red—and they sported photos from staff and patients. Some were of well-loved cats and dogs, and some of vacation scenes—beaches, mountains, forests. Others were photos of celestial events such as nebulae and meteor showers.

Karen started this, letting patients bring in photos from visions they wanted to see beyond their illness or injury. Each one was a testament to remembered wellness, and carried the charge of that energy. Karen also had an open visitor's policy, as long as the patient included a list of people who absolutely should not be allowed in. And there was good music over the PA, real music. Once, Jaguar came here and heard Springer Todd's album, *Destination Anywhere*.

Now she moved to the main desk and looked at the man behind it, who was working his computer, filing charts. Another one of Karen's innovations—filing was done by a clerks rather than medical staff, who were, she said, particularly horrible at it.

"Hi," she said, and flashed her Planetoid ID. "Looking for Karen Hackett."

He stared up at her, then pointed left. "In her office. But she just got off a rough case, so go easy on her."

"Sure thing," she said, and moved down the hall.

She knocked on the door, heard a muffled voice tell her to enter and did so, closing the door behind her. When Karen looked up, her broad, strong face showed fatigue, and a residual of anger sparked in her eyes. Her wide mouth wanted to grin but only got halfway there.

"What happened?" Jaguar asked quietly.

Karen shook her head ruefully, and spoke in her broad drawl. "I *hate* working with you guys. No privacy. You all are the worst, you know that, darlin'?"

Jaguar lifted a shoulder, let it fall. "I've heard it a lot lately." She moved to a chair near the desk and sat. "So what happened?"

"Dead man," she said. "Gorgeous young thing they insisted on transferring to the 'real' hospital, where he'd get better treatment."

"Mm," Jaguar commented. "You give 'em hell?"

"That and more," she said. "So what's up with you."

Jaguar leaned toward the desk, put a finger in the fishbowl that sat at the corner. The fish swimming within it was cobalt blue, its angelic fins tinged with red and gold. "Would you believe me if I said I came to visit your fish?"

"Sushi Two? He's worth visiting. A Beta, y'know? They have to live alone because they'll kill any other fish you put in with 'em."

"Hungry?"

"Nope. Merely vicious. Perfect pet for a single girl like me. When I had Sushi One, I asked a guy at a fish store if I could get him a mate, and he said you gotta get two or he'll wear 'em out. So I did that. Got two little girls for him. Two days later, he was dead."

"Nice," Jaguar noted.

"Yeah. I named 'em Thelma and Louise. After that old movie, right? So now we've done the fish talk, what do you need to know, darlin'?" She leaned back in her chair, dangled an arm over one side, the laid back quality of her vocal twang in contrast to the astute attention she was paying to the task. Jaguar liked that about her. Catlike, when she looked most relaxed she was actually most ready to pounce on available prey.

"I've got a prisoner who's K'aayul," Jaguar told her. "You know what that means?"

"In your terms? It means to grieve and praise, to remember and fore-see. He's a singer, walkin' between worlds. About right?"

"Exactly right," Jaguar said. "Where'd you pick that up?"

"The way you live, sooner or later, I expect I'll you in here on one of these beds. I figured I better learn what I can about your folks ahead of time. K'aayul—that's big juju. What'd your guy do to get him here?"

"He killed a bunch of kids, but he doesn't remember anything about it. We were making progress, then he went bonkers on me."

"Relapse?"

"It reads different. I think someone's either messing with him em-pathically, or feeding him drugs to get rid of his psi capacities. I'm trying to figure out which."

"Say more," Karen suggested. "Behaviors, profile and so on."

Jaguar did so, telling her about the recording studio session, about the up and down of his emotional roller coaster. Karen listened without comment, staying silent for some time after Jaguar was done. Jaguar waited, knowing she was thinking it through.

"Labile emotions, underground rage, memory loss, and uncontrolled use of psi capacities?" Karen asked.

"This is right," Jaguar confirmed.

Wheels turned in Karen's mind and Jaguar let them. When they rolled around to a stop, Karen grunted, nodded to herself. "You ever hear of Telepathine?" she asked.

Jaguar searched her memory, and came up with something. "It's the original name for the primary component of Yaje, the *banisteriopsis cappi* vine, used in making Ayawaska. Later on, researchers realized it was Harmaline, and started using that term instead."

"You get an A plus plus," Karen said. "That's what he's had, and he's had lots of it, for a long time."

"Really?" Jaguar said. "But shouldn't that help him?" She was familiar with Ayawaska and its uses. Her mentor, One Bird, used it in ceremony, to put a person in touch with their spirit guides. She also used it in a healing ceremony for something called Susto—a soul loss from spiritual fright or trauma. By all accounts it should be good for someone like Springer.

"Sure, if it's used right. Like any drug. Enough of it, mixed well, cures you. Too much, mixed wrong, kills you. And there's a lot of bad versions going around right now."

"It's not a street drug," she noted.

"Darlin' it's worse. Pharmaceutical companies are selling it. Gets rid of those nasty empathic problems, they say. And they're calling it T-phine."

"Hell," Jaguar said. "You're kidding, right?"

"Nope. The medicine geeks mixed harmaline with betademsine and found out it works wonders on schizoid affective disorder. Then someone had the bright idea to cure empaths with it." She snorted. "Cure them, right?"

"What's it do to them?" Jaguar asked.

"Inhibits MAO absorption, which is simple to fix in regular folks. But in empaths, it makes brain stem dendrites permeable to increased Lutase uptake, and that, of course, shifts neural plasticity in the amygdala, which, of *course*, creates a perfect storm of pheratin and solistate."

"Um," Jaguar said. "Translate?"

Karen grinned. "Stirs up empathic receptivity and gives it nowhere to go. Also messes with the stop and start thing, so they can't control when they're workin', when they're not. You want an even shorter version? Makes empaths go bonkers. And over time, it does cure them. Just like lobotomies used to cure people. Long term use kinda melts the down the axion function."

All of that made sense to Jaguar, given Springer's quick shifts in mood and behavior. But she prided herself on knowing all the drugs that could affect empaths, and she hadn't heard of this one. "Is it new?" she asked.

"Classified experimental, just a year ago. Not used generally, and banned here so far."

"Can you test someone for it?"

"Sure thing, sugar. You need that?"

"Probably. Then I might need access to the real deal. I mean, Aya-waska. A good mix. You got any hanging around?"

"Not me," she said. "That's classified for Indigenous ritual use. Don't you know anyone?"

She thought of Jake and One Bird, of 13 Streams, where Springer had already seen himself. Maybe they'd end up there after all. "I do," she said. "The first thing is to get him tested for the other. What do you need?"

"Skin or hair. Can you get that?"

"You bet," Jaguar said, and Karen grinned.

"Yeah, girl," she said. "Bring me the stuff, I'll take care of it. And lis-ten—if he's been eating T-phine, get ready for some nasty withdrawal."

"Specifics?" she requested.

"The technical term is wackadoodle. Erratic psi capacities—they'll go away, then shoot through the roof, then go away again. More labile emotions. And a sketchy contact with reality. How bad it is depends on his psi capacities. Probably hardest on Adepts, who see waaay too much to begin with."

"Hell," Jaguar said. "How long does it last?"

"Dissipates slowly, over the course of three to four weeks. But like I said, if he's been on it a long time, you might see permanent damage. You won't know 'til he gets through withdrawal."

"Anything I can do to make it easier.?"

"Keep him quiet. Big emotions trigger the worst symptoms. And if you can get him into some intense sweat lodges that'll help. If not, be ready for quite a ride."

"Why," Jaguar said, "am I not surprised?"

* * * *

She went straight back to the Normal house after her visit with Karen, and found Springer seated on the couch, trailing his hand back and forth in front of his eyes and watching it. He didn't acknowledge her. Just kept watching his hand float back and forth.

She looked from Springer to Scott, who sat in the chair across from him. "How's Jolly Boy?" she asked, tossing a nod at Springer. Scott shook his head, a small motion.

"Yeah," she said. "I can take it from here. Do me a favor, and let Alex know what he's up to, okay?"

"Yes, ma'am," he said, and rose to leave.

When he was gone she moved to Springer. He leaned over and ran a hand lightly up and down her arm. She felt his energy buzzing. Took time to read it. Empathic tangle? T-Phine? Could be either. She moved to him, put her hand on his head and caressed his hair. She opened mildly for empathic contact, nothing too deep. She caught the whiff of Adept space, saw images dancing within him. Blood pouring from a cut throat. Alex with murder in his eyes. Herself, alone, her hair cut short. She gave a quick gasp and closed contact. Then she twined her finger around a strand of his hair and pulled hard, yanking it out.

"Christ," Springer exclaimed, jerking away from her. "What the hell was that for?"

She held the hair in her hand, rubbed it between her fingers. "For the truth," she said, "Which nobody wants these days. Not even me."

CHAPTER TWENTY-ONE

Jaguar got the hair to Rachel, who took it to Karen for testing. Then she took a day away from Springer to try and accomplish something she didn't want to do, but had to.

She had to talk to Jeral.

It was easy enough to find out where she was staying, not much harder to grab her there, but she didn't want Ron to spot her. Didn't want him in on it in any way. So she left Springer at the Normal house in the care of her team, and drove to the Governor's Inn. She parked her car near Jeral's room, and waited.

Morning passed into afternoon and afternoon into evening before Jeral emerged, and Jaguar was glad to see she was alone. She went to her car, a brand new Galactica, got in it and drove. Jaguar started her own small Dragon and followed.

Soon enough they were downtown, and Jaguar knew where she was heading. To the bar where Springer was supposed to sing tonight. Jeral didn't know the gig had been cancelled. Jeral parked, got out of her car, went to the bar entrance. Jaguar exited her own car, strode over to Jeral and put a hand on her shoulder. Jeral turned and gaped at her.

"Surprise," Jaguar said.

Jeral eyed her with distaste. "What do you want?"

"I want to know why you're following Springer around."

"What I do is none of your business. And you can't stop me from going to public shows."

"I can't, but you're out of luck on this one. It's been cancelled."

Jeral looked back at the door as if that would either confirm or deny what Jaguar said, then turned back to her. "Is he okay?" she asked.

"Let's go inside and talk about that," Jaguar suggested. She moved her hand to Jeral's elbow, pushed the door open and entered, holding Jeral in tow.

A bartender was behind the bar, washing up glasses and checking his stock in the absence of customers. He glanced toward Jaguar and she raised a hand to him. "We don't need you. Just stepping inside for a while."

The bar was dimly lit, and he squinted at her, recognized her, went back to his work. Jaguar steered Jeral toward a table and pulled out a chair for her, then sat herself.

She gave Jeral a smile. "So who're you spying on Springer for? Alex? Is that what he asked you to do in return for the favors of his bed?"

She noted the quick pain and shame that crossed Jeral's face, confirmation of Alex's honesty. If he was having sex with her, she'd look self-satisfied, content. Shame and pain meant she wanted it, and he didn't.

"Alex isn't—we're not involved. I knew him a a long time ago. I wanted his help with Springer. That's all."

"Okay, then. You're spying for Daddy."

"I am not," she insisted. "I want to see for myself how he's doing."

"Don't tell me you have the hots for him. And you old enough to be his mother."

Before she completed the sentence, Jaguar heard her own words, saw the look on Jeral's face, and knew the truth. "Hell," she said. "Damn and hell. He's not an adoptee. He's *your* kid."

"Please," Jeral said. "Don't kill him."

That, Jaguar thought, was a helluva response. Resonant against it was Alex's words to her, his voice sharp and clear, telling her to keep him alive. "I'll try not to," she said. "And maybe you can help with that. Who's messing with him?"

Jeral licked at her lips, her eyes shifting away and back. "I don't know what you mean."

"Sure you do. Someone's either messing with him empathically, or drugging him." She leaned close to her, whispered a word. "T-phine."

"That's not a drug," Jeral said. "It's medicine. He took it before he came here. It helped."

Her automatic answer told Jaguar what she needed to know, even without test results. "It's prescribed for people with schizoid affective disorder," she said. "Your son doesn't have that."

"He's—he sees things," Jeral insisted.

"What he sees is really there, because he's an empath. An Adept. Like Alex."

Jeral's face pinched in fear. "I told you, I don't know anything about Alex."

Jaguar's heart pounded erratically, unreasonably. Alex kept appearing, in both their thoughts, in both their words. Alex, who wanted to keep Springer alive as much as Jeral did. No, she scolded herself. Stop spinning stories. Just stop.

She took a moment to reset her barometer, went back to the business at hand. "But you're giving Springer drugs. I'm sorry—medicine. How're you getting it to him?"

"I'm not," Jeral said definitively. "I'm not doing that."

Jaguar lifted her hand ever so slightly and listened in. She sensed confusion, terror, an overwhelming need to protect someone. Springer? She supposed so. But there was no information in her about how Springer was getting T-phine. She really didn't know.

"Right," Jaguar said. She relaxed into her chair. "Listen," she said. "If you want to help Springer—I mean, really help him—I need to know more. So tell me how you got him."

Her hands twisted and untwisted, and she told the story in short, clipped sentences. "I was seventeen, and I ran away from home. It was the Killing Times and my father wanted to keep me safe, but I wanted to do something. I went to Manhattan, lived in a shelter, volunteered there. I thought I was being brave and noble. I met a man, and I let him—I mean, we were lovers, for a while. But he wasn't what I thought. He was... dangerous. At least, I thought he was. I got scared and went back home. Then I found out I was pregnant. I didn't want to abort, but my father wouldn't let me keep the baby, so I left him at a hospital. Then, later, my father found him and brought him back to me."

"Why'd he do that?" Jaguar asked.

She showed Jaguar a face full of defiance. "My father loves me," she said. "He knew how much it meant to me. And, well, you know I had a brother?"

"Killed in a car accident, with your mother," Jaguar said.

"I think having Springer around helped him heal that. A second chance."

"Sure," Jaguar said. "A grandchild." Then, she took a chance on a dangerous question. "Who's Springer's father?" she asked.

"That doesn't matter now," Jeral said like she meant it. "I told you, he was a mistake. My father gave me all the help I needed."

Jaguar let these words settle in. Bits and pieces of the story were missing, her narrative jangled and untrue in places, very true in others. She reserved it for later exploration. "And Springer," she said. "When did he start showing his gifts?"

"From the start, I think. His foster parents said he saw things. Animals that weren't there. Birds and snakes and coyotes. They said he talked to them. And what he did with music—that was always in him."

Jaguar nodded. This was the first part of his art. Any one of her people would have known how to help him deal with it. "The Adept gift—when did that start?"

"It was there when he came to us. Sometimes he knew things before they happened. Then, in the last year, it got even worse. That's why he needed medicine."

Around the age of nineteen, which is when empathic gifts and insanity usually showed up. And Jeral couldn't tell the difference between the two. Jaguar bit back on angry words. "You never considered getting him guidance in the arts?"

Jeral stared at her, repulsed. "Of course not. I didn't want him to be a—a freak. I got him help—a counselor and medicine. What else could I do?"

"If he was my son, there's nothing I wouldn't do for him," Jaguar said.

Jeral's already pale skin went translucent. "That's why he loves you, and not me," she said.

There was torment in her words, but the pronoun was ambivalent. "He?" she asked.

Jeral shook her head, waved it away. "What will you do with him?" she asked.

"I'll give him some real help," Jaguar said. "Bring him to some people who have experience with his gifts."

"What kind of people?" Jeral demanded.

"Empaths. The ones who taught me. Alex will come along. Springer needs a male influence."

Jaguar watched Jeral's face tighten in anger. "Absolutely not," she said. "You can't play happy family with my son. My father will stop you."

There it was, Jaguar thought. Everything she didn't want to know. "You and your father don't have a rat's ass thing to say about it," she pointed out. "I choose his program. Me *and* Alex. And that's a good thing, since you treat your son's psi capacities like they're a terminal illness. Between that, and the drugs you feed him, I'm thinking you'd rather he was dead."

"You're wrong," Jeral replied, her face stony, "I'd rather I was dead."

She stood, turned on her heel and walked swiftly away. Jaguar, thinking she had learned more than enough, let her go.

CHAPTER TWENTY-TWO

Gerry moved his large frame uncomfortably in the chair, pushing at the arms as if he'd like to stretch them out just a little to accommodate his bulk. Or maybe it was just his discomfort at being in an office, with a supervisor staring at him. He'd never stopped looking over his shoulder, though he was seven years a team member, his days as a criminal long behind him.

"You're not in any trouble," Alex assured him.

"Yeah?" He asked suspiciously.

"Really," Alex replied. "I just wanted to hear from you how it's going." Two days had passed since his fight with Jaguar, and though he'd tried to contact her in a variety of ways, she wasn't responding. He wasn't surprised. In some ways, he was relieved, but he wanted information. Wanted to keep his finger on the pulse of this assignment. So he'd called Gerry in for a report. Not necessarily the best source of information, but it would have to do for now.

"Is *she* in trouble?" Gerry asked. Alex didn't have to ask who she was.

"You tell me," Alex suggested.

Gerry pushed himself back in the chair and tilted his head, stared at the ceiling and snorted a few times, which was his version of a chuckle. "I get it," he said. "You're worried about her, and you don't want her to know it."

Then he leaned forward, almost toppling himself off the chair. Alex waited for him to right himself.

"I told Jaguar," he said. "I like Springer—I mean, really like him. He's one of the best in the music world, and jamming with him is great. And I kinda feel sorry for him. A kid who had nothing, then everything, then, well, he went bonkers or something."

Gerry scratched at this head. All that was emotional overload for him, his instincts working against all known patterns and paradigms. And there was more. "He kinda scares me, too. He makes makes my sweat smell funny."

"Any idea why?"

"I'm pretty sure it's drugs, but I don't know what kind. Nothing I ever smelled before."

"Right," Alex said. "How do you think he's progressing?"

Gerry shook his head. "He's—rough. I mean, he can sing, don't get me wrong. But you never know who you're gonna get with him—a singer or a nutjob."

"Jaguar's managing okay?"

"The usual."

"You don't seem too sure of that."

"Well, he shoves her around. She shoves back, but not like, to stop him. Y'know?"

Alex did know. Scott said the same thing. "I'm sure it's part of her plan," he said. "But listen, Gerry. Keep an eye on it, would you? Be ready to step in."

Gerry's bulging eyes protruded a little more. "You expect trouble?"

"With Jaguar," he said. "Always."

"Well, we got those new crew guys, and that's some help. I appreciate you sending them."

Alex paused. "I didn't send them," he said.

"Oh. But he said—I think he said you put him in."

"You're not sure?"

Gerry shrugged. "Not really. I mean, they've got all their passes and everything, and the extra help's good, so I didn't, like press it. Y'know? Oh, wait a minute. Now I remember. He said he was their because of what's his face. That Pullman guy."

"You mean Schulman? Ron Schulman?"

"Yeah. That guy. I mean, it's okay, isn't it? I didn't do anything wrong did I?"

"Nothing at all," Alex said. "Not a goddamn thing."

"Then why're you so pissed off?"

"Not your problem, Gerry. Thanks for letting me know."

* * * *

When Gerry left, Alex put a call in to Paul. He didn't answer, so Alex left a message, pointed and particular, asking about the road crew Ron Schulman was paying for. When he hung up, he wondered if Paul would ever call him back.

He spent a moment drumming his fingers against his desk, then decided he should call Jaguar and let her know his suspicions, but she didn't answer her cellcom, didn't respond to her pager. He gave it up. He'd try sending her a text, see if that fared any better. If it didn't, he'd talk to Rachel, and make sure the message got to her that way.

Jaguar heard a knock on her bedroom door when she was waking up to her second day of no gigs with Springer, who was restless and sullen by turns. The lack of activity chafed him, and Jaguar thought that was good. Let him build to boiling. She might have a use for his anger. And keeping him at the Normal house was the only way to guarantee he wasn't being fed drugs. The only problem was that waiting chafed her, too. As if she didn't have enough to be twitchy about.

"What?" she snapped out.

"Rachel," the voice on the other side said.

"Come in, then."

The door opened and Rachel came to her side bearing a cup of coffee and her notepad.

"Bearing gifts," Jaguar said, holding her hand out for the coffee. "Kind woman."

"Smart woman," Rachel amended. "I've seen you before coffee." She sat down on the side of the bed. "Let me know when you're ready to talk. I've got a couple of things to tell you."

Jaguar took a sip of the coffee and stretched. "Is it about Pinkie?"

"No. And let's not go there. Work is a better place right now."

"Okay," she said. "Talk to me."

"First, the testing on Springer's hair—he's being given regular doses of a drug called T-phine. Used—"

"To treat delusional schizoid disorder," Jaguar filled in. "Derived from the Banisteriopsis caapi vine, known colloquially as Yaje. Also used experimentally to make empaths lose their gifts."

"How'd you—never mind. The second thing. I popped the bauble. What you said about pricking it. There's actually a kind of digital virus called a prick. It worked really well."

"Glad to know that. So what did you find.?"

"Ron Schulman's DNA."

She showed Jaguar her notepad, and an image appeared on it. Ron's DNA. Jaguar stared at it.

"Okay," she said. "Now what? Does it do a dance?"

"Wait a second. Look at this."

Another DNA report came up next to Schulman's. She stared some more. She knew how to read DNA code.

"Shared alleles. This is a near relative, but not a child or a sibling," she said. "Who is it?"

"Springer Todd," Rachel said, sounding triumphant.

Jaguar's response was milder. For her, this was confirmation rather than revelation. "Schulman's his grandfather," she said.

"Well, how do you know that?" Rachel asked.

"Jeral," Jaguar said. "She came clean about being his mother."

"Then I haven't told you anything you didn't know. That's disappointing."

"Sure you did. You told me she wasn't lying. Which means I know what to do next. I appreciate that more than I can say." She pulled herself out of bed, started to dress.

"You got a plan," Rachel said, recognizing the signals. "You know who's giving him drugs?"

"Sure. So do you."

"Nope. Not a clue."

"Think about it, Rachel," Jaguar said. "What's new in our cosy little world?"

"Um—lots of things. There's Pinkie, going away. There's some weird stuff going on with you and Alex. There's—I guess that's it."

"No it's not. It's something that looks so normal and practical, it's almost invisible."

Rachel chewed her lip, then shrugged. "I give," she said.

"We've got new road crew," Jaguar said.

"Oh," Rachel said. "Really? You think?"

"I think I know where I'll sit and wait for the mouse to show up. And I know it's time for Springer to sing again," she replied.

CHAPTER TWENTY-THREE

Jaguar got Alex's various messages and didn't respond. Let him feel what it was like to deal with silence. She had work to do. She'd stick to her plan, the first part of which was to let Springer do his next gig.

By that afternoon, *Moon Illusion* was rehearsing at Silver Bay, riffing on Gerry's poetic tribute to the end of styrofoam, Jaguar on synth, Springer doing vocals. He was into it, smiling for the first time in days.

"Guys, take a break," she said, when the song was done. "I need to recover from that one."

Springer gave her grin, meaning it, and headed to the Green room. Gerry started to follow, but Jaguar grabbed his elbow and stopped him. "Do me a favor. Stay away unless I call you."

His forehead knit into creases. "You sure?"

"Scott's right outside the door. The prisoner won't get past him." Gerry went back to his bass and sat with it, plucking out some random chords and humming to himself.

Jaguar stayed where she was and counted to sixty three times before she headed to the green room. She stopped briefly at the door, looked down at Scott, who nodded at her. She'd already briefed him on what they might expect. What she hoped they'd get. He'd stay put until needed, and be right on the spot when she wanted him. She opened the door, stared at the scene in front of her. Springer and Arni were on the couch, in close conversation. Springer was stuffing something into his pocket.

"That's what I thought," she said.

Arni jerked his head up, saw her, caught the anger in her face. He quickly recovered himself. "Hey, Dr. Addams," he said brightly. Springer, in his turn, showed his half grin.

She strode over to them, pulled Arni up by his shirt front and shoved him against the wall. "Did Alex okay this? Did he?"

She heard Springer laugh. "Now that's fun," he said.

"Stop it," Arni said, struggling against her. "Let me go."

She shoved him again. "How much did you give him? Some for now, some for later? And who the hell told you to give it?"

"I'm crew," he insisted. "I was assigned."

She shook him once, hard. "Bullshit. Who hired you? Oh, never mind."

She deferred any courtesies and reached into his mind, grabbed it from there. He put a hand to his head. "You can't do that," he yelped.

"I just did, asshole."

He opened his mouth to say something but she never found out what. She drew back a fist and punched him in the face. He collapsed at her feet.

"More fun," Springer said.

She grabbed his arm, pulled him onto his feet and tugged him to the door, trying to keep his hands off her as they went. Once they were in the hall she found Scott already waiting, Gerry next to him.

"What the hell?" Gerry asked.

She pushed Springer toward Gerry. "Rehearsal's done. And no gig tonight. Bring him back to the house. Keep an eye on him." Then, to Scott, "There's some garbage in the green room. Take it out. And make sure it doesn't come back." She walked to the door.

"Hey," Gerry called after her. "Where're you going?"

"Taking out some other trash," she said, and strode away.

Gerry and Scott looked at each other. Gerry gave a long, low whistle. "That's for sure," Scott agreed.

* * * *

It took Jaguar one stop to find out where Ron Schulman was, and she didn't stop again before she went to find him. He was at the Governor's Inn, in their best dining hall, having a dinner in his honor.

When she got to the hotel, she moved through the lobby like a lightning storm. A security guard tried to intercept and she flashed her pass.

"That's not adequate for this function," he said as he stared at it.

She put a hand on his shoulder. "Look at me," she said. He did so.

She tightened her hold, pushed a thought into him. "Drop," she said.

He did that as well, crumbling into a heap at her feet. She moved on.

Almost everyone ignored her as she walked fast past the tables set with white linen and fine silver. Only Paul Dinardo, at the front table with Ron Schulman and other dignitaries, gaped at her, his eyes bulging. She continued to the front of the room, where a microphone was set up for after dinner speeches. She bent her head to it and spoke.

"Hey," she snapped at the gathered assembly, and all eyes looked to her. Paul stood and glared. She turned to him.

"Shut up, Paul," she said, before he could speak. Then she moved her gaze to Ron. Within his eyes she saw a wariness of danger, and she was glad.

"While you're all busy fondling your male pride," she said, "I've been trying to get some work done. The kind we're supposed to do here. Rehabbing prisoners. But that man," she lifted a hand and pointed at Ron, "put his pride in my way. He's been feeding my prisoner drugs, interfering with a Planetoid program, which happens to be a felony offense. I'll be filing a report on the particulars, if you care to read it. Right now, I'll just remind you that what I do trumps your rat fuck pencil pushing any day of the year. So leave me the hell alone and let me do it."

Motion erupted around the room. She paid it no heed. "If you're wondering why I used the word pride instead of prick it's because I don't think there's a male member worthy of the name in the room," she said.

She strode away from the microphone and left them to it.

CHAPTER TWENTY-FOUR

Jaguar drove aimlessly for a while after she left the Govenor's Inn. Another piece of evidence harvested. One more monkey off her back. Ron was in charge of the drugs, not Jeral or Alex. Her relief was immense, but anger at the harm already done kept her neurons sparking. She asked them to subside, so she could plan the next part of her program. Or more accurately, try to figure out what the hell it was. The whiteness of her knuckles on the steering wheel told her how very much she was resisting that knowledge, never a good sign.

She was considering trying the jaguars again when she spotted her favorite dive bar, a place mostly visited by Planetoid service workers who wanted to avoid those who worked in the prison system. When she went there she never identified herself, never talked to anyone or stayed very long. A shot of tequila would be nice about now, she thought. She pulled over, got out of her car and entered the building.

It was dimly lit, sparsely filled this time of day. She went to the bar, took a seat. "Tequila," she told the bartender.

"Don Eduardo?" he asked. "Silver?"

"That's right," she said, marveling at how bartenders could store a face and associate it with a specific drink. She hadn't been here in months.

He brought her the shot and she tossed it down, let it settle in, not thinking about what came next. She was aware, peripherally, of someone taking a barstool next to her. She would have ignored it, but the person spoke to her.

"Tough day?" he asked.

She turned. Junius. "Hell," she said, before she could stop herself.

His mouth turned up in a half grin. "Yeah," he said. "I come here to be alone, too. You want me to move, I will."

She was about to request that, politely, then stopped herself. Her thumbs pricked at his presence. Clairvoyance, talking to her. "I'll be damned if I know what I want," she said.

"One of those days," he said. "How's your rock star coming along?"

"Just great," she said.

"Alex doing okay with it?"

Her hands tightened on her empty shot glass. Why would he ask that? "Sure," she said.

"No," Junius said. "He ain't. Neither are you."

She sighed. "You stopped here because you saw me, didn't you?"

"Yeah," he acknowledged. "Sorry, but you know how it is."

She did. He was an empath, seeing things he didn't want to see, compelled to say things he didn't want to say, to people who didn't want to hear it. Usually, she was on the other side of that interaction. "I know," she said.

"Sure you do. But if you want more, you need to tell me more."

Knowledge chased her like a tornado. She might as well throw herself in the funnel. "Me and Alex are making each other crazy," she admitted. "And not in a good way."

"Love'll do that," Junius agreed. He signaled the bartender, ordered a beer and another tequila for her. Then he turned back to her. "It's different, when you really love someone, and you're with them for a while. You get into the deep stuff, and the stakes get higher. I know. I was married for more than 20 years."

Whatever he'd seen, this was part of it. She'd let him take the lead, let it unfold. "And you're not now?" she asked.

"She died." Junius looked to the distance, into a different time. "I don't talk about it much."

A part of his life too sacred to share lightly. "But you're talking about it to me."

"Because it matters," he said.

Their drinks came, and Junius took a long pull off his beer. Jaguar threw her tequila down. She was about to learn something, whether she liked it or not. "What happened?" she asked.

"It was during the Killing Times. Right at the beginning, before the news started naming it, y'know? She worked at the library, and sometimes she had evening shifts. One night, she was coming home, and I was cooking supper. I looked out our window—we were up on the tenth floor, in the village. I saw her, and she saw me. She waved at me. Then there was this little girl down the street, all alone and some whacko with a gun headed her way. She moved to the girl, trying to help. It was over before I could even yell. My hand was still waving at her. I saw it all, couldn't do a thing about it."

Jaguar had heard many such stories, but had yet to grow immune from feeling them. The curse of being an empath. People's stories lived inside you, with full impact. "I'm sorry that happened," she said gently.

"Me, too." Junius didn't apologize for sharing his pain. He was here to do just that. "It's the toughest part of really loving someone. When you see what's happening, but can't prevent the pain. When you have to let them—well, you know. See who they are. Be what they see."

"Even if it's tearing them up," she said.

"Even when it breaks *your* heart," Junius answered.

The bar was quiet except for the desultory talk of two older men discussing a ball game. Traffic sounds from outside reached them dimly, like waves against a distant shore. "There must be something I can do," she whispered.

"To stop his pain? No. But you can help him face what he needs to face. That is, if he's more to you than just a sometime thing."

She considered his words. He was here to teach her what it meant to truly love. In her world, that was one of the most important lessons to learn. Was she ready for it? She didn't know, but she was certain how to answer the question he'd asked.

"He is," she said.

Junius nodded at her. "When I got married, I told my wife, there'll be times when I can't give a hundred percent, and you'll have to take up the slack. And that'll work the other way around, too. So maybe now, you have to do that for Alex. I'm guessing he's done it for you."

"He has. But I don't *know* anything for sure, least of all how to help him."

"You know," he answered. "You just don't want to."

His words hit her like an act of God, pulling together bits of information she'd stuffed in closets in her mind. There was the familiarity of Springer's voice on one shelf, and Jeral's words stuck in a back corner, next to all the facts of time and place, behind which was tucked her intuition that she smelled sex, and all of it covered with the blanket of Alex's determined silence.

Yes, she knew what she was facing. And once she admitted that, knowledge of how to deal with it coalesced. Images moved within her. She saw Alex facing Springer. Saw herself witnessing their meeting. Knew, without a doubt, how to get the meeting to occur. She licked at her lips, which felt dry. Alex had accomplished his coups on her with grace and integrity, but she lacked the Adept's capacity for manipulation. All she had was direct action, an honesty that cut the throat for blood. She would have to use that. Not fun, but nobody was here for fun.

Junius lifted his beer, drained the glass. His hand touched her shoulder lightly, then was gone. When she looked back, so was he. She waited a few more minutes, then left the bar.

Once she was outside, she stepped over the earth without any sense of her feet touching ground. She had relinquished herself, as surely as he once had for her. Now she was made of light, without substance or weight. And she moved into darkness, without regrets.

* * * *

The Planetoid had a very efficient grapevine, one that passed word of anything interesting or fun from the grassroots of the working rank swiftly. One of the luncheon staff ran into Rachel as she was getting her own lunch, and told her the latest. Rachel immediately let Alex know, so he was prepared when his telecom buzzed and, on answering it, he saw Paul's face in the viewscreen.

"Problem?" he asked.

"It's Addams," Paul replied.

"It usually is. Are you talking about what she did at Schulman's luncheon?"

"Yeah," Paul said. "That."

"She was right, Paul," Alex said. "Schulman's been slipping drugs to Springer Todd. We call that interfering with a federal program, don't we? And it's a felony."

"It's not drugs," Paul said. "Officially, it's classified as pharmaceuticals."

Alex showed him a grimace. "You're kidding, right?"

"Afraid not. And Schulman's lawyers are here, so he's good to go." He lifted a hand, let it fall again. "Alex, I didn't know. You gotta believe me. I thought he just wanted to help."

Alex nodded. "I know. But it has to stop. Even if it's legal."

Paul sighed in relief. "I'll take care of that. Listen, are you in deep shit with her now?"

"You bet," he answered. "But I was already, so that's okay. What matters is getting this assignment completed without further interference."

"I hear you. I'll keep him under wraps."

"Do so. Under wraps and as far as possible from this prisoner. It's a tough enough job to begin with."

CHAPTER TWENTY-FIVE

Having made up her mind, Jaguar acted quickly. She returned to the Normal house, and found Gerry and Rachel. "Where's Pinkie?" she asked.

"At the gym," Rachel answered. "She should be back soon."

"Call her. Tell her to stay out. And you two," she continued to Rachel and Gerry, "you stay in your rooms. Be like mice."

"How come?" Rachel asked.

"I want Springer to think we're all alone. Go. Now."

She watched them retreat, then went to Springer's room, opened the door. "No," she said, as if she was talking to them. "I can manage him. Bring me back something good to eat." She entered the room, closed the door behind her.

He was on his bed, staring at the ceiling.

"You need anything?" she asked him.

"No. Did somebody leave?"

"Everyone. I sent them out for food."

"Just you and me, baby?" he looked intrigued. "You're not scared?"

"Of what? A drug addict?"

He glowered. "I'm not a drug addict."

"Yeah you are. You had Arni feeding you T-phine."

"That's not drugs. It's medicine. To keep me from killing people."

"Right. You spew a lot of crap about music, but you're all about the drugs. You're made of sound and fury. You know—a tale told by an idiot and so on."

"That's bullshit," he said, losing interest.

She moved to him, tweaked the side of his chin. "Nope. You're an addict, and your mother's the dealer. Bad, bad, mommy. She should be in holding by now."

He jerked his head up. "What're you talking about?"

"Your mommy. Jeral Schulman. She arranged to get you the, um, medicine. Now she's looking at two felonies—dealing, and interfering with a federal program. Once we start investigating, I'm guessing we'll find out she's the one who got the live fire into your gun. Maybe when she's convicted they'll give her to me. That would be fun."

His right hand clenched into a fist, and his orange eyes sparked fire at her. She blew him a kiss and walked out of the room, made her way to her own bedroom, picked up a brush from her bureau and started brushing her hair. In short order he was behind her. She ignored him until he grabbed her arm, his hand a talon's grasp. She stood, turned and faced him.

"Leave her alone," he hissed. "She didn't do anything wrong."

"Sure she did. At a minimum she's accessory to murder, since you were on the drugs she gave you at your concert. My only question is why would she? Did she get sick of you? Or maybe her daddy didn't know what a bad girl she was and you threatened to tell on her."

His face contorted in fury. "I killed those kids. She had nothing to do with it."

"You know how many spree killers I've dealt with? Not one of them forgets what they've done, and they all want to talk about it. So explain why you don't."

He shook her arm. "She didn't *do* it," he repeated.

"Then why are you protecting her?" Jaguar demanded. She got no answer. They'd have to do it her way.

She wrenched her arm from his hold and pressed her hand against his face, shoving hard into the perpetual motion of his mind. No where to get footing, no source of stability. Inside him was all a dizzy spinning, a cacophony of sound that tossed her from thought to thought, random and confused. He tried to push her out, but she was dug in good and not about to budge.

Shifting shapes, shifting aspects, nothing solid to hold onto but she held on anyway. When one place eluded her, she jumped to the next, like leaping across moving blocks of ice on a flowing river. And sound was everywhere. The singing of all the spirits who sought his gift. The singing of his soul.

She moved beyond it. He was expert at hiding, but she was more expert at finding. She didn't look for his core. She already knew what that was made of. Instead, she sought whatever was in him of Adept, what vision he'd seen that was leading them all on this merry chase. Whatever it was, he didn't want her to see, and he didn't want it a lot.

He brought a hand back and slapped her hard. The strength of it surprised her, bringing sharp tears to her eyes, putting her off balance. She let herself fall onto her bed and rolled over quickly to see him moving toward her. He grabbed at her throat but she brought a hand up, gouged at his eyes and he released her, falling back. She scrambled to sitting, ready for him when he flung his entire body against hers. He was on top of her, his hands on her shirt and she let him proceed. All she had to do was stay conscious long enough to make sure he didn't kill her. He lifted her off the bed and slammed her onto the floor, got on top of her and held her shoulders pinned.

"Stay away from her," he said. "Say you will. *Say* it."

This. Exactly right. Just what she hoped for. Then, a shift. She felt his mind go clear, felt his own empathic contact moving in her. He went still and stared at her. He'd caught the scent of her plan. Of course he did. Apples fell close to their trees.

"This is for—for Alex?" he asked, confused.

His hesitation gave her the moment she needed. She kicked him once hard in the nuts, and roared like a banshee.

* * * *

Alex woke from a dead sleep, to the sense of Jaguar's presence. Immediately, without thinking, he got up and started dressing. He had to get to her. She needed him.

He had his pants on, his shirt over his head, and was moving to the door when his hand began to tingle. He stopped and stared at it. The lines of possibility were drawing in. Something was changing them. Something, or someone. He stood where he was, and closed his eyes.

Whatever had happened was over. Wherever she was, he couldn't get to her.

He leaned his head against the door and swore softly. He got undressed, and went back to bed.

CHAPTER TWENTY-SIX

Jaguar was someplace murky, and damp, grey mist swirling around her. Then, shapes began to coalesce. There. Alex, sitting on his bed, his head bowed in his hand.

"Alex?" she asked. He didn't answer. Instead, she heard another voice.

"Hey," the voice said. Not Alex. Gerry. He spoke with concern. "Hey, Jaguar. Wake up."

She opened her eyes and saw Gerry crouched over her. She sat up fast, and he fell back. She had no idea what was happening. Why was Gerry here, and was that Rachel with him? She looked down and saw she had a blanket over her. For shock, she supposed.

"Shit," she murmured. She tried to sit up, but Rachel put a hand on her shoulder.

"Stay down, Jaguar," she said. "Give it a minute."

She looked at Rachel, then Gerry. "What happened?"

"You don't know?" Rachel asked.

She frowned, and realized she did. At least, she knew enough. "Most of it," she said. "Fill me in on your part."

"We heard you roaring," Gerry said. "I—well, I broke the door, and I guess I'll have to pay or something, but I'm not sorry because when I got in he was—you were—well…" His words trailed off, and he looked pained.

Yes, she thought. She was. He was. But she remembered getting in at least one good kick. She remembered roaring, knowing she wasn't alone. "Be specific," she requested. As much as she didn't want to know, she had to.

Rachel took over. "Your shirt was ripped, and he was sitting on top you, screaming at you," she said. "You were passed out."

Jaguar closed her eyes, opened them again. "What was he screaming?" she asked.

"What's it matter, Jaguar?"

"Just—tell me."

Rachel pointed an index finger at her, as if to scold, then dropped it and gave up. "Something about you didn't understand. He had to make it stop. You had to help."

Jaguar considered. It didn't make sense to her. Adepts, seeing visions. "Any damage?" she asked.

"You've got a great big welt on your cheek," Rachel said. "I don't know about the stuff that doesn't show."

"Okay," she said. "So that's done."

Rachel made a tsk sound. Gerry shook his head, confused and concerned at the same time, which was overload for him.

"He should get lockdown," he said. "That's the rules for—um—something like this, isn't it? Lockdown and a new teacher assignment. Pronto."

"Did I stop him?" Jaguar asked.

"Yeah," Gerry said. "But I helped."

"What did you do?"

Rachel cut in. "He picked him up by the back of his shirt and threw him across the room," she said.

A simple but effective expedient. "I'm sorry I missed that. Must've been pretty."

"It was," Rachel agreed.

Gerry pushed himself to standing. "You need anything? Drink or shrink?"

She grinned. It was a line from one of his songs. Take a drink or see a shrink, and you'll soon be in the pink again. "Thanks, but a shower and sleep is what I need. You should get some sleep, too," she told them both.

"I think you should go to the infirmary," Rachel said.

"What for? He didn't *do* anything."

"For trauma, Jaguar. Look at your face. Your throat."

"My throat's been through worse. Where is he?"

"My room," Gerry said. "I locked him in, after I picked him up."

"Good. He can stay the night there. I'll take things up in the morning."

"You will not," Rachel said crisply. "You will absolutely not."

"Rachel, he's my prisoner. I'm not through with him."

"He *assaulted* you."

"I'm not *through* with him," she repeated. "Jesus, Rachel, I know what I'm doing."

"Don't go after me," Rachel said, stung by her words and her tone.

"Sorry," Jaguar said. "But really. We were just—tussling."

"Your shirt was ripped."

"Yeah. He grabbed it. Jeeze, Rachel. It isn't the first time this kind of thing happened. We're not dealing with buddhist monks here."

Physical violence of any kind was just another job hazard for her. All in a days work. But Rachel rarely got to see it. Her aspect remained foreboding.

"We have to write up reports on it," she said.

"Go ahead." Jaguar looked at Gerry. "Go back to your room. Stay with him. Make sure he doesn't try any other tricks tonight. And talk to him, Gerry. He's not the enemy, you get that, right?"

"Sure," he said. "I mean, I guess I wasn't much better, was I?"

She showed him a grin. "You were much worse," she said. "Get out of here. Go to work."

"If you're okay?"

"Fine," she said. He watched her for a moment, nodded, and turned to leave.

"Gerry," she said before he got to the door. "Thanks."

He turned and blinked at her. "No problem," he said, and shuffled away.

As soon as he was gone, she stood, and looked up at Rachel. "You're staying, I take it?"

"You betcha," Rachel replied.

"You can talk to me, but I need the shower," she said, heading toward the bathroom. Rachel padded after her.

Jaguar pulled back the shower curtain and turned the water on, let it flow until it got hot over her hand, then stripped quickly and stepped in, pulled the curtain shut. Rachel put the toilet seat down and sat on it.

"You really can't just ignore this," she said.

Jaguar felt the water pour over her, hot and soothing. "I'm not. I just need to think through my next moves."

She heard Rachel sigh. "You're up to something, aren't you?"

"Maybe," she replied.

"Tell me."

She thought of all the secrets surrounding this case, and how much unnecessary trouble they'd caused already. She wouldn't continue them. "Springer needs to admit to something, and this is the only way to make him do it. Also, Alex is in trouble. I'm trying to get him out of it."

"Oh," Rachel said. "Can I help?"

Jaguar smiled. Typical of her. She worried and worried, but she also trusted. And well she should. She wasn't an empath, but she had a good nose for the truth. "Just file your report," she said. "Make it graphic."

A long pause. "Really?"

"Yup," she said.

"Okay," Rachel said. "Let me know if there's anything else I can do."

"You already are," Jaguar said. "Some people ask if they should stay. You didn't ask. You just stayed."

"Well, yeah," Rachel said.

"Yeah," Jaguar agreed. She let the water wash away bad dreams, bad acts, and what would become bad memories to wake her from restless sleep in days to come.

* * * *

In the morning, she unlocked Gerry's door, shooed him out of the room and went inside. Springer was in his usual position in bed, on his back, hands behind his neck as he stared up at the ceiling. His eyes were closed, but he was awake.

"You okay?" she asked.

"Fine," he said. "I mean, I had to listen to Gerry try to explain the meaning of life, and that's always a little trippy, but I survived. How're you?"

"Peachy keen," she replied. He was clear and cogent this morning. She was glad. She needed him that way.

He opened his eyes, looked her over. "You got quite a shiner."

She touched the welt on her cheek. "Technically, it's too low to be a shiner. I won't ask about your bruises."

"I appreciate that," he said.

"What do you remember?"

"The important part. You're not going after Jeral. You never were."

"Your mother? No. But there'll be no more medicine, in case you were wondering."

"I figured. That's okay. I guess it was bullshit all along. So what're you trying to get out of Alex?"

"Same thing I want from you. Name the truth."

"I can tell you about his, if you want," he noted.

She shook her head. "Everyone thinks they can tell me about yours, too. And they're all wrong. He needs to talk for himself. So do you."

"Let's work on him, first," he suggested. "What do you want me to do?"

"Maybe you already did enough."

"Maybe, but I think you want more."

"You sure you want to play? It won't be fun."

"You keep saying I'm not here for fun. You better tell me enough so I don't fuck it up."

She drew in breath, released it slowly. Okay. She'd keep it going. "When he shows, bait him," she said. "Not too much, or he'll hurt you bad."

He tilted his head, grinned. "You think he'll show?"

"I know he will. He's reliable as death."

"Yeah. He told me he'd beat the shit out of me if I didn't respect you."

"Then that's what he'll do."

"You sure you know what you're doing?"

"Nope," she said. "I only know what I hope I'll get at the end."

"What's that?"

"You and him, alive and well."

"I thought this was about him."

"It's about both of you."

His face wrenched into a grimace and he pushed himself up to sitting. "Look, Alex is okay, so I'll help with him, but leave me out of it. I'm the guy who killed a bunch of kids."

"What if you didn't? What if someone else planned it?"

"It's still on me," he insisted. "You talk about choice—I chose to go back to Ron. Not for the money, either. I went back because I was chicken shit. I didn't know what was happening to me, so I took what he offered—his money and his drugs. That was *me*. Nobody else. Everything else happened because I chose that."

"You also went back because you knew Jeral was your mother," she said, knowing this was a truth he wouldn't state. "You went back for her."

"What's it matter? I went back. And I pulled the fucking trigger."

He was telling her almost everything, but the part he left out mattered more than anything he said. It was a whisper of distant voices that wouldn't be silenced, and couldn't be fully heard. Part of it she understood. No matter what happened, he'd witnessed horror, knew his hand as an instrument of death, and he still reeled from the shock of that. Post traumatic stress often wiped out memory of events too horrific to bear, and in a system as highly tuned as his, such stress would have even greater reverberations.

The only way he knew to deal with it was to shoulder the burden. To accept guilt, true or false, was sometimes the only way to grab back a sense of control in the midst of chaos. Also a way of showing who you really were. In spite of all appearances to the contrary, he was, in fact, a young man who shouldered burdens. It was in his nature, and she knew why. She held back from saying anything about that yet. Not time. There was more fun to come before those words were spoken.

"Pulling the trigger's nothing if you think the gun is full of blanks," she said. "You didn't load it, did you?"

He shifted on the bed, struggling with the question, with himself. "I was the ammo," he said at last.

"That's not what you're running from, coyote man. What vision don't you want me to know about?"

He lay back and closed his eyes. "You're smart. Figure it out," he said.

Damn Adepts. "I've solved worse problems," she said, and left him to his own devices.

CHAPTER TWENTY-SEVEN

When Alex got Rachel's report his first impulse was to go to Jaguar. His second was to put his fingers around Springer's throat and squeeze.

Rachel included photos of Jaguar's neck and face, which showed the marks of hands raised against her violently. And she'd been very careful to explain the exact way her shirt was torn, the exact position they'd found his son in. That any son of his could act that way.

He breathed himself into calm and asked himself what, as Supervisor, he should do. Jaguar had fielded prisoner assaults in the past, and what he usually did was call her. Confirm that she was in charge of it, make sure she didn't need back up. He might as well do so now.

He punched in her cellcom number and waited. His call went to message and he didn't leave one. She was staying elusive, giving him a shot of his own cryptic dealings.

He closed his cellcom and brooded. His thoughts chased each other like hamsters on wheels, always going back to the same place. Before long he got up, left his office and made his way to Normal House 23, where he let himself in with his Supervisor's key pass.

Gerry was immediately at the door, and blinked at him in surprise. "Oh," he said. "It's you. Is there…something?"

"Where's Jaguar?" he asked.

"She went to the store. We needed some supplies."

Good, he thought. That was good. "I need to talk to Springer. Where is he?"

Gerry tossed a nod toward one of the back doors. "In there."

Alex moved toward the room, offering no explanation. He opened the door, saw Springer standing at the window, staring out. He stepped inside the room, closed the door behind him.

Springer turned to him and grinned. "Managing it all okay?" he asked.

Alex was a big man, but he could move fast, and with the grace of a cat. Before Springer's grin dissolved he was in front of him, his fist drawn back. He hit him once hard, in the face. Springer bounced off the wall behind him, slumped onto the floor.

Alex clenched and unclenched his hand. "What did I tell you I'd do? She is not to be used that way. Not ever."

Springer felt at his jaw, offered his lopsided grin once more. "How do you use her?" he asked.

"Don't even get close."

"You *put* me close. You gave me to her."

Something red and bloody appeared in Alex's vision. He bent down to Springer and put a hand on his shirt, lifted him and pressed him against the wall. Rage raked his soul, a wild and uncontainable animal. Rage at himself, at Springer, at all inevitabilities. All he saw was red and bloody. All he felt was rage.

"If you've got a problem with me you *bring* it to me," he said, giving Springer a shake to emphasize each word. "If you threaten her in any way, if you give her anything other than absolute respect, I'll end you."

A whisper inside him, composed equally of longing and bitterness. *Promise, father?*

Not what he expected to hear. His hand tightened on the cloth he clutched. He waited to see what he planned to do next, not sure of his own intent.

* * * *

When Jaguar returned from her errand, she was greeted by Gerry's worried face.

"What?" she asked, certain something was wrong.

"Nothing," Gerry said.

Jaguar frowned. "Where's Springer?"

"In his room."

"You sure?"

"Yeah. Alex is in there with him."

"Alex?"

"That's what I said. He showed up a few minutes ago. Asked where you were, then went to see Springer."

She took in Gerry's words and his tone. She took in the energy in the room beyond Springer's closed door. She knew he'd show. She just hadn't expected him to show so soon. "Rat fuck," she said, and moved to the room, going fast.

When she opened the door she saw Alex, holding Springer pinned against the wall.

"What're you doing, Alex?" she asked, staying cool. Somebody had to.

He didn't look at her. "We're talking," he said, his voice rough and low.

"About what?"

His jaw worked. "The nature of courtesy. And it's a private conversation."

"He's my prisoner," she pointed out.

"Codebook section nine," he said. "After any serious assault report, the Supervisor will conduct an interview with the offending prisoner and determine the next best course of action."

"What's that?" she asked. "Beat him up?"

"Leave, Jaguar," he said. And he turned to her.

When she saw his face, feral was the first word that came to mind. Nothing at all of civilization in him. Just a fire held as deeply as the molten core of the earth. She thought of his guiding spirit, the wolf, who allowed no other creature near his mate. And she thought of Springer's nickname, the Wild One, and how apples fell close to their trees.

She'd worked for this, gave her flesh so they'd stand here and know each other in this essential way, troubled boy and troubled man, feeling too much and not saying enough. She'd accomplished her goal, and she tasted the joy of captured prey, held against the grief in her mouth. But she wasn't done yet. She pulled herself up for the next part of the show.

"Forty six, and eleven," she told Alex.

His brow furrowed, and his hand lost some of its impetus. She had his attention. "What?" he demanded.

"I've reported forty six prisoner assaults, and eleven attempted rapes in my time here, all of which went right to your office. This is the first time you went after a prisoner for it. You ready to tell me why, Alex?"

From Springer she heard small laughter, stifled quickly. She cast a glance at him. Empath, singer, Adept and more—he got it.

Alex's hand moved against the flesh it held, struggling to hold on, struggling to let go. With great effort of will he pulled his hand down to his side, releasing Springer. For a moment he stayed where he was, clenching and unclenching his fists. Then he turned and left the room, not looking at either of its occupants.

Jaguar let out breath, realizing she'd been holding it in. She cast a glance over Springer. He was shaken, and trying to pretend otherwise. She raised a hand, lightly touched near the welt already forming on his cheek, the mirror image of hers. "Thanks," she said.

"Yeah. At least he didn't kill me. I mean, he could've, before you got here."

"He said he'd hurt you, not kill you. He always keeps his word."

Springer chewed on his lip. "Always?" he asked.

"Without fail," she said.

His eyes went bright, his thoughts turning the notion over and looking at all its sides. "If it came down to a fight, any idea who'd end up dead?"

"Nobody. He protects what he loves."

"He loves you, too. So what if it was you or me? Who'd end up dead?"

Thanatos drive, moving him to places she didn't want him to go. Soft sorrow moved through her. "I don't want that," she said quietly. "Neither of us want that."

"Okay. But what if you can't get what you want? What if he killed me? What'll you do?"

She resisted the urge to deny what he said. It would only drive him deeper into Thanatos. What he required from her right now was just an answer. An honest answer. If he died, what would she do?

"I'd sing for you," she said. "Then I'd cut my hair."

He lowered his head, raised it again, his uncanny eyes burnished with light. Whether he'd picked it from her mind or it was some esoteric learning he'd gleaned in his travels, he knew what that meant. In her tradition, the ultimate sign of grief, never given lightly.

"You mean that?" he asked.

"I do," she said.

"No take backs," he said quietly.

She nodded. "No take backs."

Satisfied, he moved to the small mirror over the bureau, turned his face in profile to examine his bruise. "I think mine'll be bigger than yours," he said.

She grinned. "That's what they all say. I'll get you some ice."

He moved to his bed and lay down, hands behind his head, eyes open and staring at the ceiling, at visions he wouldn't let her see. After a while, he began humming softly to himself. She stayed a moment more, then walked out of the room.

CHAPTER TWENTY-EIGHT

Alex stood on a mesa, listening to the howling of wolves. They were close. Very close.

He looked toward the edge of the mesa and saw them gathered there, no more than a few yards away. Some of them worried the carcass of a deer, a fresh kill. The others faced the sky, howling out their song. Blood dripped from their jaws. As he watched he noticed an anomaly. Huddled within the pack was a human figure. A woman he knew.

"Jaguar," he said.

She looked to him, and put her hand on the head of the largest male. She leaned over and looked into his open mouth. Blood dripped from his jaw, onto her lips. Alex tasted the metallic liquid of it as she did. He was thirsty, just as she was.

He tried to move, either to her or away from this horror, but his feet wouldn't go. Something held him to the ground, stuck fast. As he stood paralyzed he felt fur brush the back of his hand. He looked down and saw a coyote skulk past him, headed toward the feasting pack. It circled Jaguar as she drank the wolf's blood in ecstasy.

Alex tensed. The coyote would go for her throat. He had to do something, but he couldn't move.

"No!" he cried out.

As he did, he woke, sitting up hard.

He reached a hand into the darkness of his bedroom, blinked around. He saw only the normal objects of his room. Bureau, nightstand, window. He recognized himself as awake, emerging from a dream. He ran a hand over his face as he listened to his heart beating hard. He was an Adept, who understood the demands of time, and he knew when it was running out on him. Knew also what he had to do next.

He sent his thoughts to Jaguar. Immediately, she spoke into him. She'd been waiting for this.

Here, Alex, she said.

We need to talk, he told her.

On my way, she responded.

He left his bed, put on a robe and walked into his living room. He stood at his window overlooking the lakeshore, waiting for her to show.

He estimated he'd been staring at nothing much for only ten minutes when she entered his apartment and closed the door behind her. He turned and faced her.

"You know," he said.

A statement rather than a question. Of course she knew. She was the most skilled empath he'd ever met. Clairvoyant, chantshaper, and more. Capable of reading the lines around someone's mouth to full conclusion. What delusion made him believe he could hide the truth from her? In asking the question, he knew the answer: He wasn't hiding from her. He was hiding from himself. She just got in the way.

She nodded. Spoke the words. "Springer's your son," she said.

His son. A coyote boy, who killed people. "Did Jeral tell you?"

"She didn't have to. I told you I smelled sex. I just didn't know if it was past or present."

"Past," he said. "Long past, and well past. Jaguar, there was noth-ing—

"—I figured that out. I'm just—I'm not very good with secrets."

He knew that about her. He was relieved they wouldn't be fighting about Jeral tonight, but he still wondered how she moved from A to Z.

"How'd you get it? Springer doesn't look like me. He looks like—like my father," he noted.

"When you're pissed, you look alike," Jaguar replied.

Certain facts fell into a cohesive whole, and he regarded her with a mixture of anger and admiration. Jaguar, master of the long con, played him?

"You set that up?" he demanded. "Pushed him to assault you just to see me pissed at him? You…hell, you did, didn't you? All that, just so you'd know I was his father?"

"Not for that. I already knew."

"Then—why?"

She turned her lucid eyes to his. "So you'd see each other. So you'd both name the truth."

Hell, he thought. That was even worse. She was treating him like one of her cases. And what a chance she took. What a God awful chance. He pulled himself up, got formal. "That was way out of line, Dr. Addams."

"So what?" she said curtly.

An appropriate answer. What the hell could he do about it? Fire her? At least he could scold her. "Jesus Christ, Jaguar, he could've—"

"So *what*?" she repeated. "It was the only way to get to both of you. Your son had to see that his father means what he says. He needed that as much as you needed to talk to me, for real."

As usual, she placed her risk against the goal and saw it small. In spite of his anger, he loved her for that. Everything in him wanted to go to her, draw her close enough to breathe in the scent of mint that always lingered around her, close enough to taste her skin. But how could he? In what way did he deserve the consolation of her flesh?

He opened his mouth to speak and found nothing to say. The complexity of his emotions defied anything as simple as words. In all his experience, she was the only person who continued to surprise him, though it almost got her killed. Though it would shred his heart with the truth.

The words of an ancient Sufi prayer occurred to him: Batter my heart, three-personned god, that I may know love. Is that what this was for? Why was he thinking that?

"Alex?" she asked. "You okay?"

He shook his head. Back to business. It was safer there. "I'll find a different Teacher for him," he said. "It might take a few days, but I'll figure something out. I should've gotten someone else from the start."

She showed him a frown. "I'd be really pissed if you did. Alex, he's your *son*."

There was nothing but love in her voice, and it hurt him more than any accusations she might hurl at him. "I didn't want you to consider that as a factor. That's why I didn't tell you."

"I know, but that's over," she said, dismissing it. "Isn't it about time you named *your* fear?"

Name it at last. He held a hand up, let it drop to his side. "There's quite a few. You want the litany?"

"I think I know some of it." She moved to him, pressed her palm against his heart and went subvocal.

You fear your courtesy and passion is perverted into charm and violence in your son. You fear you're responsible for his crime, because you made him what he is—empath, Adept, and more. You're afraid you'll become what he is, because you see yourself in his face. And he has the same fear, because he sees himself in yours. You and your son—both wild and terrified of it.

What she said was true, but there was more. "You left something out," he said out loud.

"Then say it," she suggested.

He straightened himself. "I'm afraid I'll lose him, in the worst possible way," he said.

Jaguar felt the hiss and spark of truth. "Yes," she said. "That."

Not everyone made it back from the Planetoids alive. What if she had to kill Springer? The possibility rested between them, a demon that might destroy them. It came from something he'd scented in Adept space, a possibility he was determined to avoid. The son and the father both, trying to work toward ends they wouldn't name. Alex raised a hand, pushed it away.

"I have no right to feel any of that," he said, echoing his son on the topic of what he deserved. "Aside from biology, he's just a prisoner who happened to fall in my zone."

"And when he sings, I hear your voice," she replied. "That's how I knew he was yours, Alex. I recognized your voice in his. If you don't, listen to the recording he made. You'll hear what he's capable of. He's K'aayul. He can *sing*."

She said the word as if it was the same as saving the world. To sing. To give voice to what others couldn't feel, helping them feel it. Just as she did. He knew how rare a true K'aayul was, knew what it meant, and her words ripped yet another truth from him. Whenever he imagined having a child, he wanted only hers, which was impossible. He'd accepted that, but now he understood he also grieved it, and deeply.

"I just—I wish he was ours, Jaguar."

A moment passed with breath withheld. Then, she spoke.

"He is now," she said quietly.

He jerked his head up, saw the oceans swirling in her eyes. She was right. Who had valued Springer for exactly who and what he was? Who looked beyond the evidence of his crime, beyond ego and jealousy and pride, to see his soul? Only Jaguar. Only Jaguar.

Love beat death every time. So he'd told her in a dark hour. Easy to say when he wasn't the one facing his fear. But now, but now.

"I don't know how to help him," he said.

"I do. There's a woman at 13 Springs who's the best K'aayul I know. Steady and strong. He can go there. To her, and to Jake and One Bird."

Of course, he thought. If anyone could help, they could. Just being at 13 Streams was medicine to heal the wounded soul. And Jaguar would be safe there. They'd keep her safe. Hope, that most dangerous of emotions, moved through him.

"That's a good idea," he said judiciously. "I can get you cleared for it."

"Not me," she said. "Us. Springer's not the only one with fears to work through. It'll do him good to see you deal with yours."

He remembered something he'd seen in Adept space—him and Springer, entering a sweat lodge. It was one of the better possible futures they faced. More hope, followed by the soft and deadly texture of despair. "He won't talk about what he did, Jaguar. If he can't come clean—"

"—Alex, I think he *is* clean. He says he's culpable because he went back to Schulman, but he's actually terrified his mother did it, which is why he accepted the charge."

He shook his head. "Jeral has no motive. No reason to do that."

"None we can see, but she's not the only available suspect."

He took this in, tried to make sense of it beyond his fear. "What are you saying, Jaguar?"

"I'm saying I don't think Springer knowingly killed those kids. With his empathic issues, he might kill in a moment of rage or delusion, but he's just not capable of planning a murder."

"He was on drugs," Alex said.

"Drugs that increase impulsivity, the last thing to lead to an organized massacre."

Alex licked at his lips. "Then, maybe his empathic troubles did it."

"Same thing, Alex. Any of that might make him kill. All of it also makes it impossible for him to plan killing."

Was she right? She had a very high accuracy rate—almost 100 percent, as she liked to point out, and everything she said made absolute sense. But she had issues of her own that might skew her perspective. Not something he wanted to broach right now, but he had to.

"Jaguar, is it possible your judgement is clouded? We haven't talked about this, but given your choice about childbearing, maybe you feel your own fears?"

He saw pain in her face, a flash she quickly subdued. "You mean because he's your son by another woman, and I won't have your babies? If that's a problem for you, we can talk about it, but it's got nothing to do with this case. I thought he was clean *before* I knew who he was." She stopped, ran a hand through her hair, then showed him a face both calm and certain. "It's my job to get at the truth. Where he came from doesn't change that. If you think it does, you've forgotten who I am."

He remembered a moment when she was willing to let Rachel, her best friend, die in order to finish an assignment. This is who I am, she'd told him. If you've been nurturing fantasies to the contrary, now's the time to dispel them. She meant it then, as she did now.

"You really believe someone else planned it?" he asked.

"Would I say it if I didn't? Whatever else happens, I'll be damned if I'll let this go down in lies and secrets. They've been a plague on all our houses from the start."

"Okay," he said. He moved to her, lifted a hand to her face and held it there. "I'm with you."

She brought her mouth to his and kissed him, her lips on his a reminder that this rare and precious woman had chosen him. His body responded as if he was a parched man offered water. His mouth drank from hers. Then, a moment of terror washed over him, and he pulled back.

"If we fail," he said.

She pressed closer, her body warm against his. *Why should we fear?* she said, speaking into him. *If this is our end, it still ends in love.*

He drew her close. Her hands moved over him like an unearned blessing, a miracle that could not be refused. He moved against her, heard her moan with pleasure that was no less than his. Later, there might be disaster or miracle, and if she failed, she'd go down singing. But right now, all he wanted was her skin next to his.

This implacable force of life had saved him before, and might do so again. It could save him. Save his son. It might save them all.

CHAPTER TWENTY-NINE

Jeral stood with one hand on her hip, looking at her father.

"What will you do now?" she asked. "He can't get the meds he needs. He's completely in that woman's hands."

"I'll take care of it," he said.

He sat at the desk in his suite room, working something on his computer. Since he'd been called on his attempts to get Springer his medicine, he'd avoided her, but this morning she found him and confronted him. Confrontation wasn't something she often did with him, but this was Springer, and she had to.

"It?" she said. "He's not an it."

"Not much more right now," Ron replied.

He sounded casual, as if he no longer cared. Threads of the past few weeks drew together to create a new meaning for her. Why he'd sent her to Alex. The jealousy he'd hoped to spark in Jaguar, a dangerous woman at the best of times. He hadn't come here to save Springer. He'd come here to get rid of a problem he couldn't solve.

"You—you want him to die. You *want* that woman to kill him. That's what you've been up to all this time."

He lifted a hand, let it fall. "He'll be worth a lot more once he's dead."

"He's my *son*," she said.

"Yours. Not mine."

For a long moment they stared at each other, and Jeral was the first to break eye contact. "If you hurt him, you'll regret it."

"Is that a threat? From you?" Ron said, his voice dripping with disdain.

"No threat," she said. "You'll have a great deal to regret if he's hurt. There's a lot I could say if I chose to."

"What makes you think I'd let you? I won't have you shame me any further than you have."

"Me, shame you? Your whole life is a shame and a sham. I—I hate you." She spit out the words with surprise, and found they were true. She hated him. She'd hated him for many years. Why had it taken her so long to know that?

"Fine," he said, perfectly sanguine. "Hate me all you want. Just don't mess up my program."

At that, she knew she couldn't stop him. She never could. Ron Schulman always won. What could she do against him? Nothing, except appear to go along with him, then find her own way. If nothing else, maybe she could get to an end of the madness, an end of pain. But that meant she had to find out what his plans were.

One more time she put her face on, approached him with apologetic eyes.

"I'm sorry," she said softly. "Don't lock me out. I just—I have to know what you'll do. I have to be there. I have that right, don't I? Isn't it fair?"

He brushed away the contempt he felt, and relented. Impossible not to do so with her. "We have to bring this to a close, you know that, don't you?" he said, trying to sound stern.

"Yes," she said hesitantly. "Just—don't leave me out of it."

"You sure you can manage it?"

"I am," she said. "I just—I want to be there."

He punched at keys on his computer. "Okay," he said. "I suppose you should be."

"Promise?" she asked.

He stopped his work, put a hand out and drew her close. "Of course," he said. "Anything for my little girl."

CHAPTER THIRTY

When Jaguar and Alex walked into the Normal House early the next morning, Springer was on the couch, hunched over an acoustic guitar, playing something that managed to sound both wistful and riddled with joy. He sang softly to himself, the same phrase over and over. *In his hands. I'm in his hands, and he's in mine.* Gerry, sprawled on the chair across him, added small vocal punctuations to the tune.

Jaguar and Alex stood and listened, unnoticed. When Springer's hands stopped their motion, he looked up, saw them both, and his mouth dropped open.

"Why'd you stop?" Gerry whined, and then blinked at the two new occupants of the room. "Hey," he said. "Must be time for work or something."

Jaguar turned to Alex. "I'll go to the Teacher's building, give Jake and One Bird a call." Then she nudged Gerry's leg with her foot. "Let's give them the room." He scratched at his chest, stood and followed her out of the house.

Alex stayed standing. "That was good. What you were playing. Is it new?"

"Something I'm working on," he said. He put the guitar to one side on the couch. "You here to apologize?"

Alex looked at the bruise on his face, shook his head. "You earned that."

Springer rubbed at his chin. "I did, didn't I? Jaguar told you about it?"

He was lucid, calm. Alex was glad of that. "She did. Stick around and you'll end up working here."

"That'd be something. So what's going on?"

"We're taking you to 13 Streams. Where Jaguar grew up. They'll teach you how to use your gifts."

His lips twisted around and his forehead knit into a frown. "Your idea?"

"Hers. But I like it. She said you talked about going there."

"Maybe I did," he mused. "When do we leave?"

"Tomorrow. And you'll have to stick with the protocol for the ride. We want to get you there in one piece, and it's possible someone might try to prevent that."

He grunted. "Ron," he said. He gave this some thought. "What about Jeral? She coming along?"

There were so many reasons why Alex hadn't even considered that. He mentioned the first one that came to mind. "She wouldn't like 13 Streams much," he noted. "Too many empaths."

"Yeah. Okay. But I can't leave her with Ron."

That was interesting. Alex sensed Adept space moving in and around Springer. Not active now, but a memory of some vision. One that mattered to him. "We'll get you situated first," he said. "Then I'll take care of her."

"What about Ron? You'll stop him?"

He didn't ask stop him from what. There were too many possible answers. "I'll do my best."

"I got a feeling you'll have to do your worst," Springer replied.

More Adept space. "You want to show me what you see?" he asked.

Springer shook his head. "Not yet," he said. "It's still—it's rough."

"Sure," Alex said. "And it might stay rough for a while, just so you know. Dr. Addams tells me withdrawal from the drugs you were on is pretty heavy. But I'll keep an eye on you."

Springer lifted his face to Alex, and he looked young, vulnerable, afraid. "If I get too bad, just throw me on the ground, okay? Or punch me again."

Alex's mouth twisted into a wry smile. "It won't be as much fun as the last time," he noted.

Springer chuckled, leaned back against the couch and relaxed. "Y'know what I'd like, when we get to the home planet?"

"What?" Alex asked.

"A chili dog. I haven't had one of those in ages."

Alex thought about it. When he was a little boy and he went into town, his father would always get chili dogs—one for each of them—though his mother tsked at him for it. "Me neither. Not since I was maybe twelve."

"But they were good, weren't they? My last set of foster parents, they'd take us to little league games, and there was this really old, ugly guy who made hot dogs and chili dogs at the concession stand. I hated the games, but man, those chili dogs."

Alex sat down on the couch, not too close, but close enough. "You played little league?" he asked. "You don't seem like the type."

"Hell, no," he said. "My foster brother did. I just watched. And got in trouble for dribbling my slushie down the pants of the guy in front of me. He had a big crack, and I couldn't resist."

"Jesus," Alex said. "Did I say I wished I raised you?"

"Regret those words now, don't you?"

"What else did you do to get in trouble?" Alex asked, and Springer kept talking, telling him how he snuck a kitten into one of his foster homes, even though the father was allergic, how he planted a string of firecrackers inside the mailbox of a neighbor he hated.

Alex relaxed back and listened. Stories. Just stories, but they tasted like good wine, and went right to his head. This was his son's life, and he was sharing it. Then Springer asked Alex about his childhood, and Alex told him about the horses, about his dour-faced father, the beauty and loneliness of the ranch. And Springer told him about the beauty and loneliness of the city, how the sound of it informed his music.

All of it was new, a view of this young man's soul beyond his gifts, beyond his imprisonment, and Alex accepted the gift, though he never expected to receive it. At one or two points he perceived an almost frantic quality to the telling, and felt a pinch of concern, but he wouldn't interrupt the flow of the talk with that kind of question. Let it go on, he thought. Let us just sit here together and talk, and be with each other, in some way that doesn't hurt.

He wasn't sure how much time passed before Springer stopped talking, the silence a signal of something gone wrong. Alex sat up, looked to him.

He'd gone pale, and all the muscles in his face tensed around internal pain. "I'm not sure if I can go through with it," he said.

"With what?" Alex asked.

Springer blinked at him. "Don't you know?" he asked.

Alex shook his head. "Is it a vision? An Adept vision?"

Springer ran his hand over his face. "I guess we don't always see the same things."

"No. Of course not. There's so many variables."

Springer sighed. "Then maybe it'll be okay."

"That's what we're working on," Alex said. "Making it okay. All of it."

The door to the Normal House opened, and Gerry entered the room. "Hey," he said. "Jaguar told me to come back in a hour. Is it—you want me here?"

Springer lifted his head, gestured toward the chair. "Yeah, man," he said. "We still got this song to work out."

Gerry took a seat. Springer picked up his guitar. Alex stood, and left them to it.

* * * *

Jaguar drove to the Teacher's Building and went to the secure room to make her call to Jake and One Bird, filling them in on her plans with Springer, telling them what she needed.

"We can do that," One Bird said.

Jake grunted in assent. "You can get him here okay? You're safe?" he asked.

That was typical of him. He assumed she'd take risks, and saw it as his job to to make sure they weren't too big. "I'll have plenty of back up. And I'm bringing Alex along."

"I was gonna suggest that," Jake noted. "Tell him to be careful, too."

This gave her pause. "Why?"

"This is dangerous for him," Jake said.

"Go ahead," she told him. "Say more."

"I don't *know* more," he said, petulant now. "Just—tell him to be careful, okay?"

"I will," she said, and signed off.

She left the room, and was almost out of the building, thinking through how she might prep Springer for the trip, when her cellcom buzzed her. She looked at it, saw who the caller was, and turned it off. Paul Dinardo. The last person she wanted to talk to.

It buzzed again, a special feature of Planetoid cellcoms—even if they weren't on, an emergency code could get through. She rolled her eyes, and answered it.

"Go to hell," she said amicably when Paul's face appeared on her screen.

"I know," he said. "You hate my guts and so on, but there's something you have to do. Now."

"I'm busy, Paul," she said curtly.

"Your shuttle don't leave until tomorrow morning," he noted.

She paused. "You know about that?"

"Alex called. Asked me to push the paperwork through." He shrugged. "Not much I wouldn't do to get this monkey off my back. While you're waiting, Ron Schulman wants to talk to you."

"Rat fuck," she said.

"Sure," he said. "Just go see him. He's in the bar at the Governor's Inn, waiting for you. Listen to him and smile nice, then walk away. It won't hurt anything."

"Any idea why he wants to see me?"

"He didn't tell, and I didn't ask. I just said our people are always glad to oblige. Maybe he wants to dig an apology out of you."

"All the way to China and back won't get him that."

"Yeah. Just go."

She was curious now, and her curiosity overcame even her deepest rage. Besides, she might learn something from him. "In the interests of your ass, I'll do it," she said. "Just don't forget me in your will."

"Like you'll outlive me," he said, and signed off.

* * * *

The bar at the Governor's Inn was sparsely populated and she spotted Ron easily at a table toward the back of the room. He also spotted her. He stood, leaned toward her in a small bow, let one corner of his mouth turn up in a smile. His well-known boyish grin, his famous charisma at work, a legacy he'd given to Springer, as if he needed it.

"Dr. Addams," he said. "It's an honor."

She gauged him. The air around him was pulsing with energy, all of it saying she was just the kind of person he liked to know. A special person, as he was, smart, determined, a worthy opponent or a valuable ally. Everything in him suggested he would court her as an ally, feel privileged if she would be on his side. Because, of course, they both understood the world in a different way than other people. They were both above the common lot.

And it was all a lie. He called her here to find out what she was up to, so he could prevent it. As Springer said, he liked to stay in control.

She took in a deep breath, tasting what he projected and how he projected it. She smelled telepath, and a slight touch of hypnopath. She smelled secrets and lies, long nurtured. She smelled a hypocrite.

"Put it away," she said.

He tilted his head at her. "I don't understand," he said, still courteous.

She pointed a finger toward his crotch. "Keep it in your pants. We won't be using it."

She sat in the chair across from him and watched as his polite smile was replaced by brief anger, a flash there and gone. He sat down. "I had no intention—" he began, but she cut in.

"Don't bother," she said. "Just tell me what you want, and we can both get on with our day."

He picked up his drink, took a long swig. When he raised his face to hers, it was all business. "I hoped we could reach some kind of accord about Springer's treatment, and undo your bad impression of me. Just so you know, I was trying to help him. If I was mistaken in my approach—well, it worked for a while."

She had to play this right and she was not a player. She pulled in her horns as best she could. "If you mean that," she said, "will you answer my questions?"

He waved a hand at her. "Go ahead and ask," he said.

She dove in. "When did you start giving him T-phine?"

"About a year ago. When he started having—difficulty controlling himself."

"Visions?" Jaguar asked. Ron nodded. "What visions, specifically?" she requested.

Ron shifted, uncomfortable. "It's a private matter."

"If it's about your daughter being his mother, I already know that."

Ron lowered his head, but lifted his eyes to her. Abashed. That, at least, was the impression he wanted to project, though she doubted he felt anything near. "He said he knew who his parents were. That he saw things happening. Violent things. He asked for my help, to stop him."

There was limited truth in this. Springer saw visions, and told him about them, but she doubted he asked for Ron's help, or said anything about violence. "And since you've got some psi capacities yourself, you believed him," she said.

"I don't—"

"—Skip it," she cut in. She wasn't here to argue about that. "What did you tell Springer?"

"That I'd help him. Of course."

"No. I mean, about his parents. Did you tell him the truth?"

"I didn't," he admitted, his face projecting guilt which Jaguar didn't believe. He'd never known guilt in his whole life. "I thought it best not to to disturb his emotional equilibrium. But Jeral told him she was his mother. She couldn't hold back."

Jaguar tapped a finger against the arm of her chair. "Thanks," she said. "That explains a lot. Next question—who helped him plan his killing spree? How'd he get the live fire?"

"He did it," Ron said quickly.

"He did not," she said. "He couldn't plan escape from a paper bag, even if you gave him scissors. And I think someone plugged infrasound into his act, to distract the kids. Not a lot of people know how to do that, so who're you protecting? Your daughter?"

"There's no way you can prove anything of the kind, Dr. Addams," he said.

A small twitch at his mouth. Satisfaction. He wanted her to believe Jeral was involved, and he was the good father, protecting his daughter. But it wasn't the truth.

"Maybe I can't," she said. She leaned back and stretched her legs out in front of her. Her next move was risky. Ron liked a challenge, a place to prove himself, and she could use that. But if she didn't nail him good, he'd find a way to kill her. That's what he did.

"Wanna play?" she cooed at him.

He tilted his head at her, curious and on guard. "What did you have in mind?"

She felt him using capacity for telepathy, and that gave her the opening she'd hoped for. "This," she said, and swiftly, effortlessly, she moved into his mind, making empathic contact.

She was well in before he even realized her presence, and for a few seconds she roamed freely, going directly where she wanted before he closed against her with no small finesse. Not only a telepath, but a practiced one. At the same time he made a stab at her mind, but she'd prepared for that. No entry for him today. When it was done, silently and with very little motion, his hands closed and opened, making fists and releasing them.

"I think that round goes to me," she said.

He waved it away, not at all anxious. In fact, he was quite satisfied. Less than an inch away from smug. "You still don't know who helped Springer plan his crime," he said.

"That's not what I was looking for," she answered.

Ron's lips went tight, and his face lost some of its color.

"Well, well," Jaguar said. "Ron Schulman blinks first."

He recovered, offered a stern glance. "Dr. Addams, if you think—"

"—I *do* think," she cut in sharply. "I think all the time. I've got a very busy brain. Lately it's been working on a hypothesis. Springer gives no motive, isn't up to planning this level of mayhem, so someone else made it happen. Someone who wanted him here, and then dead."

"My daughter is not the kind of person to do anything like that," Ron said firmly.

"She's not. I considered her, but in spite of all her hard-earned neuroses, she actually loves Springer. So I went to the next on the list, which is you, but I couldn't figure out why you'd want him dead after you went to so much trouble to get him. That's what I was looking for, and that's what I got." She paused, waited for reaction.

"I think you should stop," Ron said, but his words lacked the energy of a real protest.

"No you don't," she said. "Your nuts are perspiring to know. I'll oblige them." She leaned forward, reached her long arm across the the table and pressed a finger against his forehead. In quick flashes, she played back what she'd seen in him. Jeral, pregnant, and his solicitous care of her. What he said to her: *Ours, Jeral. All ours.* Then, another scene of him with Jeral, when she was a teenager. He was undressing her. She was demure, though her eyes spoke of horror.

Jaguar pulled back, let him take it in. "There's my motive," she said. "You thought Springer was your very own baby boy, until he came back from his small rebellion and told you he knew who his mommy and daddy were. That's why you wanted him dead."

He worked his face into righteous anger, but he couldn't hide the blood leaving his lips. He was shocked. Not that she'd say this, but that she knew. He recovered quickly.

"How dare you?" he demanded. "How dare you accuse me of this—this—"

"Evil?" she filled in for him. "Sputum of perversion? Effluvium of a disintegrated soul? I dare because it's true. When I enter someone's thoughts I'm not looking for what they want me to see. I'm looking for what they're trying to hide. Pretty fucking easy with scum like you, arrogant enough to believe no one would ever suspect you."

She let Ron work on this. She didn't need his confirmation. She just wanted to know how he'd fight back. After he had enough time to consolidate a position, she went on.

"When Jeral ran away and came back pregnant, she told you the baby was yours, said she thought about having an abortion and changed her mind. You—well, you were thrilled. It gave you the perfect family. The son who died returned to you. Your compliant daughter for your wifey, all completely owned by Schulman Enterprises. You couldn't claim Springer publicly, but you could get him into your house. You had to kill a few people, but what the hell. They were in the way. Everything was hunky dory, until Springer—empath, Adept and more—had a vision of his real parents. In all innocence he told you about it. I'll just bet," she said, "that didn't tickle."

She eyed him. He said nothing, so she continued. "I'm guessing you got a DNA test about then. Better late than never, but you were too damn conceited to imagine your daughter would lie to you. Once you knew better, you set out to punish Jeral, get rid of the false son. Maybe you knew he'd figured out what you did to his mother, too. You fed him drugs to drive him over the edge, and got live ammo for his final act. Brilliant, really. He'd be arrested, destroying your faithless daughter, *and* increasing sales. And he'd land here, to destroy Alex as well. And

Ron Schulman lives happily ever after, his wretched excuse for honor avenged."

She leaned back in her chair, held his gaze, waited for his response.

"Are you finished?" he asked, icy cool.

"Sure," she said. "Your turn."

"There's not much I care to say about the pile of filth you just spewed at my feet, except that I feel sorry for you. You've been working with perverts for so long, you see nothing but perversion. And you shouldn't try your hypothesis on anyone else, because I have lawyers who deal with slander quite efficiently."

She brushed back the silk of her long dark hair, gave him her best smile. "All those words," she said, "and you have yet to say it's not true."

His pupils dilated, his eyes widening briefly. Fear. She laughed. It was quiet laughter, but he knew what it meant. She was on to him, and having got on, she wouldn't get off.

"It doesn't matter. No one will believe you," he said. "I know how to deal with your kind."

"No you don't," she replied.

Ron held eye contact. She'd gotten one blink out of him. She wouldn't get another.

"I'll win anyway," he said at last. "I always do."

He stood, moved around her and left the room. She stayed where she was, contemplating the nature of arrogance.

CHAPTER THIRTY-ONE

After she left the bar at the Governor's, Jaguar went directly to Alex's office. When she arrived, he lifted his head from a report he was reading, took one look at her, and stood.

"What?" he asked.

"Let's take a walk," she answered.

He got it. Whatever she had to say was too private to risk anyone overhearing, and something made her shy away from empathic contact. He followed her out of his office, down the hall, out of the building. They'd walked about a block before she started talking.

"The reason," she said without preamble, "is that Schulman's a telepath, among other things. While I doubt he's good enough to listen in without us knowing, I didn't want to chance it. And I certainly wouldn't put it past him to have your office bugged."

"Okay," he said. "Keep going. Full report."

She took a breath and dove right in. "Schulman thought Springer was his child. He planned the killing spree to get to you, and he's still out for blood."

Alex shook his head, unable to absorb something as unexpected as snow in July. "That's impossible. Jeral is Springer's mother." He let the sentence fade to silence, hissed in breath through is teeth. "Jaguar, no," he said.

"Yes," she replied. "I'm afraid so."

She put a hand to Alex's heart and gave it to him in full, showing him everything she'd seen concisely and with an absence of emotion, though he could feel her blood boiling beneath her skin. She was humming like a live wire. In short order, so was he.

By the time she was done, his fury was too great to be accommodated by words. He pulled away from her and walked fast, staring straight ahead, saying nothing. They covered three blocks that way, and then Jaguar put a hand on his arm.

He came to a full stop, turned and looked to her. "I'll kill him," he said.

"Not yet," she answered.

He appreciated her use of words. Not that he shouldn't kill Schulman. Just not yet. "Why not?" he asked.

"Too risky," she said. He laughed wryly.

"I know," she said. "Strange notion, coming from me. But Springer needs you. We have to get you both to 13 Streams alive, and I'm worried about that. People have a tendency to drop dead around Schulman's interests."

He gave a curt nod. She was right. Nothing mattered more than healing Springer, who might know about this already. It would certainly explain his reluctance to leave his mother with Ron. He called his mind to order, used his extensive capacity for self-discipline to cool his own fire. He filled Jaguar in on his conversation with Springer, which made her dig her hands into the pockets of her jeans and scowl down at the sidewalk.

"You think he knows?" she asked.

"At the least he suspects. Maybe he saw it in a vision, and he's still denying it. What else is bugging you?" he asked, knowing her signals.

"I'm worried he's inherited his father's capacity for self-sacrifice to protect the greater good," she said.

"I don't think that's genetic," he noted.

"You never know. Anyway, we have to be like bubble wrap, swaddle him down tight."

"Extra security for the Normal House tonight," he said. "Four good house guards. Scott inside, and he sticks to you like glue until we're at 13 Streams. Rachel, Gerry and Pinkie do the same. Have Gerry call in a bouncer friend or two for supplement. He'll know the best ones. When you travel tomorrow you'll have a car in front and behind you, and I'll have some people checking the shuttleport before you enter."

"That's all good," she said. "But what about you?"

He frowned. "What about me?" he asked.

"Alex, most of the blood Ron wants is yours. I'm thinking you should go to 13 Streams now. Get out of the line of fire."

"And leave you to negotiate the shuttleport without me? I don't think so."

"You can't help Springer if you're dead."

"I won't be. I'll take Paul out to dinner tonight. Fill him in. Schulman won't touch me if I'm with a governor."

"And after dinner?"

"I'll get a hotel room. Stay invisible." She opened her mouth to protest, but he was adamant. "I'll be *okay*, Jaguar. Tomorrow's the problem. You know the protocol for bringing Springer through the shuttleport under these conditions?"

She rolled her eyes. "Now you're being ridiculous. Of course I do."

This pulled a small smile from him. Then he had another thought. "Jaguar—what I saw in Adept space. Springer might go after you again."

He touched her lightly on the forehead and showed her the image of bared teeth lunging toward a female throat. Showed her Springer with a gun held to her face.

"Maybe," she said when he ended the contact, "if you leave now, it won't happen."

"And maybe something worse will," he pointed out. "Jaguar, in what universe do you imagine I can *not* be there?"

She understood. She'd feel the same, even if all her intuition was against it. "Okay," she said. "I know you'll watch out for Ron, but don't disregard the damage Jeral might do."

"Jaguar, I never—"

"—I don't mean that. She's a victim, and they're dangerous."

"A victim?"

"She was abused. That means either she's a victim, a perpetrator, or a protector. And she chose victim so far. She had you—gold in her hands—and she tossed you away. She had the chance to raise a fine son, and wouldn't do it. Right now, what she really wants is to die. That makes her the most dangerous person in the pack. We can't let her near this."

"Okay," he said. "I understand. Jaguar, will you stay safe? I need you with me."

She touched his face and he felt her intent. Mountains would melt and seas burn before she would let him down.

"Ze Adalak," she said softly.

A Mertec phrase, used to express love, though the more accurate translation was along the lines of 'you are the eyes of my soul.'

Heat stung his own eyes. Swiftly, he leaned down and kissed her. An empathic kiss, sharing the core of his emotions with her. Just as quickly, he pulled away.

"Let's get this rolling," he said. He pulled out his cellcom and started making arrangements. They turned back toward the Teacher's Building and walked.

CHAPTER THIRTY-TWO

The night went quietly, though Jaguar remained on high alert. At the Normal house they slept in shifts, with two awake at any given time. She risked empathic contact with Alex a few times, just to check in briefly.

First, *How's Paul?*

Fine. All on board.

Meaning, he was prepared to back them.

Then, later, *All is well?*

Yes. No trouble.

He was safe. Nothing else mattered.

At dinner, Springer was brooding and silent, gone entirely interior. She tapped his hand as they ate their Chinese take out. "You okay with what's next?" she asked.

He startled, blinked up at her. "Yeah," he said. "We're going where there's only singing." As he spoke, she felt the texture of the landscape he longed for. It was smooth as silk, and the light touching it was beyond human yearning.

"That's what I planned on," she said.

"Maybe I'll get there ahead of you," he said.

"What's that mean?" she asked, but he turned away from her, didn't answer.

Either he was getting himself ready for what he'd find in New Mexico, or the withdrawal process was moving along, pushing and pulling at him. She was relieved he wasn't showing any of the worst symptoms. No howling, no roller coaster of emotion or psi capacities. Not yet. After dinner he went to his room and lay on his bed, his face turned to the wall.

Sometime around midnight she went in to his room to check on him. He hadn't moved at all. As she stood next to his bed, she smelled Adept space.

"Springer?" she asked quietly. No response.

She reached out slowly to make empathic contact, but before she could find his thoughts he rolled over, shot upright and grabbed her arm. His orange eyes were wide and wild. She tensed for trouble, but it didn't come. He was clear headed, focused and grim.

"You talked to Ron, didn't you?"

She nodded.

"You know what he did to my mother?"

She drew her lower lip through her teeth. Alex was right. He did know. He'd picked it up from Adept space, from somewhere, a boy who loved his mother, facing horror. Not something she wanted him to have to deal with right now, and not something she could lie about.

"I know," she said. "That's why you went back to him, isn't it? Not for money. To protect your mother. You suspected what he did."

A shudder ran through him, and his grasp on her tightened. "I told Alex. You'll have to take care of it. You and him. And you have to stay with Alex. Don't leave him. No matter what. That's important."

Not the response she expected, and not one that made sense. "I don't understand," she said.

"You will," he said, cryptic as his father.

"Tell me what you see," she insisted.

He made a sound between a growl and moan, released her and lay down again, turning his face away from her. She put a hand to his head, tried for empathic contact, but felt only the shifting motion of many shapes, all working to hide his intent, his vision, from her.

* * * *

He was still quiet when they left in the morning, dark and cryptic as his father could ever be. They got him in the car with no trouble, and moved on.

Scott drove, and she rode in the back seat with Springer. Rachel and Gerry had a car behind them. Pinkie and two of Gerry's bouncer friends had a car in front. Traffic was light, and they moved forward quickly. She was glad. She'd be even gladder when they boarded the shuttle.

Her greatest worry was the walk through the shuttleport, and she rehearsed it several times in her head, blocking out moves to anticipate any trouble. Once they arrived and got the all clear from Alex, Scott would exit first, open her door only when the others were out of their car and ready to form a phalanx around Springer. Typical protective maneuver, but she had some special help today because both Alex and Scott would be reading the people around them, ready for any sign of trouble. She hoped it went easily, and well.

"You're all good, Scott?" she asked as they drove.

"Yes, ma'am," he said, and she believed him.

But at her side, Springer began to laugh. It wasn't a pleasant sound. She looked to him, and he turned his orange eyes to hers. "Not for long," he said.

The tingle of Adept space moved through him, to her. "What is it?" she asked, but he ducked his head down, started humming softly. Once again she tried for empathic contact, and found only static, and indecipherable motion. They came to a crossroads, and the light was green. She saw Scott turn his head slightly both ways as he slowed, looking for trouble. He proceeded through the intersection.

The next thing she felt was the impact of another car against theirs.

It threw her against the door, and then they were rolling, the world going wrong, righting itself. She had time to wonder what the hell hit them. Time to feel her head smash into the door and time to view the strange angle of the world as the car rolled, slid, righted itself. Time to wonder if they were all about to die.

Then, all motion ceased. She touched her face. It was wet. She looked at her finger and saw red. Blood. She looked to the front seat, saw Scott slumped against his door, blood pouring down his face. A noise disturbed her and she looked out the car window, saw a man kneeling by the hood of her car, fiddling with something underneath. What was he doing?

She had no time to figure it out. A hand pulled her roughly, and she was out of the car. She whirled, ready to fight, then saw Springer's terrified face. He pushed her away from the car. "Go. *Now!*" he roared at her.

The wheels in her mind began to turn. An accident. A man at their car. The accident was planned. The other driver was one of Ron's minions. What did he do to their car?

"Scott," she said hoarsely, and lunged toward him.

Springer lifted her off her feet, tossed her away as if she was a rag doll. She landed hard on her hands and knees, pushed herself up and saw him dragging an unconscious Scott to the other side of the street. Saw Rachel and Gerry jogging toward them and Springer gesturing, yelling something she couldn't hear. His voice was distant, heard through the ringing in her ears. She rolled away, covered her head.

When the blast came she was out of range, but the concussion, the roar of fire that followed, kept her glued to the ground. She tried to think, found it impossible. Then she heard Alex speaking within her, panic in his voice. He'd been in light contact, of course. He'd know.

Jaguar—what the hell?

Sabotage, she answered, and showed him the scene.

She felt him subduing panic. *Damages?* he asked tersely.

Scott's hurt. Call it in.

You?

She sat up, pushed herself to standing. She was dizzy, and blood ran freely down her face, but her legs held up, and everything moved when she asked it too.

Fine. I'm fine.

Springer?

She turned to where Springer had dragged Scott and saw Gerry, Pinkie, Gerry's two bouncers huddled over what she assumed was Scott. Gerry, Pinkie, two bouncers. No Springer. She moved to them, grabbed Rachel's arm.

"Springer," she demanded.

"There," Rachel pointed, then lowered her arm. "He was there," she said, her eyes wide. "Right there."

Jaguar sucked in breath. "Not anymore." She fumbled at her belt, checked her implant recorder, saw him going north, three blocks over already.

Jaguar, what's happening? Alex's voice demanded within her.

Springer took off. I'm going after him, she replied.

Silence. Fear. For the first time since she'd known him, he focused on something other than her protection.

Where's he headed?

North on Spodina, near seventh, she said.

On my way. If you get to him first tell me where he lands.

She would. She was closer. *I know what to do*, she said.

What?

Hold on, she said. *That's my job.*

No words. Heaviness. A dark place. With great care, he ended contact, and she was alone.

Heaviness. A dark place. Alex leaving without the courtesy of a goodbye. Jaguar kicked off her shoes. They'd only hamper her, and she had to move fast.

The outlook was worse than she'd thought.

* * * *

Alex was already on the move when his cellcom buzzed. He answered it, and was surprised to hear Jeral's voice.

"Something's going on with Springer," she said.

"I know. We're after him," he answered.

"So are we," she said.

"We?" he asked.

"Me and my father."

Alex didn't ask how they knew. It was Ron's doing. He had a plan of his own. Not good, he thought. "Don't," he said. "Stay out of it. Both of you."

"I can't stop him," she said. "I never could. I just—you need to know."

"Does your father know where he's headed?"

"I think so, but he won't tell me."

"Right," he said, and was about to hang up, but she kept talking.

"Alex, what I tried to do to you—I was wrong. But I'll do what's right this time. I'll take care of him."

He was about to ask her what the fuck she was talking about, but she hung up. And he had more important things on his mind right now.

Saving his son's life. Keeping Jaguar alive. He hoped to accomplish both.

CHAPTER THIRTY-THREE

Jaguar would always remember that run down the streets of Toronto's replica city as nightmare. She felt blood coursing down the side of her face and the street tilted under her feet, but adrenalin coursed through her, blocking any pain. She thought of commandeering a car, but what if Springer ducked into a building, or went down an alley? She couldn't lose him. Her vision strayed in and out of blurriness, which made reading the implant a problem. After a few blocks she tossed it aside and sought him empathically.

For the first time, he allowed the contact without blocking. In fact, he was drawing her to him, and she followed. What wouldn't she do for Alex's son, K'aayul who sang the song of the earth? In short order, she knew where he was going. To the recording studio. Good, she thought. That was good. Two blocks. Just two more and she'd be there. She made contact with Alex.

Recording studio, she told him briefly.

Got it, he replied.

She sensed him rushing toward Springer just as she was. But there was half an hour between shuttleport and studio, and though he'd go fast, break every law he could, she'd still get there first. She'd have to deal. She thought of random matters. Today was Sunday, so the studio was closed. They'd be alone. She didn't have a key, but she could break the lock. She could do this.

When she got to the studio she found the door open, its handle blown off. Did Springer do that? How? Scott's gun. He'd taken Scott's gun. She breathed herself into what she could find of calm, and entered the building. All was quiet in the lobby. She moved deeper in, to the engineering room outside the recording area. And she saw him.

He was in the recording room, his back to her. She saw a gun stuck in the back of his pants. Scott's weapon. Would he use it? And if so, who would he use it on?

He was wearing headphones, swaying back and forth, singing. She couldn't hear him, but his posture, everything about him, spoke to her of love. Love beats death every time, she thought. So Alex said to her in a dark hour. That time he'd been right. She hoped it was still true.

Springer, she whispered into him.

Without turning, he held up a hand for her to wait, and kept singing. She didn't interrupt. Nothing was more important than this. His song must be sung, regardless of any agenda. In one sense she was satisfied that she'd completed her job, because he knew who he was now, and lived it. Now she just had to keep him alive.

She saw his foot keeping time, his hand lifting and falling with waves of sound only he could hear. Then he tilted his head back, shuddered. He took off the headphones, let them drop to the floor and turned to her. His eyes were clear and shone with a light that went well beyond happiness, into the realm of the ecstatic.

He opened the door, left the recording area and moved toward her. "It's almost over," he said. "I can do this."

As far as she could tell, he was fully in himself, singer, empath and Adept. But the calm in his face read as a danger signal to her. He'd gone beyond her, and she had to grab him back.

She lifted her hand, reached out to him. "Tell me what you see," she requested.

He gave a twitch of his head. "Too late," he said. "Do what you promised."

The door behind her opened, and two people entered the room. Ron and Jeral.

She whirled to face them. Emotion was Springer's enemy, Karen said. And they would certainly draw emotion from him. "Get out," she hissed. "Leave him alone."

"You leave us alone," Jeral spit back. "He's nothing to do with you." She turned her attention to Springer, spoke more quietly. "Come with us," she said, lifting a hand to him. "We can get you out of here. Just— come with us."

Springer's eyes sparked with rage "Us?" he demanded. "*Us?*"

"Yes," Ron said. "Us."

Springer laughed raucously, his voice a coyote braying, but his laughter became a gasp and then twisted into a screech of agony. He clutched at his head, as if demons did fire dances inside his skull. Not good, Jaguar thought. She made empathic contact and felt rage boiling in him, more than he could manage. And twisting around it like a thin thread flaying flesh, a smooth, calm, voice. Ron, messing with him at the worst possible moment.

She tried to cut him off, drown him out, anything, but it was too late. Springer bared his teeth and launched himself at his grandfather.

Almost over, he'd said. Jaguar knew what came next. He'd go for Ron's throat, using his teeth as proof against evil. Sacrifice himself on the altar of his mother's protection. But it wasn't a male throat Alex saw. Not a male throat waiting for them all in Adept space. Cold crashed through Jaguar's veins. Not that. He'd never survive it. She pushed herself to him as Ron took one small step to the right, and nudged Jeral forward. Full willing, she stepped out to meet the death her son offered, knowing it would be his as well.

Springer, lost in rage and errant visions, propelled by momentum, caught his mother at the thorax and bit down, not seeing whose throat he held. Jeral wrapped her arms around him and pulled him close, an ecstasy on her face, an ecstasy of blood escaping her, the victim's way out. She would die and he would die, and they would be together forever, her ultimate fantasy.

Jaguar flipped out her knife and forced herself between them, slashing at Springer's lips, feeling the slice of glass through skin. If she could get him to let go in time, she could salvage this. She still could.

Without turning, Springer backhanded he and she was tossed away, landing hard on her back. He whirled to her, blood pouring from his dessicated lips, his eyes chasing torn skies. Through vision blurred with rage, he saw the terror in her eyes. He turned back, saw his mother's body on the floor behind him, Ron standing over it, not looking down, a half smile on his face. I always win, he did not say, because he didn't have to.

Soundlessly, Springer turned again to Jaguar. What was left of his lips parted in horror and blood ran down his teeth. She heard his voice inside her.

Tell him I'm sorry.

He pulled the gun from the back of his pants, raised it and pointed it at her. She didn't understand. He'd saved her life. Made sure Scott was safe. Why was he doing this? And what should she do? She could kill him, and that would kill Alex, kill their love. Or she could die, which would do the same. Before she could call it, a familiar figure entered the room, silent and reliable as death. Just in time, as Springer knew he'd be.

Alex, still and contained. He kept his gaze on Springer. "Don't," he said. One word, spoken with the weight of the universe behind it. Cold and true as the darkest star.

Springer twisted around, showing his bloodied face to his father.

Stop me, he whispered back subvocally, an urgent command. Then he jerked back to Jaguar, aimed the gun at her face, pulled back the trigger.

Alex moved faster.

He had no weapons, and he needed none. He strode forward, grasped Springer by his collar, cracked him like a whip and threw him down on the floor. The gun clattered away from his hand. His body was still, teeth bloodied, eyes empty, voice gone.

Alex lifted his hands and stared at them. He dropped to his knees, rested a finger against Springer's throat and listened.

"Springer?" he asked, and shook him lightly.

When no answer came, his face collapsed into grief. He reassembled it quickly, brought his mouth close to Springer's and breathed in the last taste of life, the first taste of death. Then he stood, turned, and walked out of the studio.

In the wake of his exit, a clatter of noise occurred. Planetoid security and medics arriving, Gerry, Pinkie and Rachel close behind. Jaguar ignored them all. Ignored the belated demands of Ron Schulman for a doctor to tend his daughter, who was well beyond saving.

She took one step toward Springer, and another. She dropped to the floor next to him, the silk pool of her shirt dipping into the stream of his winding blood, wicking it up to her skin. She wrapped her arms around her shoulders, hugged herself and rocked back and forth.

Rachel started to move to her, but stopped when she raised her face and began the thin, wailing cry of the Mertec death chant.

The singing wind rises. Only the singing wind remains.

Blood and breath left bodies. Jaguar's voice was luminous in the narrow moment.

The singing wind rises. Only the singing wind remains.

The living and the dead stopped to listen to her song, its long, high keening cradling them in the untamed arms of its curled embrace.

CHAPTER THIRTY-FOUR

The paramedics clapped hands on Jaguar as soon as she finished singing, and dragged her to the infirmary to check her for concussion, though she protested every step of the way.

"Just let me talk to Alex," she insisted, but they shut her down.

"Lethal incident, Dr. Addams," they said. "You can't talk to him until after the interviews."

After she was cleared for injury they let her leave the infirmary, but they escorted her to the secluded rooms of the Teacher's building, keeping her away from Alex. When she next saw him, it was in the conference rooms of the Teacher's building, in the company of many others who gathered to give testimony on the death of Springer Todd and his mother, Jeral Schulman. She sat across the room from him, viewing him from that distance. His face was tight and pale. He spoke his piece without emotional inflection.

"The prisoner threatened deadly force against a Teacher," he said. "I moved to stop him, my intent to subdue." He stopped, the muscles in his throat moving. "Unfortunately, the prisoner died," he concluded.

Beyond that his answers were brief, monosyllabic. He said little, heard even less from the island of grief he occupied, very far away.

There was no doubt this was a necessary kill, so most of the questions centered around where Springer got hold of a gun, how the initial accident happened. In spite of what Jaguar knew was true, this group found more palatable answers.

The accident was a drunk driver, like the one who killed Ron's wife and son. He'd been breathalyzed, and charged. Springer grabbed the gun from an unconscious Scott. And the explosion was a result of the accident. No evidence of foul play. Jaguar wondered how much Ron doled out for it all, but she could accuse him of nothing.

He attended all the meetings, and was offered a great deal of sympathy for his loss. He accepted it with dignity, responded with clarity and confidence to questions about the allegations that illegal drugs were used on Springer.

"They were experimental, not illegal," he noted. "I wanted to make sure Springer had the best. I'd do anything to help him."

So, Jaguar thought. Ron Schulman always wins. She listened in smoldering silence, keeping an eye on Alex, who looked stunned.

After the questioning, Ron made a formal statement. He took the high moral ground, saying this was a tragedy, asking the Planetoid to respect his privacy as he mourned. He added that in spite of what happened, he'd continue to support Planetoid operations. He only hoped they'd be more mindful of the programs they chose, and who they chose to run them. When he said this, he looked directly at Jaguar. The Board governors who were present did the same.

His message was clear, and his complacency palpable. If the Planetoid kept its mouth shut and let Jaguar take the fall, he'd keep sending money. Jaguar scanned him with a venomous eye, then put her head back and laughed long and hard, until everyone in the room was embarrassed.

"Dr. Addams," A governor said at last. "This is no laughing matter."

She glared at Ron. "Next time you want to kill someone, hire your own help. We don't get paid for assassinations around here."

With no break in motion, in absolute grace and certainty, she stood and left. When the door closed behind her, everyone talked at once, but Ron's voice rose above the others.

"You're lucky I'm not suing," he barked at Alex. "You put Springer with her. She's not safe."

"She's not," Alex agreed. "She keeps no secrets and accepts no lies. That's as dangerous as it gets." He made his own exit, following Jaguar's more quiet energy out of this noisy space.

* * * *

He wasn't surprised to find Jaguar already at his apartment when he arrived. He thought she'd have a few things to say.

She was sitting in his rocking chair, staring out his window at the darkening of the evening sky. He took off his jacket and tie, went and stood behind her.

"Everything that happened, Springer wanted to happen," she said, not looking up and not looking back. "It's what he saw in Adept space."

"What happened is I killed him," Alex said.

He stopped speaking. She raised her head to stare into the reflection of his eyes. His pupils were wide and dark as a frozen night sky. And he was shaking, a fine trembling he couldn't control. She pushed herself out of the chair, sending it skittering as she whirled to face him.

He stared down at the tremor in his hands. "What is this?" he murmured.

"It's grief, Alex. Yours, and Springer's. You took his in. I saw you. And you have to let it go." She put a hand on his arm, but he tossed it off.

"No," he said sharply. She stayed where she was.

She felt the pounding of his will, held beneath the iron wall of his capacity for stillness. He hated his grief, hated what he'd done to cause it, hated that she saw him this way, hated himself. He was an Adept who read all possibilities and moved events toward the end he wanted. He hadn't wanted this ending. He couldn't accept it. All his capacity for endurance worked against acceptance. And then, in a millisecond, the molten core of his earthlike center erupted into fire.

He swept a hand across the room and roared out, "*No!*"

He pushed her away, picked up the rocking chair and threw it down again. Picked it up once more and flung it across the room. Jaguar stumbled back and he whirled on her, pointing an accusing finger at her.

"*This* one, Jaguar?" he demanded. "You couldn't save this one? You won't have children and your gods won't let me keep mine? Is that it?"

He moved to the chair, picked it up and flung it in the other direction. It cracked against the wall and he was screaming at her why, why why couldn't she save his son?

Jaguar stayed silent as he poured out words he wouldn't remember saying. Cursing Ron Schulman, cursing her Mertec gods, cursing himself for a killer. When words ran out he roared incoherently, the sound of a wounded animal facing death, as he slammed the chair against the floor again and again.

She rode it out. What was wild in the son came from the father, and now the father gave it voice, as if he needed to do this for his child whose voice had been stilled. She'd never seen him lose control so thoroughly, but she wasn't afraid. At least, not afraid of his loss of control. She was more afraid of what he'd do when he regained it. She stayed silent while he shattered the frame of the chair until there was nothing more in it to break.

He stared at the remnants, breathing hard. "I killed him," he said dully. "I wanted to stop him, and I killed him. Did I want him dead?"

"No," Jaguar replied calmly. "You're feeling what he wanted. He was an Adept, too. He saw something beyond your vision."

Alex held up a hand to ward off her words, made a rough sound in the back of his throat. She moved to him and touched his shoulder. He jerked away, then blinked at her, not seeing, not feeling anything except what was in him. She didn't ask him what he wanted. She knew he wasn't capable of responding. She put her hand on him again and led him to his bed.

"Lie down," she said, a command rather than a request. He did as she said.

She sat next to him, moved a hand softly over his forehead, over his heart, smoothing energy around his frayed and tangled soul, seeking a crack in the cold wall he was already building around himself. She watched as he retreated further and further from her.

"I apologize," he said after a while, courteous and formal. You didn't need to see that."

"Maybe I did," she said, and continued soothing him.

After a while he closed his eyes. His breathing became regular and deep. He was asleep.

She waited until he was deep in, and then she spoke quietly into his dreams, a confusion of images, dark and sharp as shards of obsidian. He wouldn't remember her words when he woke, but later they might recur to him, when he was ready to hear them.

Alex, you didn't fail your son, she said. *You did exactly what he wanted. You saved his soul. His singer's soul. He chose you, knowing you'd see it done. Never forget that. You did what your son needed most, when he needed it. And you'll do more. You have more to do for him.*

She stayed next to him through the night, and for the next two days she remained at his apartment. They didn't speak much. She'd ask if he was hungry. He'd say no. She'd ask if he needed anything. He'd shake his head.

"Do you want to know what he told me?" she asked him.

"It doesn't matter," he said, firm and final. "This is my responsibility. I have to deal with it."

She sighed. That's what she was afraid of.

On the third day he told her she didn't have to stay. "You don't have to babysit me, Jaguar. I'm fine on my own," he said.

"No, you're not," she answered. "You're a wreck."

"Then you should let me be a wreck on my own," he said.

"Not a chance," she said. She bit at her lip, took a chance on saying more. "Not until you release Springer's grief."

"My business, Jaguar," he said crisply.

"Mine, too," she replied, just as crisply. "Alex, you have to let it go. It's his, not yours."

He turned away from her, cast a glance around the room with the look of a wild animal caught in a trap. "Not here," he whispered.

She didn't push it. She understood the parameters of his grief. She'd been through similar. But she stayed with him, sleeping on his couch to give him space, silently entering his room to check on him as he slept. Sometimes she caught him in the middle of nightmare, groaning out words in the language of dreams. The language of Old Man Coyote.

She'd touch his forehead, find a chant and sing it into him until he subsided into silence.

A very worried Rachel called a few times to check on them and report. She said Ron was working the media, which was carrying nasty stories about the way Planetoid empaths killed people. Scott wanted to know if he could kill anyone, and Paul was having a shit fit.

"Tell Scott not just yet, but thanks and I'll let him know. Tell Paul to go fuck himself. Wait. I don't want him having that much fun. Tell him to pour antifreeze down his throat and swallow."

"You mean that?"

"I sure do. If he asks, that's your answer. In the meantime, there's something you can do. Do *we* have any media friends left? Anyone interested in the truth?"

"I know a few," Rachel said.

"Good," she said. "They might enjoy a leaked report from Planetoid Three about how Ron Schulman fed drugs to Springer Todd, who happened to be his secret grandson. They might also like to look into all those attempts at adoption for Springer that failed."

"Oh," Rachel said. "That's good. I'll get right on it."

That, at least, was a source of satisfaction for her. And she found one more. She put a call in to a lawyer she knew, one who specialized in civil litigation, and suggested he contact the kids who had friends killed by Springer. They might want to pursue a civil suit against Schulman Enterprises, since it was the drugs that made Springer crazy. Not necessarily an easy case, but she could get certain pertinent information to him, and the payoff could be hefty. None of this would help Alex, but it might wound Schulman, and at least it relieved a little of her own rage, her own untended grief.

She stayed for another day and another, keeping watch over Alex, afraid of what the remnants of Springer's spirit would do to him. Afraid of what he'd do with his grief. He had no more outbursts. He'd regained all his superb discipline and went silent, sleeping a great deal, speaking only in the most courteous and formal ways. The best and the worst of him, she thought.

On the fourth day, while he was sleeping, she took a break to go home and get some clothes. When she returned to his apartment the first thing she saw were two bags, packed and parked in the middle of the living room.

She stood looking down at them. Something cold moved through her.

Alex emerged from his bedroom, dressed, shaved, his jacket on. He saw her, and went still.

"When are you leaving?" she asked.

"Now," he said. "There's a shuttle out in twenty minutes."

"And what? Not even a post-it note to let me know?"

"There's a letter on the table," he said.

She looked toward the table, saw the envelope with her name on it. "What does it say?"

"That I have to go away for a while, figure this out. That you shouldn't worry about me."

She couldn't fault him. She'd done the same to him, and not that long ago. She supposed he hadn't liked it any better than she did now. But there was one thing she had to know, and to find out she'd have to trip him up one more time.

"If you're going after Schulman, you should let me help," she said.

"That's my job," he said too quickly, his voice too low and too rough.

That told her everything she needed to know. "I guess that's a yes, then."

"It's not," he amended quickly. "Not yet. It's one of the things I have to think about."

"Take your time," she said. "Getting him could be complicated, and you'll only get one shot. Besides,you're in no condition to make big decisions right now. You realize that, don't you?"

"I'm in no condition to stay here," he said. "I've got nothing to give."

"Maybe," she said, "you've got something to receive."

He opened his mouth to speak, closed it, started over. "Jaguar, this isn't about you. I just—I have to think it through. What it means to me, and to him. What I have to do."

She wanted to remind him he should be grieving and not thinking. Time enough to think when the tears began to dry. She realized it was futile. Right now, for him, grief was the enemy, and the only warriors that would take it down were action and thought. "Where will you go?" she asked instead.

"New York, first."

"Why there?"

"It's not here. And it's a hub city. I can go wherever I want from there."

They both paused for the time it took to remember they'd had this exact conversation once before, only it was Jaguar who was leaving then.

She stepped forward, breathed a thought into him. *I'll go with you.*

His response, another repetition of their past. *No. I have to be my own.*

She sighed, left his thoughts. Yet another Karmic return. "How long will you be gone?" she asked out loud.

"My leave of absence is good for a year," he said.

His words hit her with a shock. He'd applied for a leave of absence. He'd made it official. The implications weren't good. She bit at her lip to bring blood back into it.

"Are you coming back?" she asked.

He tensed, the muscles in his jaw working hard. "I'm not sure," he said. "This work—what it does to us. To me. What I've become. I'm… not sure."

There were a few questions she didn't ask. What about us? What about me? Instead she thought of all he'd done for her, what he'd tried to do for his son, and what it cost him. Thought of the ten thousand miles of the heart they'd traveled together. She held silent converse with herself, traversing those miles. When she reached a conclusion she looked at him with her sea clear eyes.

"I'll wait for you," she said quietly.

"Jaguar—"

"I'm *telling* you."

Not open to discussion. Just what she would do. Mountains would melt and seas burn before he'd move her from her stance. He nodded, stayed silent.

"You'll call me if you want me, right?" she said.

A grim smile. "There's not a moment since I met you that I haven't wanted you," he said. "Only moments when I tried not to."

He picked up his bags, headed toward the door.

"Alex," she said to his back.

He stopped, but didn't turn to her.

"Don't try too hard," she said.

He gave her nothing. Nothing at all. He just left, without looking back.

www.ingramcontent.com/pod-product-compliance
Lightning Source LLC
Chambersburg PA
CBHW050729250626
47155CB00005B/1719